TRULY DEVIOUS

MICHAEL OLIVE

Other novels by Michael:

The Death Whisperer Series
The Death Whisperer
The Magician
An Impolitic Solution
Easier Killed Than Forgiven
The Fury of a Silent Man
Black Widow's Bite
Tears of the Betrayed
Color Me Deadly
Tenebrae
SybrKombat
Lunatic Fringe
Asp
Puppet Master
Checkmate
The Tree Remembers
The Street of Regret
Night Dancer
The Black Rose of Death
A Deadly Compulsion
The Kingdom Where Nobody Dies

Guardian Series
The Guardian

Non-Fiction
A Scientist's Search for God

Acknowledgements

Any author knows that his or her work cannot be completed without the help of others. Thanks to my Lord and Savior Jesus Christ who has graciously blessed me. Next, thanks to my wife Sandy for putting up with my whims. I'm indebted to Doc Chaves for his editing, proofreading, and discussions. I truly appreciate your efforts.

As you may have noticed above, I am a Christian. Because of that, some readers may find the profanity used by some of the characters in this book odd. I have tried to keep the dialogue realistic, even though I may not approve of the kind of street language the characters might use. For example, a killer would not use the phrase "oh my goodness." He or she would probably use something more colorful. Please forgive me if some of you find it offensive. The world is what it is.

"Look! A riddle! Time for fun!
Should we use a rope or should we use a gun?
Knives are sharp and gleam so pretty
Poison's slow, which is a pity
Fire is festive, drowning's slow
Hanging's a ropy way to go
A broken head, a nasty fall
A car colliding with a wall
Bombs make a very jolly noise
Such ways to punish naughty boys!
What shall we use? We can't decide.
Just like you cannot run or hide.
Ha ha.
Truly,
Devious"
— Maureen Johnson, Truly Devious

Chapter One

Wednesday, March 1st; Dubrovnik, Croatia; The E65 Coastal Road

Jacob Novak took the curve dangerously fast. The Peugeot 208 barely managed to hang onto the oncoming lane before he pulled it back to the right. The Croatian coastal highway was a narrow two-lane road. With nothing resembling a shoulder or safety barriers, the blind corners and sharp turns had taken many inexperienced drivers off the cliff's edge. It was not a road for the faint-hearted. But Jacob didn't have a choice.

He was being hunted.

He and his partner, Janice Kovač, were CIA field agents, investigating rumors of a Russian assassination plot to take out several U.S. ambassadors and diplomats. The flash drive he had in his pocket contained a list of names of the targeted people, their positions, places of residence, and travel schedules, and it was critical that it get to his handler.

But their plans hit a snag. Jacob and Janice had finished their work in Dubrovnik and were getting ready to drive to Trieste to hand off their information. They left the Pub Dubrovnik after having a quick lunch and a beer and headed for their car. As Jacob unlocked the car, he heard a hissing sound, and blood splattered his face. When he'd looked up, a crossbow bolt was bisecting Janice's neck. He would never forget the horrified look on her face as she touched her throat and then toppled over backward. The crossbow bolt was the signature of the assassin known as Enigma. Very little was known about her other than she was mysterious, invisible, and deadly.

Jacob hadn't waited. Instead, he hopped behind the wheel, fumbling with his keys. He'd managed to get the car started then floored the gas and rocketed away from the curb, leaving his partner's body lying in a puddle of her blood. After weaving through the streets, he headed for the Franjo Tudman Bridge over the inlet of the Adriatic Sea. He shot across it and sped away along the coastal road. But he cursed himself when he saw he had less than a quarter tank of gas. He pulled off in Zaton and filled the tank.

Standing at the pump, Jacob realized getting to Trieste with his information might be problematic, meaning he might not make it. He checked his cell phone and saw there was a DHL office in Zaton. When he finished paying for the gas, he drove to the DHL and dropped the flash drive in a padded envelope. He addressed it to the U.S. Embassy in Athens, paid, then returned to his car, hoping he could make it to Trieste before Enigma caught up to him.

He performed an elaborate surveillance detection run before hopping back on the coastal road, heading north to Trieste and he thought he was clear until five minutes later when he noticed a white VW GTI closing on him. The sound of a horn snapped his eyes back to the road in front of him. He swerved to the right, barely avoiding another car coming at him around a blind curve.

A bead of sweat dripped into Jacob's eye from the white-knuckle driving. He had to concentrate all his attention on the road in front of him and couldn't worry about the GTI. If it came down to a confrontation, he had an HK VP9 loaded with fifteen rounds in the center console.

God, he wished Janice was here. A wave of remorse swept over him as he remembered the look on her face with the crossbow bolt sticking out of her neck to the right of her trachea. The bowman was an expert because the placement of the arrow took out her jugular and carotid. She would have bled to death in minutes, so he left her. Instead of fighting, he ran.

Looking back, he justified his actions because he was able to mail off the flash drive to his handler. He came around a curve and saw he had about a kilometer of straight highway ahead of him, so he fished out his cell phone and called his handler in Trieste. The woman answered on the fourth ring.

"Jacob, are you on your way in?" she said.

"Diana, Janice is dead. Shot with a crossbow."

His handler was silent.

"Are you there?" Jacob asked.

"Shit, Enigma?" Diana asked.

"I think so, and someone is following me in a white GTI. I'm coming up the E65 coastal road, but I can only go so fast without flying off a cliff."

"What about the flash drive?"

"I found a DHL office in Zaton and mailed it to the embassy in Athens. It has information on the planned assassinations.

"Get off the coastal road ASAP. If Enigma is following you, you'll never outrun her on that road."

"I'm almost to the 25. I'll take it east then I'll pick up the E71 and continue north. I'll pick up the E65 again at Senj then follow it to Rijeka where I'll join the E61 and take it to Trieste."

"You're booked into the Hotel Riviera. It's away from the city. I'll contact you tomorrow and set up a meeting. And Jacob…I'm sorry about Janice."

"Thanks." He disconnected. The turnoff for the 25 appeared and he headed east. The road was much more drivable, and he made good time to the E71. He kept checking his mirrors, but the GTI was no longer behind him. Thirty minutes later he merged onto the E65. Ten miles in, the road turned into a series of switchback curves that force him to drop his speed to thirty kilometers per hour.

Jacob maneuvered through the curves and came out onto a straight section. He shook out his hands after making it through the crazy hairpins. Traffic on the road was negligible so he stretched his back and relaxed.

While this section lacked curves, there were mountains on his right and a sheer two-hundred-foot drop-off on the left.

As his car came out of a gentle S-curve, Jacob swore. The GTI was parked on the edge of the road up ahead. He'd barely noticed the car when the windshield shattered, and a bullet took him through the right eye. The car pulled hard to the left and plunged over the cliff's edge, exploding in a ball of flame two hundred feet down.

A tall, solitary figure scrambled down the mountainside, tossed a rifle in the back, and slid into the driver's seat. Seconds later, the only evidence that someone had been there was the black smoke drifting up from the inferno below. By the time they recovered the body, it would be nothing but an oversized charcoal briquet. No sign of the bullet that sent the driver to his death.

Chapter Two

Friday, March 10th; London, England; Jack Stevens' Home

Dan Andrews slouched behind the wheel of a dark blue Mini Cooper parked five cars down from a palatial home in Kensington. His partner, Jack Stone was in the passenger seat scrolling through something on his phone. Both were CIA agents and had been scrambled here to watch the house where Jack Stevens, the U.S. ambassador to the U.K. resided with his wife. Intel off a flash drive sent to the U.S. embassy in Athens detailed a Russian plot to assassinate several top U.S. diplomats in response to the sanctions placed on the country following their invasion of Ukraine.

Stevens was a retired United States Navy admiral and a past chairman of the Intelligence Oversight Board. He was instrumental in successfully getting British Petroleum to sell its nearly 20 percent stake in Rosneft, the Russian state-controlled oil company. BP wrote off about twenty billion pounds on the transaction, but that charge was considered a paper loss by analysts, with little relevance to the company's continuing performance. However, while it didn't hurt BP, it was devastating to Rosneft because BP sold its holdings at a bargain price, tanking Rosneft's valuation and royally pissing off the Russian government.

They'd been watching the house for the last twenty-four hours, looking for any signs of unusual activity in the neighborhood. The Agency thought that if an attempt was made on Stevens, it would be at his home. He had tight security surrounding him to and from work and at the embassy, and while he had two members of the Diplomatic Security Service or DSS in the house, the two CIA field agents were better trained to notice potential threats.

Steven's home was one of the most impressive they'd ever seen. Formerly an artist's studio, it was an expansive 3,350-square-foot house typical of palatial London living. It was tucked down a private lane in South Kensington, just a three-minute walk from the Gloucester Road station.

According to Jack's online research, the house had five bedrooms, three with marble-clad *en suite* baths, a chef's kitchen, and a Sonos sound system throughout. The property had a secluded patio and garden in the back hidden behind a ten-foot ivy-covered brick wall. The house was also furnished with heated floors and central air conditioning, the latter unusual for London. The home was further distinguished from its neighbors in that its style was very contemporary with a lot of glass. It would have been easy to break into it had Stevens not had a top-of-the-line security system in addition to the two DSS agents. On the surface, he would seem to be a difficult target, but Dan and Jack had identified a half dozen points in his routine where they could have killed him.

"He's heading for work," Dan said.

They watched the iron gates slide open and Stevens' Mercedes-Maybach S cruised out of the drive and took a left. The two agents knew it was heavily armored.

"You want to get breakfast?" Dan asked.

"Let's hang out a bit and monitor the activity around the neighborhood," Jack said.

A half-hour after Steven's left, the gates opened and a Mercedes transit van with Pennyworth's Maid and Cleaning Services printed on the side pulled into the drive. The male driver and four women began unloading buckets, mops, and vacuum cleaners out of the van. Three of the women were short and plump while the fourth was tall and slender. All of them wore aqua-colored scrubs and safety glasses and pulled on green rubber gloves. Stevens' wife was in the States to watch their son graduate from law school and Stevens didn't look like the type to take out the vacuum and clean the house himself. The cleaning people carried their equipment into the house, but the male driver returned and sat in the van listening to the radio.

"I'm going to check on the driver," Jack said. He slipped out of the car and approached the vehicle from the passenger side. He crouched low, but as he crept forward, he heard soft snoring. He reached up and carefully moved the outside mirror so he could see inside. The driver had reclined his seat and was napping. He debated entering and checking out the house, but deemed it too dangerous, so he returned to their car.

"The guy's sleeping," Jack said.

Two hours later, the cleaning ladies came out of the house, carrying their equipment. One of them rapped on the driver's side window.

"Wake up, Tommy. We're finished, so help us load up," she said.

Tommy the driver climbed out of the van and helped stow the vacuum cleaners in the back. The women reentered the house and emerged five minutes later.

"All set. Everything is out," one of the women said.

They piled into the van and the driver backed out. Seconds later, they were gone.

"Let's get something to eat," Jack said.

Dan pulled out and headed for the Scarsdale Tavern. He found a parking space and they got a table in the outdoor dining area. Both men ordered a smoked salmon platter and a pot of coffee. They lingered over their food when it was delivered, thinking about the task facing them.

"I checked my email, and our handler says the assassin is someone called Enigma," Jack said.

"That's it? No information on him?"

"He says Enigma is a female."

"How does he know that?" Dan asked.

"This babe isn't new. SOG and MI6 have been hunting her for several years. She's taken out over two dozen high-value targets, but one of her hits got a little sloppy. She was wounded and an analysis of the blood left behind indicates Enigma is a female."

"How do they know it was her blood?"

"Can't answer that, but for now, let's assume the intel is solid."

They paid their check then Dan dug the keys from his pocket as they walked back to their Mini Cooper. They stopped off at their hotel, the Griffin Belle Vauxhall to relax before they had to get back to watching Stevens' house. They met in the lobby three hours later and stopped off at a coffee shop where they bought a couple of large, black coffees before returning to their surveillance. They drove back to the house and parked on the opposite side of the street three cars up from the property. With nothing more to do, they reclined their seats and settled in to watch. Jack opened his email to check for any further communication from their handler while he sipped his coffee.

"Nothing," he said.

"So how are we supposed to find this gal if we don't know what she looks like?" Dan asked.

"I don't know. I guess we just look for anomalies."

Rain started to fall as they sat in their car.

"Shit, I didn't bring an umbrella," Jack said.

"Well, hopefully, we won't have to get out of the car."

Around seven-thirty, they'd finished their coffee as Steven's limousine pulled in. Two DSS agents accompanied the ambassador into his house. When they were inside, the limousine backed out and drove off.

The CIA agents watched lights come on in the back of the house where they assumed the kitchen was located. They watched the street for another hour and a half, as lights came on and off in different rooms.

"Do you think we should check around the house?" Dan asked.

"Hang on, someone's approaching on the other side of the street," Jack said, adjusting his mirror so he could watch the person.

A tall figure in a hooded raincoat wearing a backpack approached from behind their car on the opposite side of the street. The figure had a black cocker spaniel on a leash and was walking fast probably to get out of the rain. Jack couldn't see the figure's face as it was buried inside the rain jacket. The figure turned in at the third house down from Stevens' and disappeared.

"What the hell?" Dan said.

The cocker spaniel streaked around the front of the house and made a beeline down the block. As Dan turned around to watch the dog, a bullet punctured the windshield, spraying Jack's brains on Dan.

"Son of a bitch!" he yelled.

A second round just missed him as he ducked below the dashboard. He opened his door and rolled onto the sidewalk. A third bullet hit the car's hood. Dan hadn't heard the sound of the shots, which told him the sniper was using a suppressed rifle, probably with subsonic rounds. That meant that the police wouldn't be called for a while, if at all.

Another round slammed into the Mini Cooper. Dan knew he couldn't stay behind the car any longer because if the shooter moved, he was a dead man. He started backing away from their car, using the other parked cars as shields. He got to the corner where a seven-foot, ivy-covered, brick wall surrounded a house. He dove for the cover of the wall and rolled to his knees. He turkey-peeked back toward the car, but with the darkness and rain, he couldn't see a thing. He needed to get away from the scene and call his handler.

He took out his cell phone and turned to walk away when he noticed a dark figure rise between two parked cars. A dark hood covered the figure's head, but what drew Dan's attention was the black basilisk eye of the barrel of an FN P90 pointing at him. He barely had time to register the threat when the first two rounds hit him in the chest, causing him to stagger backward. He sank to his knees and put a hand on the pavement for support. His eyes widened as he looked up at the approaching gunman. The shooter fired a two-round burst to his face, ending his life.

Chapter Three

Sunday, March 12th; Paris, France; Palais Garnier

Alison Burton's train arrived at midday from an Eastern European country where she'd been on assignment for the CIA. She had to scramble to get a ticket to a dance recital by the Paris School of Ballet where Georges Toussaint's daughter was performing. Toussaint was the U.S. ambassador to France. With the EU aiming to cut off gas and oil imports from Russia, they needed to find alternative sources of energy. One of France's major industries was the energy sector. Its leading power company, *Electricite de France,* or EDF was the largest utility company in the world. The company supplied approximately 20% of the total electricity in the European Union and was the world's largest producer of power. It operated fifty-six nuclear reactors spread out over eighteen sites. Toussaint managed to broker a deal to get the French president to cut off gas imports from Russia and work with EDF to increase their production. It did not sit well with the Russian President and Georges Toussaint was on the list that Jacob Novak supplied before he was killed.

After checking into the Maison Astor Hotel, Alison had to run out and pick up something more appropriate than cargo pants and Doc Martin combat boots. She was now dressed in a black silk tee shirt under a light gray pinstriped suit coat and pants. She had an FN Five-seveN in a suede Miller Crossbody bag and a Benchmade Infidel knife clipped to her right front pocket. Her shoes were black Nisolo all-weather Amalia boots.

The annual dance spectacle of the prestigious Paris Opera Ballet School presented a patchwork of ballet excerpts performed by the students and was designed to show off the wealth and breadth of their training. Toussaint's sixteen-year-old daughter, Marie had been studying at the school since she was eight. It was a rigorous curriculum, and the company had a lofty goal for each student at the end of their time at the school. By their last year at the academy, they expected the students to be capable of dancing any principal role from any of the ballets in the company's large repertoire. Even then, only two or three from a graduating class of twelve would be lucky enough to enter the company. Marie had two more years before she would graduate and try to obtain a spot as a dancer with either the POB or one of Europe's other ballet companies.

Alison had checked online for the entry requirements. Most of the students entered like Marie at a very young age. The school preferred to have children untainted by other teachers and methods so they could train them in the "French" way. It was far more difficult to enter past the age of twelve because applicants were expected to try out and demonstrate a level of proficiency equal to the currently matriculated students. Not an easy task.

The actual school was nestled in a large park just a short train ride away from the center of Paris. The campus featured three distinct areas: the academic wing, complete with classrooms for study; the dance wing; and the dormitories, where students slept two or three to a room.

In all the dance classes, the French style was ever-present. Its trademarks included the clarity of the *épaulement* and *port de bras* that were slightly rounder than the Russian style, yet not as round as the Danish. Elegance and strength were emphasized as well as the precision of the footwork.

But the signature of a French dancer was the *petite batterie*, a term used to describe rapid steps or steps with beats. A *jeté battu* and a *cabriolé* were examples of *batterie* because there was a beating of the dancer's legs when performing them. The steps were difficult to learn because of the lightning speed at which they were executed.

But although she was interested in seeing the performances, Alison was concerned because the recital would be packed, the perfect situation for an assassination, and it would be difficult for her to keep track of Toussaint. Her mission brief described a female assassin who went by the moniker of Enigma, and she was excellent at improvisation and adapting her methods to the situation. That meant Alison was going to have to stay near Toussaint, something that would be difficult since her seat for the recital was nowhere near the box where Toussaint would be sitting. Fortunately, it was common practice to bring a pair of binoculars to the ballet and opera. Granted, Alison's Steiner's Safari UltraSharp models were a little overkill for the ballet, but they had impressive clarity and low light capability.

She dropped the binoculars in her crossbody bag and headed out to get a cab to the Palais Garnier. She had an hour and a half before the performance began, but Paris traffic meant she'd get there with about forty-five minutes to spare. When the cab dropped her off, she trotted up the stairs and showed her ticket to the doorman. Her seat was in the front row of the main mezzanine, which was perfect for watching both the performance and the balcony box where Toussaint would be sitting. But the problem was, he was wide open and there was nothing Alison could do to protect him from where she sat.

The main lobby faced a double stone staircase that led to the upper levels. Her seat was up one flight of stairs, but she loitered in the lobby admiring the frescos painted on the vaulted ceiling that was illuminated by enormous ornate chandeliers created during the reign of Louis the XIV. Twenty minutes before the start of the performance, Toussaint entered, trailed by a single bodyguard. Alison's research indicated his wife died three years ago from metastatic breast cancer. Toussaint lingered in the lobby, greeting friends before heading up to his box.

Alison followed him up the stairs but had to stop at the mezzanine when one of the ushers asked to see her ticket then handed her a program and directed her to her seat. The main hall was spectacular. The seats were red velvet, and the balustrades were painted gold. The stage was enormous and cloaked with a red velvet curtain. Alison took her seat and drew her binoculars from her bag. She scanned the stage first then moved to the first balcony where she saw Toussaint and his bodyguard enter. His protector was an idiot. If someone wanted to kill Toussaint, they could easily appear at the entry to the box, fire a suppressed pistol at both men, and be gone before anyone knew what happened. It's how she would do it.

The hall filled up quickly and the headmaster came out and introduced the performances. Marie was dancing the *pas de deux* from Sleeping Beauty, quite an honor for a sixteen-year-old. The first dances were excerpts from Giselle, including the *pas de deux*. Alison kept one eye scanning the concert hall and another on Toussaint, but the place was huge, so there was no way she had any hope of finding an assassin.

The next number was a performance of excerpts from the Nutcracker. It brought back memories of her childhood because her parents took her to see it performed in New York where she grew up. But Alison couldn't enjoy it because she needed to watch for the assassin. She scanned the upper balconies across from where Toussaint sat, but it was about an eighty-meter shot at the closest point. Extremely difficult for a pistol and a rifle would never make it past security.

The number ended and after a brief break, the music began, and the curtain rose on Marie dancing the *pas de deux* from Sleeping Beauty with her partner. Alison had a horrible thought that the killer, in an act of sheer cruelty, might take out Toussaint while his daughter was dancing. Alison slipped out of her seat and stepped out of the hall. The ushers were gathered on the main floor getting ready for the intermission that came after Marie's number. That gave her an opening to climb the stairs to the first balcony level. She crept down the corridor, past a lady's restroom, and continued to the emergency exit just beyond his box where she waited for the intermission.

The sound of clapping signaled the end of the performance and people started streaming out of the balcony boxes, heading for the lobby and a champagne reception. Toussaint joined the flow with his bodyguard on his right. Alison fell in about twenty feet behind them as they moved slowly toward the stairs. Toussaint was only five and a half feet tall, which made it hard to see him, so she focused on his taller bodyguard, straining to watch them. They were almost to the stairs when she froze, her eyes went wide, and she grunted. She felt a sharp pain as a stiletto pierced her back and ripped into her heart. No one noticed because she was the last person in the crowd.

She sank to her knees and felt the assassin remove the blade that had done its damage. She gasped as blood filled her lungs and dribbled down her chin. A tall woman passed by her and smiled. Alison slumped over on her face and quietly died.

Chapter Four

Monday, March 13th; Paris, France; Café Voltaire

It was a perfect evening for an assassination. Raindrops acted like tiny prisms, refracting the lights of Paris into subtle colors as a steady rain fell. With the temperature in the mid-fifties, Brook Nathans was the only person out walking along the Seine. She looked like a typical Parisian woman in a black, belted, below-the-knee Tanner trench coat, black wool pants, and black Doc Martin lace-up boots. Her shaggy chestnut hair cut in a shoulder-skimming style was tucked under a claret Donegal waterproof hat. But the features that sent shivers down the spines of those who faced her were her eyes. Looking into them was like looking past the event horizon of a black hole.

She walked east along the Quai Malaquaise, heading for a date with Farzad Majidi. After the death of Qasem Soleimani, Majidi took his place as the commander of the Quds Force, the IRGC division responsible for extraterritorial and clandestine military operations. He was the country's most powerful commander, a celebrity, considered the most important person in Iran after Supreme Leader Ayatollah Khamenei.

During the Syrian civil war, Majidi coordinated attacks, trained militias, and set up an elaborate system to monitor rebel communications. His command worked closely to coordinate the Russian support of Syria and plan strategic attacks against Israel. He was also the one who instigated the use of nerve gas on Kurdish rebels. But recently, he began overseeing the Iranian nuclear program with particular emphasis on developing weapons of mass destruction. Like his predecessor, Majidi was the personification of evil—and tonight Brook was going to kill him.

She was an assassin and a distinguished member of the CIA's Special Operations Group, a subgroup of the Special Activities Center. The SAC provided the United States Security Council with alternative options when overt military and/or diplomatic actions were not viable or politically feasible. The SOG was a department within SAC responsible for operations that included clandestine or covert operations with which the U.S. government did not want to be overtly associated. There were only 100 SOG operators, far fewer than most of the other special mission units such as the U.S. Army's 1st Special Forces Operational Detachment-Delta or the SEALS. And they were the most secretive and highly trained operatives in the U.S. military force.

Brook Nathans was the epitome of their motto, *Tertia Optio*, or the Third Option. When diplomacy failed and direct military action wasn't feasible, she was the one they called. One of her best-known exploits occurred in Afghanistan where disguised as an Afghan woman in a burqa and abaya, she approached a meeting of a dozen Taliban leaders and killed them with an HK MP7a1 and fragmentation grenades that were hidden under her clothes. When she finished, she simply walked away and disappeared.

Majidi was staying at the Hotel du Quai Voltaire that was up ahead on her right. It was a middle-of-the-road hotel, probably because Majidi didn't want it known that he was in town to meet with a local cell of Quds force operatives tasked with removing Iranian dissidents and organizations dedicated to the overthrow of the Iranian government.

She'd watched Majidi for four days, noting his daily routine that included dinner every night at Café Voltaire. The restaurant was an upscale bistro that served traditional French cuisine. It was named after the writer François-Marie Arouet, also known as Voltaire. It was an interesting choice for Majidi because most of its patrons were well-heeled members of English society or English-speaking tourists. While concierges at the city's high-end hotels frequently recommended it, she found the food to be hit or miss.

But tonight, Majidi was dining with Yaroslav Semenov, a Russian GRU colonel who was involved with Russia's nuclear weapons program. Over the past two months, the two had been meeting here in Paris and the CIA strongly suspected the Russians were supplying the Iranians with enriched uranium and technical support for the Iranian nuclear program.

They were a contrast in terms of appearance. Whereas Majidi was approximately five-feet-eight with a growing paunch that hung over his belt, Semenov was a trim six-feet-two, two hundred pounds. Brook knew the Russian wore a shoulder holster with an MP-443 Grach 9mm pistol under his sport jacket.

Killing Majidi had to be done in such a way as to deflect suspicion away from the United States. For that reason, Brook was carrying an FN 502 .22 tactical pistol with a fifteen-round magazine and a Bannish 22 suppressor. The gun was loaded with CCI Stinger ammunition. The Stingers were copper-plated 32-grain hollow point bullets, that were fast, accurate, and deadly. Israeli kidons were known for using .22 caliber pistols for their assassinations and since they were sworn enemies of Iran, the use of a .22 to kill Majidi would point the finger at them rather than the United States.

Brook wasn't concerned about a .22 bullet ending Majidi's life, but Semenov was a different story. If the .22 didn't kill him, she had an FN 509 tactical loaded with 15+1 rounds of 115-grain Speer Gold Dot full metal jacketed bullets in a Craft quick draw holster threaded through her belt at the back of her waist.

She checked her watch. She knew Majidi left the hotel at 8:15 every night and would be walking to the restaurant with Semenov for their 8:30 dinner reservation. They would spend the next two hours eating, drinking, and planning until they left at approximately 10:30. Brook timed her walk so she would reach the two men just after they passed the Rue de Beaune.

A smile tickled the corners of her mouth as she saw them approaching. She kept her eyes averted and hugged the buildings as they approached. Both men eyed her but didn't see her as a threat. Semenov bumped her as he passed, and he and Majidi laughed as they continued toward the restaurant. Brook drew the FN 502, turned, and aimed at Semenov.

"Excusez-moi, messieurs."

She fired three quick shots into the spot where Semenov's head met his spine, severing his spinal cord and dropping him like a bag of cement. The gun was Hollywood quiet, so anyone in the vicinity wouldn't be alarmed. Majidi didn't realize what happened before Brook put three rounds through his left temple. He joined Semenov on the pavement. Brook walked quickly to the two men and shot Majidi twice through his left eye. She nudged Semenov's head with her toe and did the same to him.

She lowered the gun and held it by her right side then walked briskly to the Pont du Carrousel. She disassembled the gun as she crossed the bridge, dropping the pieces into the Seine. She cut through the Jardin des Tuileries, exiting onto the Rue de la Paix. She continued to the Rue Saint Honore and went west to the Mandarin Oriental where she was staying. She walked through the lobby leaving a trail of water droplets and took the elevator to her floor. She entered her deluxe king room and hung her coat and hat in the bathroom to dry.

Brook took a hand towel and went to the small desk. She removed her FN 509 and holster, placed it on the desk then covered it with the towel. She picked up the phone and ordered white asparagus with hollandaise, and a half bottle of Chateau de Villeneuve Saumur Blanc. She kicked off her shoes and changed out of her damp clothes, pulling on a pair of gray sweatpants and a Cambridge University sweatshirt. She took out a copy of Frederick Forsyth's novel, *The Day of the Jackal,* and set it on the desk. A knock on the door indicated her food had arrived. She took her gun and tucked it in the back of her sweatpants then checked the peephole to verify it was the hotel staff. She had the man set the tray on a small end table and then signed the check.

When she'd poured herself a glass of the wine and savored a sip, she took out an ultra-secure Kerberos cellphone and sent a text to her handler.

"No one can jump high enough to escape death."

Mission accomplished.

Chapter Five

Wednesday, March 15th; London, England; Stratford Station

Brook sat on a bench in London's Stratford station people-watching. She looked like a typical Londoner in khaki cargo pants, black Ryder sneakers, and a black cotton turtleneck, under a dark gray Arc'teryx Beta LT jacket. The shoes were impregnated with military-grade Kevlar and sported steel toes. Stratford was a major multi-level railway station that was served by the London Underground, London Overground, the Docklands Light Railway, and the West Anglia Main Line of the National Rail. It was rated as the busiest station in Britain, which served her purposes perfectly. It was easy to come and go without being noticed.

Her organization often gave her mission instructions the old fashion way. Emails could be hacked, and phones could be tapped, so she was waiting at the station to rendezvous with her contact. She'd be given an envelope containing a new ID, a set of credit cards, and instructions on where to find her mission brief. Often her contact would hand her a key to a locker in one of the stations or a post office box in the city where she was residing. The delivery methods varied to avoid setting a pattern that could be intercepted.

Her phone buzzed with a text that read, *"left"*. She looked left and spotted her contact, a man wearing black wool pants, a gray turtleneck, and a black knee-length raincoat as had been described in an encrypted text message yesterday. Brook stood and began walking toward him. Neither looked at the other. As they passed, her right hand brushed the man's left, taking a card-size envelope from him. She headed for a coffee kiosk and as she joined the line, she pocketed the materials and ordered a small coffee. She took it to a two-top table and checked for anyone who might have observed the exchange. When she was confident no one was watching her, she took out the envelope and examined its contents—a small key to one of the lockers in the station and a note that said "Sea Containers Hotel".

She pocketed the key and envelope and finished her coffee. When she was done, she tossed the cup in the trash and headed for lockers that were located outside the station. She circled the area several times looking for watchers and when she was sure it was safe, she went to her locker and took out a small crossbody sling backpack. She looped it over her head and adjusted it, so it rode under her left arm. She checked for observers and then headed for the Underground Station. She didn't open any of the compartments because it would have drawn attention. She hopped on a train heading toward Liverpool Street and took a seat in the corner.

After several train changes, she reached the hotel located on the south bank of the Thames River. She entered the hotel and took a seat in the lobby then unzipped a small outside pocket on the backpack. The pocket contained a British passport in the name of Susan Emery and Chase Sapphire Preferred and American Express Gold cards that matched her new identity. She placed all three in one of her cargo pockets and approached the front desk. A reservation for a room in the name of Susan Emery was waiting for her.

The hotel's design was reminiscent of a 1920 transatlantic liner. Her Riverview Balcony Suite was one of the hotel's most sought-after accommodations. It was positioned above the Thames with wall-to-wall windows that provided a breathtaking view of the London skyline. The suite had a king bed and a marble *en-suite* bathroom. The living area was divided into three sections, one for relaxing and TV viewing and another with a desk and work area. The third area was a private, fully furnished balcony.

She walked the suite, looking for anything out of the ordinary, but it was doubtful anyone knew she was coming, especially in her new identity as Susan Emery. When she was satisfied that the suite was secure, she set the backpack on the desk and sat in the desk chair to review its contents and her instructions. Brook took out a black book-sized case and opened it. Inside was an FN Five-seveN pistol with a GSL57 suppressor, three extra twenty-round magazines, and a Craft quick draw holster. She set the case aside and removed two A4 size envelopes. One of the envelopes contained £5000.00 and €5000.00 in cash. The second detailed her mission, so she spread its contents across the desktop.

The first page contained a synopsis of the problem. Two CIA field agents had retrieved a flash drive containing a list of names of a half dozen U.S. ambassadors and diplomats targeted for assassination. Both agents were killed but managed to mail the drive to their handler. It included information on the daily routines, places of residence, and travel schedules of each target. Two of the targets were the U.S. ambassadors to the U.K. and France. The CIA sent operators to watch over both targets and stop the assassin from achieving her goals. But while neither ambassador was harmed, the three CIA operators were assassinated. One of the men watching the U.S. ambassador to the U.K. was killed by a sniper's bullet while his partner was gunned down with an automatic rifle. The female agent assigned to the U.S. ambassador to France was stabbed through the heart from behind while she followed him to the intermission cocktail party at a performance of the Paris School of Ballet at the Palais Garnier. The ambassador wasn't harmed.

Thus far, none of the targets listed in the flash drive had been harmed, but three CIA agents were dead. The agency concluded that the list was intended to draw their agents into a known theater of action to assassinate them. However, they couldn't discount the danger to the diplomatic personnel, so they still had to guard them.

The assassin thought to be responsible for the killings went by the moniker Enigma. The only information the agency had on the assassin was based on a blood sample found at a previous hit attributed to her. She was a female of Slavic origin with dark hair and brown eyes. Brook knew the CIA used a system called HIrisPlex to reliably predict human eye and hair color from a DNA sample. The HIrisPlex system was a single multiplex genotyping assay that targeted 24 eye and/or hair color predictive DNA polymorphisms and provided individual prediction probabilities for eye and hair color categories. Personally, Brook discounted the information on hair and eye color because hair could be dyed and contact lenses could change the visible eye color.

Very little else was known about her other than she was mysterious, invisible, and deadly. She was adept at adapting her killing method to the situation, and one of her signature methods for killing her prey was a crossbow.

Even without any information, if Enigma was anything like her, then she could surmise several things. While the assassin would be an expert with knives, handguns, and rifles, she would be an ardent believer that her body was her primary weapon. If it wasn't honed to a fine edge, everything else suffered. It was the only weapon that could never be discovered going through TSA, customs, or by a police officer. Their profession required them to be strong, quick, flexible, and precise. That meant taking care of their bodies was of paramount importance.

For Brook that meant keeping her joints flexible by starting the day with a half hour of Hatha yoga. It built endurance, strength, and breath control. Along with yoga, she took care to stick to a healthy diet, focusing on lean protein from fish or chicken and vegetables, particularly the leafy green varieties, which meant she could forego vitamins and supplements.

Brook had one other rather unorthodox practice that she felt was critical to her own proficiency. From her childhood through her teen years, she'd studied ballet and still made it a critical part of her training regimen. It was important for balance and movement and helped her develop total control over her body. Combining ballet with various fighting forms that she'd studied allowed her to develop a unique style.

Her assignment was to find Enigma and eliminate her. Brook chuckled. That was all well and good, but how the hell was she supposed to find and eliminate a ghost? Yet while the CIA was stymied as to the identity of Enigma, Brook had some contacts that she could mine for information. The first one on her list was Arseny Balakin, the owner of a small pub just south of the Tottenham Hotspurs stadium. He was a tough old buzzard left over from the days of the Soviet Union's KGB who'd come to appreciate the capitalist West and never returned after the fall of the wall. Tomorrow, she'd visit him. Then, as the Russian saying went, hopefully, she'd gain some insight into where the dog was buried.

Chapter Six

Thursday, March 16th; London, England; Little Russia

Brook never stayed in the same place for more than two nights, so she checked out of the Sea Containers Hotel and moved to St. Martins Lane Hotel in Covent Garden. It was a five-minute walk from Trafalgar Square and close to the Piccadilly line tube station on Leicester Square.

The hotel was concealed inside the bland wrapper of a 1960s office block. As Brook entered through London's tallest revolving doors, she was reminded of Alice in Wonderland. The hall that led to the reception desk was flanked by oversized chess pieces, ceiling-high mirrors, and molar-shaped chairs. The whole thing presented an intriguing medley of whimsical design features.

Brook's superior room had clean white lines and modern material choices set off by floor-to-ceiling windows that framed central London. It had a floating bed and brushed aluminum teardrop lights hanging from the ceiling. At night, the monochrome furnishings could be illuminated in a variety of fluorescent LED colors from a bedside control panel.

First on her agenda was a visit to an old acquaintance. Little Russia was formerly an area of Tottenham, London. It was on the northern boundary of the London Borough of Haringey, adjoining Edmonton, and bounded by Pretoria, Durban, and Lorenco Roads. During the early 20th century, it was the center of an influx of Russian immigrants. Nowadays it was little more than a residential area with a small industrial estate halfway up Pretoria Road. Traces of the bustling Russian community were next to nothing.

Brook stepped off the Abellio Greater Anglia service to the White Hart Lane station. The station was only a five-minute walk from her destination, the Bell and Hare Pub located just south of the Tottenham Hotspurs Stadium. The pub's owner, Arseny Balakin was a former KGB agent, although he was still plugged into the Russian grapevine. He knew her as Phoebe Dixon and although he didn't know her actual affiliation, he did know she was extremely dangerous.

She wanted to get to the pub after dark, so she stopped off at the Milcana Ethiopian and Eritrean Café. She took a table inside with her back to a wall where she could see the whole restaurant as well as anyone approaching outside. She ordered beyainatu, a vegetarian dish that translated as "a bit of everything." It arrived as a pile of colorful vegetables, potatoes, curries, and a lentil stew on top of injera, a giant gray spongey pancake-like bread. To accompany it, she asked for a glass of spriss, made by pouring layers of three types of fruit juices on top of each other. There was no added water, sugar, or ice, just unadulterated, pureed juice topped with a lime squeezed over the top.

She lingered over the food savoring the beyainatu and conversing with the owner. His wife was the cook. She ordered a cup of coffee to finish off her meal and watched the area for anyone who might be lingering a bit too long. She wanted to be alert for anyone who might be hunting CIA and SOG operators. In her line of work, you only made one mistake. You weren't around long enough to make a second. She went back over the scenarios in which the agents were killed. While the stabbing of Alison Burton could be ascribed to a single assassin, the deaths of the two CIA agents watching the ambassador to the U.K. could not. It had to be a two-person team. Did that mean that Enigma had a partner? Or were the CIA agents killed by someone else? Regardless, someone had a definite hard-on for the CIA. She would be more cautious than usual on this one if that were possible. And hopefully, Arseny could shed some light on Enigma.

She finished her coffee, paid her bill, and thanked the owner for a delightful meal. The Bell and Hare Pub was two blocks west. It was a modest place with a couple of dart boards on the walls and a small outdoor area behind it. She stepped inside and scanned the place for threats. She was gratified to see the bar was only a quarter full. A group of four young guys wearing Hotspurs jerseys was sitting at a table in one corner. Based on the number of empty glasses on their table, they'd already tossed back a few pints.

Brook found a two-topper in a dark corner and melted into the shadows. A young girl waiting tables saw her and smiled as she approached.

"Evening, ma'am. what can I get you?"

"Do you have Samuel Smith's oatmeal stout?" Brook asked.

"Sure do."

"I'll take one of those, thanks."

The girl headed for the bar and placed her order. Two barkeepers were working, one of whom was Arseny. He hadn't seen her, so she kept her head down as her beer was delivered. Brook poured the beer down the side of the glass and then finished it off by giving it a creamy head. It was a silky-smooth ale with a complex palate that hinted of chocolate.

She watched the waitress as she went to check on the four Hotspur dudes. They started making lewd comments about her, but when one of them grabbed her butt, she slapped his face. He was on his feet in a second and grabbed both her arms.

"You little bitch, how about I take you out back and slip you nine inches?"

"I don't think you can get it up three times, asshole."

He turned and saw Brook standing ten feet from him.

"Fuck you, you want some of this?" he said humping the air.

She laughed. "Dude, the only way you're gonna get laid is to crawl up a chicken's ass and wait."

Brook smiled as he let go of the waitress and advanced on her. He reached for her but never made it. She shot a spear hand strike to his throat that dropped him to his knees, gasping for air. The other three guys stood up but froze when Arseny came around the bar holding an axe handle.

"You boys pay up and get your mate out of here."

They looked at each other then two of them pulled switchblades. One of them lunged at Brook. She sidestepped his thrust and grabbed his wrist. She used her free arm as a fulcrum, bent his arm down, and drove the knife into his thigh. He screamed and dropped to the floor clutching his leg. She heard the second guy's knife hit the wall as Arseny smashed his wrist with the axe handle. The loud crack meant the kid's bone was broken. The Russian followed up with a smack to his head that dropped him like a rock. The last guy put his hands up and patted the air, signaling he was through.

Arseny stared at him and motioned to the other barkeeper who appeared carrying a bottle of ice water. The two prostate boys were startled and sputtered as he dripped the ice water on their faces. The one Arseny had cuffed sat up rubbing his ear, but the one Brook punched in the throat coughed and wheezed while he held his throat.

"One of you take him and the other pick up your buddy with the knife sticking out of his leg. Might want to get him to a hospital and in the future find another pub."

They struggled with their friends and left the pub. Arseny turned to Brook and shook his head. "An uninvited guest is worse than a Tatar."

She cocked her head at him. "What does that mean?"

"You showing up unannounced is always like a bloody invasion."

"Why Arseny, I'm hurt."

"You never make social calls, so what do you want, Phoebe?" Arseny asked.

"I'd like to finish my beer and have a chat."

"About?"

"An enigma."

His face scrunched into a puzzled look. "An enigma?"

"Yes, in fact, I believe it's *the* Enigma."

"Vot der'mo," he whispered.

"Oh, shit is right. Let's sit and talk."

Arseny motioned for Brook to sit while he retrieved a frosted bottle of Zyr vodka and two ice-cold glasses from the bar. He took a seat opposite her and poured a shot for each of them. He raised his glass.

"Na zdorovje"

"Yeah, to my health," Brook said.

"You're going to need it if you're facing Enigma. So, what happened?"

"Without getting into specifics, my organization got wind that an assassin called Enigma was going after U.S. diplomats to retaliate for the sanctions on Russia."

"You're sure it's the Russians?"

"I'm not sure of anything. The point is two men were watching the house of the U.S. ambassador to the U.K. and one was shot with a sniper round while the other was hosed with a machine gun. Then, another agent was expertly stabbed in the heart from behind at the Paris ballet. What puzzles me is that these had to have been carried out by two different groups rather than a single assassin. I was told Enigma was the one contracted for the assassinations, but does she have help?"

"Why do you say Enigma is a woman?"

"DNA analysis on her blood that was left at one of her assassinations. What can you tell me about her?"

Arseny sipped his vodka. "First of all, the one who stabbed the woman was Enigma.

"How do you know that?"

"Because Enigma works alone. She never uses an accomplice."

"Can you tell me anything about her?" Brook asked.

"Not really. She works freelance and no one knows what she looks like. No one even knows her nationality, but I do know that if you're a first-call assassin, you'll most likely work through a particular broker."

"You gotta name for the broker?"

He poured himself another shot and offered the bottle to Brook, but she declined.

"The top broker for these kinds of jobs is known by the handle Circe. She's been brokering for several assassins for a long time, matching the right killer for each job, but she's also an expert at staying off the grid. No one knows who she is but be careful. She handles some of the most accomplished assassins walking the earth and is extremely well-connected to corporate, government, and criminal entities who might need the services of one of her clients. If you hurt or, God forbid, kill her, it would remove a major income resource for her clients, and they might decide you need to die."

"You got a location for Circe?"

"Paris. But you won't find her. Go to the Darkweb and search for her. Tell her you're looking for a broker. If she's interested and has a potential match with one of her clients, she'll answer. That's the only chance you have of getting close to her."

"What if she wants me to do a job?"

Arseny emptied his glass. "Then I recommend you complete it."

She finished her drink and stood. "Wonderful."

Chapter Seven

Saturday, March 18th; Paris, France; Hotel d'Aubusson

Brook's hotel, the Hotel d'Aubusson in the Saint-Germain-des-Prés neighborhood, was originally a townhouse built in the 17th century. It was known for its Old-World charm with exposed beams and parquet floors. Located a short walk from the Pont Neuf, it gave her excellent access to the entire city via the metro trains. Ironically, it also happened to be close to where she'd assassinated Farzad Majidi and Yaroslav Semenov.

First on her agenda was finding and contacting Circe. While she intended to take Arseny's advice and offer her services as a contract assassin, she was also hoping to lure either the broker or one of her people to the Hotel Dauphine Saint-Germain two blocks away where she had two rooms set up to trap them. In one of the rooms, men's clothes hung in the closet, the bed was rumpled, and there were toiletries set out in the bathroom, but the real bait was a laptop sitting on a small desk.

She'd placed several cleverly disguised mini cameras in the room that she could monitor through a second laptop. One was disguised as an HD WiFi streaming USB wall charger. A second was hidden in a clock radio next to the bed that was also equipped with night vision.

Arseny said to search on the Darkweb, but she wasn't going to do that anywhere near her hotel on the outside chance that someone could track her. She chose Milk Montparnasse for her work because it was across town and a popular spot since there were a lot of business travelers that stayed in the hotels in the area. To further cloak her location and hopefully draw Circe or an associate into her trap, she had software on her working computer that routed her searches through the laptop in the room at the Hotel Dauphine Saint-Germain, making it look like that was where her dark web search was conducted.

She got off the subway at Courcelles and adjusted her crossbody bag, so it rode across her back. An M2 MacBook Air laptop fit snuggly in the largest pocket while several small outer compartments contained protein bars, an FN Five-seveN with a threaded barrel, an FN 57 suppressor, and an extra twenty-round magazine. A Benchmade Infidel OTF auto knife was clipped to her pocket.

As she exited the station, she began looping through alleys and cross-streets, performing a series of surveillance detection runs or SDRs to pick up anyone following her. She stopped at a coffee shop and bought a large black to go then headed for the internet café across the street. She paid for an hour at one of the empty workstations and sat down to begin her search.

Brook took out her laptop and placed a small piece of tape over the camera. She booted the TOR software and then connected to the dark web through her military-grade VPN network. Although the security it offered was not absolute, it significantly decreased the chances of an unwanted party hacking into her computer.

The TOR software further increased the security level by using "onion routing," so-called because of the way it worked. Each packet of information that traveled through the TOR network was wrapped in multiple layers of encryption, like an onion. To understand how TOR worked, Brook thought of it in terms of Russian Matryoshka dolls. If she wanted to send a message that only her handler could access, TOR would place it in the smallest doll and assemble the nested set. She would send the set to a hypothetical Agent One who could only open the largest doll where a message would tell him to send the remaining nest to Agent Two. Agent Two could only open the second largest doll where a message would tell him to send the remaining nest to Agent three. Eventually, the last agent would be instructed to forward the smallest doll to her handler who was the only one who could open it.

As the number of dolls or "nodes" increased, more layers of security were added with each agent knowing only where to send the next smaller doll. In theory, it was an extremely secure system, but as the best hackers always said, nothing was 100% secure.

She connected to the remote computer and slipped into the dark web. Entering it was like stepping into a macabre version of Alice's Wonderland. You could buy credit card numbers, drugs, guns, counterfeit money, stolen credentials, and software that helped you break into other people's computers. You could hire hackers to attack businesses for you, or even an assassin to kill someone, which was why you wanted your access to the dark web to be as secure as possible.

Brook set up a search for assassins offering their services and a list of sites appeared. Many of the listings claimed multiple spectacular kills. Others promised no collateral damage or that they used methods that made the kill look like an accident. But one innocuous listing made no claims for anything. It simply billed itself as a problem removal service.

Circe.

She opened the website and saw two questions. The site operator wanted to know the target and the timing required for the hit. It stated that if the job was accepted, the information for an account would be sent to the buyer who was to transfer $250,000 into it. Once payment was received, the hit would be executed. After completion of the job, a second payment equal to the first would be expected.

Brook composed a message, ignoring the questions, and said she was an ex-Israeli kidon looking to go freelance. She left an email address where she could be contacted and laid a trail back to her honeypot hotel. Seconds later, she received an automated reply that said she would be contacted within forty-eight hours if the task was acceptable. It was an automated system set up to answer inquiries for hits, but someone would read the message and either ignore her or contact her.

She logged off the internet and packed up her laptop then zipped up her jacket and performed another set of SDRs before heading to the subway. She expected someone to follow the trail to her room at the Hotel Dauphine Saint-Germain at which point she hoped it would be Circe herself or someone who could lead her to the broker.

Chapter Eight

Sunday, March 19th; Paris, France; Hotel Dauphine Saint-Germain

Brook was usually fastidious about her diet, but she had a weakness for *pain au chocolate* when in Paris. The croissant oozed with butter, and they didn't skimp on the dark chocolate filling. She bought two earlier that morning along with an American-size cup of coffee to enjoy while she watched her laptop, monitoring the room down the hall.

If Circe or one of her associates decided to visit her room, Brook figured it would be during the day when business people were at meetings. She watched as a cleaning person finished tidying up the room. As she went to leave, a woman who bore a distinct resemblance to Natalie Portman in her role in *V for Vendetta* slipped by the cleaning woman. She was a petite five feet but appeared trim in the way a gymnast looks. The stranger said something to the cleaning lady that must have reassured her that it was her room. The stranger closed the door and pulled on a pair of plastic gloves as she scanned the room. Brook watched her go to the closet and check the clothes then went to the desk and shuffled through the stack of papers Brook had left. She took a seat at the desk and pulled a small, black device that resembled a portable hard drive from her pocket. She opened the laptop and plugged the device into the Thunderbolt port. After typing a command, she sat back and watched as presumably, the drive-like device broke the password protection. Minutes later she leaned forward and began scanning the files. After five minutes, she removed the device, pocketed it, and closed the laptop.

Brook took a microdot tracking device from her pocket and peeled off the adhesive back. She stood and cracked the door to her room, watching for the stranger to exit her honeypot. As soon as the woman stepped out, Brook left her room and made a show of checking to make sure her door was locked then followed the stranger to the elevator. She purposely hung back so the elevator would arrive before she reached it. As soon as the doors opened and the stranger stepped in, she took off to catch it before the doors closed.

She timed it so the doors closed on her shoulders then stumbled forward, bumping the stranger, and knocking them both into the back wall.

"Oh my gosh, I'm so sorry," Brook said. "I guess I didn't time that right."

"*Aucun problème,*" the stranger said. "You are American?"

"Yes, it shows, huh?"

The stranger laughed. "No, I can tell by your accent. Are you here on business or pleasure?"

"Pleasure. It's a kind of celebration. I came here for my honeymoon, but it wasn't a very pleasant memory because I found out my husband was having an affair the whole time we were engaged. My divorce from his sorry ass was finalized two weeks ago, so I decided to treat myself to the vacation I should've had, but this time without anyone to drag me down."

The stranger clucked her tongue. "Men can be such, how do you say, assholes?"

"Ya got that right."

The elevator doors opened, and they stepped out.

"Well, I hope you enjoy your stay this time more than the last," the stranger said.

"I'm sure I will."

The stranger climbed into a cab while Brook walked north toward the Seine. She checked her cellphone and saw that the tracker she'd placed on the back of the Stranger's jacket was working.

Whoever she was, she had a certain elementary degree of spy craft by fooling the cleaning woman and getting into Brook's honeypot room. The device she used to break into the laptop was also something that spoke of more experience than just answering emails and inquiries about representation.

Brook noticed that the red dot representing the stranger was now behind her. She continued past the Hotel d'Aubusson toward the Quai du Conti. As she turned left, she caught a glimpse of the stranger following her.

"Ah, so you're the suspicious type, huh?" she whispered.

Brook kept walking west until she came to the Musée d'Orsay. She stood in line briefly and bought a ticket. As she entered the museum, she checked to her left and saw the stranger continue walking west, apparently having decided Brook was not a threat.

The museum happened to be one of her favorites because it housed an impressive collection of impressionist and expressionist art, particularly the paintings of Georges Seurat, her favorite. After an hour of browsing, she checked her phone to see where the stranger was. It appeared she was no longer on the move and had stopped in the fashionable Marais district in the 4th arrondissement. The area was filled with hip boutiques, galleries, and gay bars. The grassy Place des Vosges housed elegant arcades and the Musée Victor Hugo where the writer used to live. Apartments in the area were pricey, but when you work for people who pull in a half million Euros or more per hit, your commissions were probably more than enough to afford it.

Brook left the museum and headed east down the Quai du Conti back to the Hotel d'Aubusson. She changed into black, six-pocket pants made of stretchy Freeflex material and a black cotton turtleneck then threaded her Craft holster through her belt. She checked her FN Five-seveN, positioning it behind her right hip, and dropped its suppressor in her left front pocket. She slipped into a dark gray zip-front hoodie and clipped her Benchmade Infidel knife to her right front pocket then headed for the Saint-Michelle Notre Dame subway station. She took the train, switching several times, looking for tails, and finally got off at the Rambuteau stop. She checked her phone as she climbed the stairs to the street then checked left and right before starting a series of SDRs.

The Marais was one of the most popular *quartiers* in Paris. It was famous for old-world charm; narrow cobblestone streets; hidden courtyards with tranquil gardens; a multitude of mansions called *hôtels particuliers*; and a thriving gallery and cafe culture. Historically, the area, built over marshland, was the neighborhood of choice for the aristocracy from the 13th to the 17th centuries.

What the Marais district didn't have were the *grand boulevards* or the big parks found in much of the rest of the city. It was all small, maze-like streets and gave a glimpse of what Paris looked like two to four hundred years ago and made it the perfect place for an assassin or an agent to hide.

The tracker took Brook to an impressive two-flat on the Rue Charles V. The stone exterior looked like it had been sandblasted to reveal its original white color. Brook checked the street then crossed to the stranger's building and skipped up the stairs to the front door. She studied her cell phone while checking for observers then took out a small device the size of a pack of playing cards and held it against the door's locking mechanism. A buzzing followed by a click indicated it was open.

There were only two apartments, so Brook stood next to the first-floor unit while watching the app. Before she could check it, she heard a door above her open and close. She faded into the shadows under the stairs and pressed her back against the wall. Light steps descended the stairs and then pushed through the door. Brook stepped out of her hiding place and checked to see who'd left. She smiled because it was the stranger. She had a messenger bag over her shoulder.

Brook crept up the stairs to the second-floor unit, stepping on the outside of them to minimize creaking, and stopped before the stranger's door. She flicked a switch on her cellphone-like device, which converted it to a portable EMP generator that could send a transient electromagnetic disturbance, radiating outward from its epicenter, disrupting electronic devices like security systems.

She took out a set of lock picks and had the door open in thirty seconds. The one drawback to using the EMP generator was that it would fry all the electronics in the apartment, including the burner phone in her pocket, so Brook cracked the door and checked to see if the stranger had a security system that if fried by the EMP might alert the stranger to an intruder. Thankfully, she did not, so Brook pulled on a pair of plastic gloves and a black balaclava and entered, closing and locking the door behind her. She began exploring the apartment and hopefully, getting one step closer to finding Enigma.

Chapter Nine

Sunday, March 19th; Paris, France; A Le Marais Apartment

As Brook expected, the apartment was spectacular. The black slate floor contrasted with white walls. A bright pink chaise lounge next to a set of tall windows faced a white sofa and flanking chairs. Throw pillows in the same shade of pink gave the décor some pop. The apartment even had a working gas fireplace. A desk was next to a window and black shelves lined with books covered one wall. An unopened bill addressed to Ms. Elise Garnier lay on the desk. She checked the room for weapons, but the only thing of note was a letter opener that Brook hid behind the books.

Beyond the living area, a six-person dining table divided it from the kitchen where a black marble counter was set off by white cabinets and stainless-steel appliances. A bottle of white wine was one of the few things in the fridge. She removed the knives from the drawers and dropped them behind the books with the letter opener. While the oven was empty, the microwave held a Glock 26. She dropped the magazine and cleared the chamber. She removed the bullets and pocketed them then shoved the empty magazine into the gun and set it back in the microwave.

Brook climbed an open staircase to a loft where the bedroom and an *en suite* were located. A king bed with an enormous white headboard dominated the room. The wall behind it was black with a broad ribbon of black and white floral wallpaper running along the top. The bathroom was typical with a shower, tub, toilet, and dual sinks. She went through the bathroom drawers as well as the nightstand and found another Glock 26 in each. She repeated the process of removing the bullets and replacing the empty magazines in the guns then put them back in their original places.

She returned to the living area and checked the closets. One was for coats, but the other housed a vacuum cleaner, buckets, and a mop as well as cleaning chemicals. Brook stepped into the closet and moved the vacuum to one side, clearing a space for her to stand. She screwed the suppressor on her Five seveN and shoved it into her waistband. She closed the closet and went to the windows overlooking the street to watch for the stranger.

The thing that stood out about the apartment was that there was no indication the person living here had a job. No briefcase or backpack, no file cabinets, and just a couple of pens and pencils in the desk drawer. Of course, if she was an agent for top assassins, she wouldn't need any other employment, nor would she need any office supplies, rather just a few weapons in case of an emergency. Everything would be on her laptop which Brook assumed was protected by some heavyweight encryption.

An hour later she saw the stranger whom she now knew as Elise Garnier coming down the street. Brook moved to the utility closet and closed the door. Minutes later she heard Elise enter and relock the door. Her footsteps clicked on the slate floor as she passed Brook's hiding place and went to the kitchen. A sucking sound indicated she was getting something from the refrigerator. The clinking of glass told Brook she'd retrieved the bottle of wine and a glass. Elise's footsteps passed by again and Brook heard her climbing the stairs.

Several minutes later, Brook heard the shower running, so she left her hiding place and crept up the stairs. Steam rolled out of the bathroom and Elise's naked body was silhouetted behind the frosted shower door. Brook pressed herself into the wall outside the bathroom and waited.

Ten minutes later, Elise came out of the bathroom naked but unaware of Brook until she grabbed her by the throat with her right hand and squeezed. Her eyes widened when she saw Brook and her mouth opened to scream, but it clamped close as she squeezed tighter and pushed her back into the bathroom.

Once inside, Brook slammed the woman against the wall and, using her left hand, thrust the tips of her locked fingers against her abdomen, an inch below her sternum. Elise gasped at the intense pain and instinctively tensed her stomach against the attack, but it was to no avail. Brook's fingertips were pushing against the *linea alba*, the narrow strip of connective tissue that ran vertically down the center of the wall of the abdominal muscle and she knew from experience how debilitating the resulting waves of agony and nausea could be. Elise's hands tried to grip Brook's arm, but the pain weakened her, and she didn't have the strength to push her away or fight.

Brook held her for a few more minutes then shoved her onto the toilet. The pressure of her finger thrust weakened her more than she expected because the woman slid off the stool onto the floor and pulled her knees to her chest, curling into a fetal position. Brook drew her suppressed gun and aimed it at Elise's forehead.

Elise raised her hand, palm out, toward her. "Wait, please."

Brook leaned against the wall, careful to stay out of range of a kick even though the woman looked incapacitated.

"Hello, Elise."

"Who…are you," she asked, grunting in pain.

"Someone you don't ever want to meet."

Elise pulled herself upright and lifted herself onto the toilet. Brook expected panic to warp her features, but aside from the pain of her blow, she looked angry.

"Va te faire foutre, Chienne. Qui es-tu et pourquoi es-tu ici? "

"Ooo, such language. To answer your questions, my name is inconsequential but I'm here to get a few answers to some questions that I have. In the meantime, be polite and speak English."

"Va te faire enculer!"

Brook aimed the pistol at Elise's right ankle and pulled the trigger. The woman screamed and grabbed her leg.

"First of all, telling me to go fuck myself is impolite and secondly, any, more outbursts like that and I'll put bullets in your shoulders and hips where they won't kill you, but they'll leave you crippled for life, *Capisce?*"

Brook took a towel off a rack and tossed it at Elise. "Use that to wrap your leg."

She gave Brook a murderous look. "Ask your questions and get out."

"Sure. So, Elise, or should I call you Circe?"

"Circe…?" She grit her teeth and groaned. "You're pissing on the wrong tree, lady."

"And why is that?"

"Because Circe is the broker for some of the deadliest people in the world and you don't want them coming after you."

"True, but I'm only looking for one of her clients. The assassin is called Enigma and if you know anything about her, it might be in your best interests to tell me.

Elise frowned. "Enigma?"

"Hmm, maybe your English isn't so good. *Parlez-moi de l'Enigma.*"

Elise winced. "You think I know anything? All my communications with the one you called Circe and people like you are done through the dark web. But if I were you, I'd drop your search and get out of Paris fast. You don't want to piss off Circe."

"Ah, well poking the bear is part of my job. You have a nice apartment. They must pay you well," Brook said.

She grunted from the pain. "They pay me well to screen inquiries and forward the ones that pass my initial inspection to them."

"So, you've never seen Circe or Enigma?"

"Of course not. That's not how these things work. This way, as you are now learning, I can't help you, nor can I betray them."

"How do I contact Circe?"

"You can't." Her breathing had transitioned to panting. "I send… potential contracts to a blind site…then check back…to see if the contract's been accepted. If so, I…forward the bank information to the client and…drop a message on the site when payment's been received."

"Well, just tell them I'm looking for them."

Brook removed the suppressor from her gun and dropped it in her pocket. As she turned to go, Elise reached behind the toilet tank and used her left hand to draw a Beretta nano. She raised the gun to fire, but Brook was faster and kicked the gun out of her hands then followed with a kick to her stomach that knocked the wind out of her. Brook grabbed her arm and pulled her off the toilet onto her stomach. She put her knee on the back of her neck and pulled a pair of flexicuffs from her pocket then secured Elise's hands behind her back.

Brook rolled her onto her back and grabbed her chin. "Your tradecraft leaves something to be desired. You're lucky I don't kill you, but I need you to send a message to your colleagues. Just tell them that I'm looking for them."

Brook left her lying on the bathroom floor and descended the stairs. She left the apartment but didn't remove her balaclava until she was at the door to the street in case there were CCTV cameras. Darkness had fallen as she checked the street through the window in the door. She pulled a ballcap from her pocket and tugged the brim low over her face then left the building.

Brook started a complex series of SDRs on the way back to her hotel. She hadn't learned anything useful from Elise, so she was no closer to finding Circe or Enigma. The only thing she could do was wait for instructions from the agency. Hopefully, they could provide more information the next time they contacted her.

Chapter Ten

Monday, March 20th; Paris, France; Les Deux Magots

Les Deux Magots was one of the oldest and best-known cafés in Paris. Located in the Saint-Germain-des-Prés area of Paris, it played an important role in Parisian cultural life. In the past, it was frequented by many famous artists and writers including Louis Aragon, Jean Giraudoux, Picasso, Fernand Léger, and Hemingway. It was a past meeting place for existentialists like Sartre and Beauvoir. Its name meant "two Chinese figurines" and originated from a sign over a novelty shop that occupied the same location a century and a half ago.

Brook grabbed a newspaper and took an outdoor table against the windows at the café. She draped her hooded trenchcoat over the chair next to her. A dwarf man with a full black beard and hair that was longish on top and faded down the sides, and wearing a green apron appeared and gave her a stylish bow.

"Bonjour Eliana. Comment allons-nous aujourd'hui?"

"I'm doing fine, Henri," Brook said. She leaned over and let him kiss her once on each cheek. He knew her as Eliana Azarolla.

"How is your novel coming, Ms. Eliana?" he asked.

"Still pitching it to agents. No luck yet."

He leaned forward, put his hand next to his mouth, and spoke conspiratorially. "Les Deux Magots is a hot spot for literary types. I can drop your name to several of them if you like?"

"A reviewer said I need to polish it a bit more, so I'll do that and then tell you when to pass my name around.

"But of course. Anything for one of my favorite customers. Are you doing anything exciting today?"

"I going to spend some time in the Musee d'Orsay. I'm partial to the impressionists and I find it's a great place to find inspiration to break through writer's block."

"Yes, yes, and the French impressionists were the greatest. My favorite is Henri de Toulouse-Lautrec. He spun around and motioned to himself. "He, too, was one of the little people, and I am named after him."

Brook grinned. "I love his color palette."

"Will you be having your usual café crème and *pain au chocolate*?"

"Yes, please, Henri."

"Excellent. I will be right back."

Brook always enjoyed the delightful little man. She'd been coming to Les Deux Magots for five years he'd always waited on her. He was a beloved fixture at the cafe.

Henri returned with the food and drinks. "You have a glorious day to enjoy your breakfast and the museum. Will you spend your whole day there?"

"Most of it, but I may wander over to the Louvre."

"You must also visit the Musée de l'Orangerie in the gardens of the Tuileries. It's within walking distance of the Louvre. It has a fine set of Monet's water lilies, as well as works by Renoir, Cézanne, Rousseau, Matisse, Picasso, Utrillo, and others."

"Thank you, Henri. I'll make a point to visit it."

Brook took a bite of her croissant and sipped the coffee, thinking about what started this hunt. The initial impetus for sending CIA agents to watch over U.S. diplomats was the flash drive that indicated they were being specifically targeted by Enigma, who was supposedly hired by the Russians. These days when someone wanted to kill you, there wasn't much you could do to save yourself. With the kinds of rifles available on the black market, nobody in the world was safe against an assassin's bullet. But in this case, the only person killed by a sniper's bullet was one of the CIA agents guarding the U.S. ambassador to the U.K. All of those on the list retrieved by the two CIA agents were still alive and there were no indications attempts had been made on their lives.

Enigma's call sign was appropriate. The word was defined as a difficult problem that baffles and cannot be explained. It was never truer than with this assassin. And with the paucity of information on her, it meant Brook had to be doubly vigilant.

As she sat sipping her coffee, it began to rain. It started as a soft patter on the awning protecting the outdoor seating area but gradually crescendoed into a silvery downpour that sounded like steel balls hitting the fabric. Most of the patrons scurried inside, but Brook stayed at her table.

Henri appeared with a frown on his face. "Eliana, don't you want to come inside?"

"I don't know, Henri, I've always liked the rain and the sound of it as it beats on the roof and windows," she said. "It's like a cleansing shower for the soul of the city."

"Ah, you are a poet."

"No, it's just something left over from my childhood."

"Something good, I hope."

She smiled at him. "Yes, Henri, something very good."

"Do you want me to call you a cab to the Musay d'Orsay?

"No, my coat and shoes are waterproof, so when it lets up a bit, I'll walk."

Henri pulled out a chair and sat across from her. "Where did you grow up?"

"Cambridge, England. Both my mother and father were scientists with Pfizer, working on vaccine development."

"Doctors?"

"Yes, they left Pfizer and moved to Chicago where they started their own company. They're credited with developing a pan-SARS CoV-2 vaccine."

"*Mon dieu,! Ils sont célèbres!*"

"Yes, I suppose they are famous, but it came with a cost."

"How so?"

"The anti-vaxx movement came out against them. My father was murdered by two of them and my mother eventually sold her shares in the company and left the country."

"I'm so sorry. Where is your mother now?"

Brook smiled. "Good question. She made over one billion dollars from her stock sale, so now she travels around the world visiting interesting places."

"I think it must be healing for her," Henri said. He glanced at the street. "The rain is less now so you are sure you want to walk?"

"I am, Henri. It was good to chat with you."

Henri took her hand. "And with you." He rose and disappeared into the café as Brook walked toward the museum. It was a perfect day to peruse the paintings and sculptures. Certainly better than standing in the rain waiting for her agency's next communication.

Chapter Eleven

Wednesday, March 22nd; Berlin, Germany; A Flea Market

Brook had been sipping her room service coffee when her Kerberos phone buzzed with a text. The message simply said *Gare de l'est* station; SNCF to Berlin; 10:20; fourth car. It meant she would receive an update on her assignment on the train. Brook preferred trains for international travel because they gave her more options. Air travel was faster but was also the most-watched, regulated, and best way of getting picked up by undesirables. While no one was going to kill her on a flight, boarding and deplaning were choke points that she avoided.

She field-stripped her gun and ditched it in several trash bins before heading to the train station. She didn't want to cross a border carrying a gun in case she was stopped. She had no idea why the agency was sending her to Germany, but hopefully, they had more information on Enigma.

But oddly no one approached her on the train. Brook got a room at the Garden Living Hotel, about a mile north of the Brandenburg Gate. It was also about a quarter of a mile from the Berlin Main Station and only six hundred feet from the Naturkundemuseum Underground Station. There were plenty of restaurants, cafés, and bars along Oranienburger Straße, just a half mile away. But its main attractiveness was that it was off the beaten path where fortune-hunting assassins might look. And for the sake of security, she also had a room at the Westin Grand that she didn't plan on using.

She traveled light. A backpack or a small rollaboard were her preferences. A change of clothes and some toiletries were all she required. Her practice was to change clothes often and wear items bought in her area of operation to help her blend in. While she carried cash, she also used expensive watches and jewelry that could be worn across borders without raising suspicions and then sold them for cash at her destination. She had safe deposit boxes in London, Paris, Zurich, Amsterdam, and Brussels that the agency didn't know about. Each held extra passports, cash, and weapons that were for emergency use. Procuring weapons and cash was not difficult for someone with her connections. But regardless of how well she might know one of her contacts, she trusted no one. She expected to be betrayed at any face-to-face meeting and took appropriate preparations to avoid injury or death.

She'd stopped by the Paris bank where she had a safe deposit box that contained a Swiss passport in the name of Dylan Payne with a photo that showed her with a blond crew cut. Before she left Paris, she picked up a Cold Steel Nightshade knife with a four-inch blade made of Grivory, the latest in fiberglass reinforced plastic and stronger than even super tough Zytel. They were UV and heat stabilized, making them impervious to the elements. Most importantly, they were undetectable by X-rays and magnetometers if she had to go through security.

But a knife wasn't going to protect her from other assassins that might be hunting her, so she needed to contact an old acquaintance. Brook found what she was looking for in a flea market located in a seedy area of the city. It was a place that sold fake designer clothes, knock-off watches, bootleg movies, cheap shoes, and electronics. There were three stalls selling what she wanted, namely mobile phones that the owners had sold for cash to buy the latest model or that had been stolen and unlocked so they could be sold. She kept her Kerberos for communications with her handler. She found one she liked. It was a cheap flip phone. Anything fancier risked compromise. She liked secondhand phones with minutes that she could prepay for because they were close to untraceable. She paid cash for it and a beat-up charger then stopped off at a coffee shop to charge it. She bought a large black and sipped it slowly while she watched the young people around her staring at their laptops. By the time she'd finished the coffee, the phone was charged sufficiently for her needs.

She had one call to make and would ditch the phone as soon as she finished. While Brook had few friends outside the agency, she did have access to many individuals around the world who could offer skills and services to her. All of them had been developed during her professional career. One of them was a supplier who went by the moniker of Hanna, even though it was a man.

She dialed a number she hadn't called in two years. Eight rings sounded before the party answered.

"Who is this?"

The male voice that answered sounded like someone who'd smoked two packs a day for decades, but Brook knew it was because two years ago he'd taken a bullet to the throat during a deal to supply her with needed armament. She'd saved his life after she'd eliminated the three men who tried to take her equipment and money for themselves. The man she knew as Hanna was five and a half feet tall and skinny enough to dodge raindrops as he ran across a parking lot in a storm and still be dry by the time he reached his car.

"This is a woman to whom you owe your life," she said.

"I don't owe anyone anything," he said.

"Then search your memory for one who dialed the emergency number while keeping you from bleeding out until the medics got there."

"Oh, geezus," he whispered. "I hoped I'd never hear from you again."

"Not a very nice thing to say about your savior, Hanna."

"I don't go by that name anymore."

"Regardless, I need some equipment."

"Why would you think I'm still in that business?"

"Because I know you, Hanna. Your real name is Alain DuBois, and you have a very nice apartment in Kreuzberg that didn't come cheap."

"*Scheisse*," he whispered. "What do you want?"

"Not much. Just an FN Five-seveN with a GSL57 suppressor and three extra twenty-round magazines. I'd also like an FN P90 with an extra fifty rounder, a suppressor, and two boxes of two hundred rounds for the FNs."

"Not much, my ass. But you're in luck. You did save my life and removed a major pain in my arse by killing those assholes, so I can get you the FNs."

"Ah, Hanna, you're a wizard. How soon can you get the equipment to me?"

"Where are you?"

"I have a room at the Westin Grand."

"I'll drop a key to a locker at the Hauptbahnhof station at the front desk tonight. For security reasons, the lockers are located in the car park outside the main building."

She disconnected, dropped the phone on the ground, and crushed it with her boot. She hopped on a tram that would take her near her hotel and took an aisle seat. It had been a long time since she'd been in the city. She was five years old when the wall came down and graffiti-covered remnants of it were spaced around the old border. Her eyes roved constantly over the passengers, looking for threats, but no one stood out. Most were fixated on their phones or reading newspapers.

But then the door to an adjoining car opened and a man entered. Everything about him was wrong and said trouble. On Brook's checklist of telltale threat signs, he ticked every box. He was in his late thirties or early forties and in shape but not bulked up. His hair was short and graying at the temples and he had a three-day stubble of beard. He was just shy of six feet tall and went about 175. He wore clothes that looked to be a size too large but gave him freedom of movement and allowed him to hide a weapon. His shoes had a decent tread for running or fighting and his hip-length leather jacket was partially unzipped. But the real tell was the pair of thin, black gloves made of supple leather that he wore. The weather was cool, but no one was wearing gloves.

The man wasn't aware that he'd been made, because there were dozens of people on the tram distracting him. By the time his gaze reached Brook, she'd already assessed the threat and diverted her eyes to look out the window watching his reflection as he approached. He wouldn't shoot her on the tram, nor would he use a knife with so many witnesses around. The only weapon Brook had was her ceramic knife, but she was an expert at knife fighting, so she felt she had a slight advantage…as long as he didn't pull a gun and shoot her.

Brook waited as the train stopped at Alexanderplatz and when the trainman announced the next stop, she darted out the door and jogged across the plaza toward the entrance to the underground station. As she reached the stairs, she glanced behind her and saw that the man from the tram was following her. She took the stairs down two at a time and ducked into the women's washroom. She drew her knife from its forearm sheath and waited. She knew she had to end this quickly because her opponent was bigger and stronger than her, and knife fights could devolve into a bloodbath, which would make it hard to get back to her hotel unnoticed if she was bleeding from a dozen cuts.

Several minutes later, the door burst open, and the assassin shot into the room holding a suppressed Glock 19. He didn't expect Brook's sudden attack as she sliced her blade across the wrist that held the gun. It clattered to the floor and before he could react, she grabbed the front of his jacket and stabbed him four times in his stomach then spun him around and slashed his throat. She kicked him behind his knee and dropped him to the floor. His blood fountained across the tile away from Brook. His unseeing eyes wore an expression that said he never expected a woman to kill him.

Quickly, she grabbed a paper towel and wiped off her blade then sheathed it. She grabbed the suppressed Glock and took an extra magazine from his shoulder holster. She stuffed the gun in her waistband behind her back and dropped the suppressor in one of her cargo pockets. She pulled her jacket over the gun and left the washroom. She took a series of trains then went to the surface and took a tram followed by two cabs before returning to her hotel.

She checked her clothes for blood and, after confirming they were clean, headed straight for the restaurant where she ordered a light dinner and a glass of Courvoisier XO cognac. She sipped, trying to calm the adrenaline rush that was gradually leaving her system after the altercation in the subway washroom. How the hell did that assassin know who she was and that she'd be there? Had someone breached the SOG servers? The identities of their agents were closely guarded secrets, but the fact that the guy she killed knew what she looked like and where she'd be was a major concern. Her salmon salad was delivered, and she picked at it, thinking about the situation.

She raised the snifter to take a sip of the cognac and frowned. A man wearing a charcoal gray suit, white shirt, and black oxfords with thick rubber soles approached her table. He was a shade over six feet with a lean physique, medium-length gray hair, and dark eyes behind black non-prescription glasses. His face was unremarkable, and his overall appearance was forgettable, designed to blend in.

He took a seat opposite Brook and when the waiter appeared, he pointed to Brook's drink.

"I'll have what she's drinking."

His lips quirked in the beginning of a smile. "Hello, Zealot."

"Hello, Dasher. What brings you to Berlin?"

His cognac was delivered. He waved the snifter under his nose and arched an eyebrow at her. "I've been sent to help you find Enigma and protect your fine ass."

"Protect my ass? Really?" Brook asked. "Why do I need you to protect my ass?"

Like Brook, Dasher was a SOG operator. He was five years older than her and very experienced. She knew him from her work in Afghanistan and Iraq. Several times he'd made a pass at her, but she rejected him every time. She also knew that while he could be a boorish ass, he was one of the best.

"Are you not aware that Enigma is targeting people like us?"

"Why would the powers that be think I need your help with this?" Brook asked.

"Mine is not to reason why. Mine is but to do and try not to die. Do you need equipment?"

"I'm picking it up tomorrow."

He nodded. "What time do you want me here tomorrow?" Dasher asked.

"I'll leave here about seven to pick up the locker key where my equipment is stored."

"I'll be outside and follow you." He stood. "You be careful, Zealot."

"I will."

Brook watched him leave. He didn't finish his drink, so she combined it with hers, leaned back, and decided this called for a conversation with her handler. She lingered over her dinner for another half hour then retired to her room. She took out her Kerberos phone and input a series of numbers. Her handler answered after four rings.

"Input?" he asked

"Charlie, Echo, Foxtrot, Sierra, Victor, X-ray. Counter?"

"Whiskey, Tango, Golf, Lima, Oscar, Mike. What's up Zealot?"

"Just wondering about this next assignment I was supposed to be given."

"We're working on some new information. Just stay in Paris until further notice."

"Paris? I got a text that sent me to Berlin. In fact, I met up with an assassin earlier today and barely escaped with my life. He wasn't so lucky. And tonight, Dasher showed up and told me he was sent to assist me."

Her handler was silent.

"Hector, are you there?" she asked.

"Get out of there now, Zealot. No one sent you to Berlin nor was Dasher sent to help you. Don't take a plane or train. Rent a car. Use one of your private IDs and credit cards that the agency doesn't know about."

"Shit," Brook whispered.

"Go! Now!"

Chapter Twelve

Wednesday, March 22nd; Berlin, Germany; The Garden Living Hotel

She took the stairs to the lobby then went to the concierge's desk and inquired about renting a car tonight and the location of any all-night pharmacies in the area. He said he'd have a car brought around for her then directed her to a nearby pharmacy She found the drugstore and grabbed a shopping basket. She picked up a Wahl Clipper Self-Cut Compact Personal Haircutting Kit, bleach, a set of brushes and combs, plastic garbage bags, the lightest blonde hair dye she could find, and a small, hand-held, cordless vacuum. She paid for her purchases and returned to her hotel room.

She spread two of the garbage bags on the sink and floor and stripped to her underwear. She took the haircutter and settled on a number six guard that would leave her hair three-quarter-inches long on top and tapered it to a four on the sides. Leaning over the sink, she used a pair of scissors to trim her hair down to a manageable length for the clippers. She started with the number six guard and did her whole head. Working slowly, she used the number four clippers to begin the taper on the sides and back to complete her new cut.

She gathered up the hair and placed it in plastic bags then went over the sink, floor, toilet, and towels with the vacuum. Next, she used the bleach to turn herself into a blonde. Last of all, she used the blond hair dye on her eyebrows. It was safer than the bleach and gave her the result she wanted. When she was finished, she looked like Dylan Payne, the woman in the passport she retrieved from her Paris safe deposit box.

She changed back into her khaki cargo pants, a black tee, and her Ryders. She packed up the bag with her hair clippings, towels, and pharmacy purchases and stuffed it into her rollaboard and then gave the room a once-over to make sure it was clean. She shrugged into her gray Arc'teryx weatherproof jacket and pulled a black slouchy beanie over her head. She checked out online, grabbed her suitcase and backpack, and then took the stairs to the lobby. As she approached the concierge he smiled and handed her the keys to a VW Golf that was parked outside. She handed him a fifty Euro bill and pushed through the doors.

She blipped the locks on the doors, tossed her backpack on the passenger seat, and slipped behind the wheel. She cruised out of the hotel's drive and headed for the A9. She stopped at an all-night gas station and bought two large, black coffees for the road. It was a nine-hour drive to where she had an apartment that contained a stash of weapons. Before she left the station, she pulled out her Kerberos and dialed her handler.

He answered and they input their codes and counter codes.

"What the hell, Hector? What's going on?"

"I don't know, Zealot. I've contacted Langley and alerted them to the possibility that we've either been hacked, or we have a mole. I also inquired why Dasher was sent to back you up. At this point, I don't know anything. Did you get out?"

"I'm on the move right now," she said. "I'm going to turn off my phone and pull the SIMS card so the agency can't track me. I'll be going to burners, so don't ignore a strange number."

"I won't," he said.

"I gotta ask you something."

"Fire away."

"Earlier today, I was attacked by an assassin who knew what I looked like and where I'd be. How does that happen?"

"How do you know he was looking for you?"

"Because he got on the tram I was riding and was obviously searching for me. He followed me when I got off and tried to kill me in the lady's washroom."

"How would he know what you looked like?"

"You tell me, Hector?"

He was silent for a few seconds then swore. "Shit, we have a mole."

"I think that's the only answer that makes sense. I mean, it's not like I go around advertising who I am."

"I'll bounce this upstairs ASAP."

"One more thing," Brook said. "The information on the flash drive you guys are concerned about is strange."

"What do you mean?"

"Well, you guys think the list was intended to draw agency personnel into killing fields, but I think your conclusions may be oversimplifying things."

"How so?"

"Think about it. Have you considered the possibility that there may be two separate contracts here?"

"I don't get it."

"One of the contracts is for the deaths of CIA operators, but it's embedded in the contract for the diplomats. The diplomatic contract does two things. It draws the CIA into a killing field, but then when the agents scatter to avoid getting killed, the second contract kicks in, which is for the diplomats. So, I think you still need to watch the diplomatic targets."

"Interesting theory."

"It's more than fucking interesting, Hector. Our agency is under attack and it's my life that's on the line. Is anybody guarding the ambassadors?"

"Just DSS agents."

"Which means they're unguarded. Diplomatic Security Service agents are more like close protection bodyguards. They have no experience protecting their charges from killers of this caliber. So, I predict you're going to see those on the list start dying, probably at the hands of the one called Enigma. She probably has the diplomatic contract. But agents like me are being hunted by the whole assassin community. And they have information on our movements and what we look like. The key questions are where they got their information on us and who issued these contracts because we need to find them and take them down."

"I'll discuss it with Langley as soon as we finish our conversation."

"There's more. Something felt off when Dasher approached me tonight. I need you to check out his handler and see if he was sent to partner with me. It could be he's being duped too. Alternatively…"

"He could be a rogue," Hector said. "But why? I'll look into that, too."

"I'm going dark now. You won't be able to contact me, but I'll check back in a day or two and see what you've found out."

"Good luck, Zealot, and stay safe."

They disconnected. She scanned a hotel app and made a reservation at Zurich's Storchen hotel for a week in the name of Dylan Payne, even though she had no intention of staying there. She had an apartment in a town forty kilometers south of the city.

Aarburg, where Brook's apartment was located, was a picturesque town on the banks of the Aare River, a tributary of the Rhine. It was considered one of Switzerland's most beautiful villages. The town was dominated by a narrow, elongated ridge of rock, on which the fortress of Aarburg sat. A reformed church sat on the same terrace as the fortress. The town's location was convenient for Brook because it was only a fifty-minute trip to Zurich by train or car. And her apartment's purchase price was considerably less than something similar in Zurich.

Her apartment was a second-floor two-bedroom flat with a living area furnished with a pale blue sectional on a burgundy and blue patterned carpet. A matching easy chair was off to one side. The kitchen had cherry cabinets with a stove and oven, a microwave, and an espresso machine. The master bedroom had a king bed and closets that stretched across one wall. A quarter of them held clothes, but the rest were devoted to storing her weapons which included an FN P90 personal defense weapon, a .22 FN502, and a 9mm FN509 with matching suppressors for both the pistols and the P90. The closet also contained a Nemesis Arms .308 Valkyrie rifle disassembled and stored in a backpack along with flash-bang and pepper spray grenades.

Brook checked her watch and estimated she'd get into Aarburg at about eight AM. When she arrived, she planned to take a nap, shower, and get something to eat. Then, after arming herself, she'd take the train to Zurich to check into the Storchen hotel. Afterward, she'd pay a visit to the bank where one of her safe deposit boxes was located and remove a new passport and credit cards. There was a café on the bridge over the river next to the hotel that led to the city hall building. She planned to sit there and sip café crème while she watched for anyone showing unusual interest in the hotel. The life of anyone showing too much curiosity would be shortened by several decades.

Chapter Thirteen

Thursday, March 23rd; Zurich, Switzerland; The Storchen Hotel

Tomas and Karel Bozik were twin brothers and as identical twins, were as close as two people could be. They liked the same foods and sometimes spoke in unison. Often, they even wore the same clothes. Today, both were dressed in dark gray suits with white shirts, rep-striped ties, and black leather Oxfords with thick rubber soles. Each was an inch short of six feet and went a trim 175 lbs. Their medium-length hair was professionally cut with Tomas' parted on the left while Karel's was on the right. Karel had a brown leather crossbody messenger bag at his feet while a black leather computer bag sat next to Tomas. They even choose the same careers.

Both were assassins.

They received a tip from their broker, Circe, that one of the targets for a rather lucrative contract was here in Zurich, posing under the name Julia Laurent. They split up the hotels and called four dozen of them, asking to speak with a guest by that name, but their search came up empty. She must have ditched the Laurent identity for a new one. But for the money involved, they wouldn't give up their search easily.

As they sat at an outdoor café, sipping espressos, Tomas checked an email confirming that there was a one hundred thousand Euro bounty on any MI6, CIA, or SOG operator while Karel continued to watch the passersby.

"Do you think we missed her?" Karel asked.

"I don't know. The intel was good," Tomas said. "I'm thinking she's using a different name, but she's here somewhere."

"Do we have any idea how solid this contract is?" Karel asked.

"You mean might the contract's sponsor renege on the payment?"

"Yeah, I mean, does he or she have the funds, because an unlimited contract of a hundred thousand Euros for any CIA, SOG, or MI6 agent is huge."

"Well, I don't think they'll welsh out of paying," Tomas said. "After all, we *are* assassins. Defaulting on payment means they default on their life."

"Ya got that right."

Tomas put away his phone, rolled his neck, and stretched his arms over his head. "You wanna get some lunch?"

Karel's eyes widened and he raised his hand and inch off the table, signaling Tomas to hold. "No sudden moves, but there's a tall woman wearing a beanie with a black leather briefcase over her shoulder walking toward the entrance to the Storchen Hotel. She's wearing black cargo pants, a black leather jacket, and boots with thick rubber soles. Move casually and check her out."

Tomas pulled his arms in and twisted like he was still stretching. He saw the woman and then turned to his brother. "She's supposed to have long brown hair, but she must have it stuffed up in the beanie. That's got to be her."

"She just entered the hotel," Karel said.

"We've got to find out what room she's in."

Karel nodded. "Follow her. I'll wait here for ten minutes then meet me in the hotel's restaurant."

Tomas stood, shrugged his shoulders, and cracked his neck then looped his computer bag over his shoulder and followed the woman into the hotel. She was approaching the desk clerk as he picked up a newspaper and casually stood ten feet behind her acting like he was waiting to talk to the clerk.

"Hi, I'm Ms. Payne. I'm just checking if there's any mail for me?" the woman said.

The clerk checked her computer then shook her head. "I'm sorry, Ms. Payne, I don't see anything for you."

"Thank you."

Tomas lingered for a minute then followed the woman to the elevator. She pushed the button for three while he pushed four. When she got off, he kept his finger on the open-door button. When he heard a door unlock and open down the hall, he stepped out and walked in its direction.

"324," he whispered.

Tomas turned away and took the stairs to the lobby then headed for the restaurant. He took a table for two overlooking the Limmat and waited for his brother.

Karel joined him a few minutes later. "Well?" he asked."

"She's going by the name Payne."

"Room number?"

"324. Do you want to take her now or later?"

"Let's watch her for a bit. Tonight might be better. If she goes out, we'll take her when she returns. Otherwise, we'll wait until late tonight and get her while she's asleep."

"I'm hungry," Karel said. "Let's order lunch."

"Do you think it's safe to eat here?" Tomas asked. "What if she comes down here and sees us?"

"She doesn't know us and the way we're dressed, we look like a couple of businessmen."

Karel ordered leeks with potatoes and sausage while Tomas had the ragout of veal and mushrooms. They had a couple of Falkenbrau Hell beers to go with their food.

A group of businesspeople entered and split up, taking tables along the windows and toward the back.

"So, who do you think these intelligence agencies pissed off to have a bounty placed on their heads?" Tomas asked.

"I don't know, but the fact that it's a blanket order for MI6, CIA, and SOG operators tells me a government is sponsoring the contracts.

"Well, Circe brokers for a lot of the top assassins, and she certainly has the resources for this kind of operation, but I think you're right. It's not one of her usual clients. It's got to be a government."

"Yeah, and they would have deep pockets," Karel said.

"On a more professional note, how do we want to do this?" Tomas asked.

"A silenced gun would be my choice," Karel said. "Go in fast, shoot her before she knows you're there and get out. Any other way might risk her screaming and alerting hotel security, and we don't want collateral damage on this one."

"Don't forget we have to take a picture of her corpse. We gotta send it to the broker to collect the reward," Tomas said.

"I won't forget. If she goes out, you sit in the bar and watch for her to return. I'll take the stairs to her room and be in and out in under a minute."

"I'll meet you outside over by the café where we had coffee this morning," Tomas said. "We can call a cab back to the Sheraton and send the pictures to the broker then catch a train out of here tomorrow."

They finished their dinners then paid and left the restaurant. Neither noticed the woman with crewcut blond hair sitting in the back reading the newspaper and watching them.

Chapter Fourteen

Thursday, March 23ʳᵈ; Zurich, Switzerland; The Storchen Hotel

Tomas sat at a back table in the Storchen hotel restaurant, finishing his beer. He watched a woman with brown hair in a bob cut finishing up her dinner. They'd identified her as their target. When she left her table and headed for the hotel lobby, Karel rose and followed her. He passed her and kept walking toward the hotel exit as she stopped at the elevators. He glanced back and saw her get on then pulled out his cell phone and called his brother.

"Where are you?" Karel asked.

"I just left the hotel. Payne just went up to her room," Tomas said. "Where are you?"

"I'm at the Aelpli Bar directly across the river from you. I've saved a seat for you. We can kill time here until it's time to move."

"I'll be there in ten minutes."

Tomas disconnected and walked toward the Weinplatz past the café where they'd sat earlier today and continued past the Rathaus. He turned right and walked two blocks south then made a left and entered the bar. His brother was sitting at one end, nursing a beer.

The ceiling and bar were framed by rough-hewn beams and the bar itself was a single long piece of oak. Strings of lights hung from the ceiling and assorted bottles of various kinds of alcohol lined the shelves behind it.

Tomas slid onto the empty stool next to his brother and pointed to his brother's beer as the bartender approached. A minute later, a stein of beer sat on a coaster in front of him. He picked up the beer and turned to face the rest of the bar. A girl with a guitar was singing, accompanied by some guy playing the accordion.

"Damn, Karel, I swear the only instrument allowed in hell will be an accordion. And the girl's voice is quite pitchy."

"Yeah, it's not my favorite, but this was the only bar near the hotel that was open late."

"And people like this kind of music?" Tomas asked.

"You might want to keep your comments to yourself and just drink your beer." He flicked his head toward the bartender who was glaring at them.

"Sorry, it's just not my kind of music."

The bartender moved to talk to a big guy sitting at the other end of the bar. His head was shaved and his nose was flat like he was a fighter. His beady eyes fixed on Tomas as the bartender talked with him.

Karel clucked his tongue and shook his head. "Looks like someone is going to want to have a musical discussion with you, so it's probably a good idea to finish your beer and we'll find some other place to kill time."

Tomas tossed down his beer and wiped his mouth with a napkin. "Ready anytime you are."

Karel left twenty Swiss francs on the bar, and they threaded their way through the tables toward the door. The big guy and one of his friends followed them out.

"Hey, scheißkopf, die Musik hat dir nicht gefallen?

The brothers turned to face the two guys. The bald guy was well over six feet but had a serious paunch hanging over his belt. His buddy had the same out-of-shape build but wasn't as tall and had a salt-and-pepper crew cut.

Tomas tilted his head at baldy. "No, I didn't like the music. My tastes run to anything that doesn't include an accordion and a girl who sings off-key."

"Maybe I teach you to like it," Baldy said.

"Not likely, fat boy. Now, I suggest you go back inside the bar and try to enjoy the kind of music that will be prominent in hell."

As Tomas turned away, the big man reached out with his right hand and grabbed Tomas' right shoulder. The assassin spun to his left looping his left arm over Baldy's and locking it then sent an open-hand strike to the guy's chin. He moved his leg behind him and pushed him so that he fell on his back. His head hit the pavement hard but before he could move, Tomas stomped on his face, breaking his nose and a few teeth.

Karel looked at the second guy. "I suggest you call a doctor for your friend. He may have a concussion."

The second man's eyes went from Tomas to his buddy then to Karel. He nodded and pulled out a cell phone as the two assassins disappeared into the darkness.

"Well, that wasn't something we needed," Karel said. "Did you have to hurt him like that?"

"Eh, they don't know us, and we'll be out of here by morning." He checked his watch. "I think you can pay Ms. Payne a visit. I'll wait for you by the city hall."

"This shouldn't take more than fifteen minutes," Karel said.

They bumped fists.

"Good hunting," Tomas said. He walked over to the city hall and sat on the steps in the shadows.

As he walked toward the hotel, Karel checked to make sure there were no observers then drew his Glock 19X and attached a suppressor. He shoved the gun in the back of his waistband and minutes later entered the Storchen. He walked straight to the elevators and pressed the button for the third floor. It was late and the hotel was quiet, but he checked left and right as he got off the elevator and moved smoothly to room 324. He listened at the door but there was no sound. He took a small black box from his suitcoat pocket and inserted the attached keycard in the slot. A soft click indicated the door was unlocked.

Karel cracked the door and peered inside. The room was dark, so he drew his gun and slipped through it, closing the door softly behind him. The room was a junior suite with a separate bedroom. He moved through the suite with his gun pointed in front of him in a two-handed grip. The light from the outside partially illuminated the room, revealing tarps thrown over the furniture and several paint cans lined up against one of the walls. He checked the bedroom, but the bed was stripped of sheets. As he turned, he saw rolls of wallpaper and a ladder leaning against the wall. He shoved his gun back into his waistband and called his brother.

"Is it done?" Tomas asked.

"There's no one here and I think the room's being redecorated."

"What the…get out of there! It's a trap!" Tomas hissed.

Karel pocketed his phone and hurried to the door but when he opened it to leave, he found himself staring into the cyclops eye of a suppressed pistol. He had no time to react as the gun spit twice and he fell backward as his brain functions shut down.

****

As the assassin found out too late, the room Brook sent the assassin to, was unavailable because they were redecorating it. She'd bumped one of the bellhops and took his master key. She tucked the suppressed .22 in a shoulder holster under her jacket and booked it down the stairs and out a side door.

Her clothes were black, which made her invisible as she moved through the shadows to where she could watch the assassin's twin. He checked his watch to see how much time had passed since he talked to his brother in the hotel. She smiled as it dawned on him that something was wrong. He stood up and walked past her, heading for the hotel. As he passed, she stepped out and called to him.

"Hey, dickhead."

When he turned to face her, she pointed the suppressed .22 FN 502 tactical pistol at his face.

"Wrong room."

She fired two shots that penetrated his head and sent him tumbling over backward. She stepped next to his body and put two more through his heart then disappeared.

Chapter Fifteen

A McMillan CS5 subsonic sniper rifle fitted with a matching suppressor and an HD 4-32x50 Sightmark Wraith digital riflescope was aimed at the back of the head of Jack Stevens, the U.S. ambassador to the U.K. The sniper cradling the rifle on a roof a hundred meters away made a slight adjustment and then settled in to watch the target. With the buttstock and suppressor detached, the CS5 was only 23 inches in overall length. The infinitely adjustable buttstock fit any operator, regardless of height, build, the bulk of clothing, or shooting position. It stuffed neatly into a backpack, yet it delivered the stopping authority of a .308 projectile. Using McMillan's match-grade 200-grain subsonic .308 Winchester ammunition, the rifle would deliver 0.5 minute-of-angle or MOA performance or better at this distance. The shots would sound no louder than someone snapping their fingers.

The sniper was ecstatic over the way the plan was working out with the flash drive and the list of targets. It was a contract within a contract. The one on the diplomats served two purposes. The first was to draw CIA and MI6 agents into known locations. Then she and her partner, Circe, had leaked information to Elion Kastrati, the new head of the

Odessa mafia that his brother was killed by either a CIA or MI6 special operation. It was like pouring gasoline on the hothead's fire. He put out a hundred thousand Euro bounty on the head of any of their agents and with them being called to guard the diplomats, it became a killing field for any assassin, especially those working with Circe.

Two CIA agents were dead at the hands of those looking to collect a bounty. The assassin killed a third CIA operator with a knife at the Paris Ballet. The whole operation led the foreign intelligence services to conclude the diplomatic list was bogus and caused them to scatter their agents, fearing for their lives at the hands of some very competent killers. But the irony of the whole plan was that the list of diplomatic targets was real, and the contract had been given to the woman with her rifle aimed at the U.S. ambassador's head.

The last bit of sleight-of-hand was that the American and British intelligence agencies were looking for an assassin who went by the call sign of Enigma, but, in fact, wasn't involved. It all served to confirm something the assassin already knew.

There were none better than the one whose moniker was Paradox.

She'd worked with her lover to set up the deception and it was working like a charm. But to accomplish the goals of the contractor, Paradox had to work quickly. Tonight, Jack Stevens would die. Tomorrow, it would be Georges Toussaint and Sunday a soiree was planned at the home of the U.S. Chargé d'Affaires for the U.S. Mission to the Netherlands. However, the *pièce de résistance* was General David White.

White was the commander of the U.S. European Command and NATO's Supreme Allied Commander Europe or SACEUR. He was responsible for one of two U.S. forward-deployed geographic combatant commands whose area of focus spanned across Europe, portions of Asia, and the Middle East as well as the Arctic and Atlantic oceans. The client was very nervous about NATO's mutual defense treaty that meant if a NATO member country was attacked, they would face an overwhelming force opposing them. And while her client had nuclear weapons, the U.S., the U.K., and France also had nukes and you could bet your ass that several U.S. boomer submarines were parked off the coast of Russia.

Paradox wasn't naïve. The client thought that by taking out White, they could cripple the alliance. That wasn't true. White's death certainly wouldn't cripple NATO, however, his death would be a bonanza for their propaganda machine. But that didn't concern her. The assassin's job was to kill the targets without regard for the reasons behind the assignment. If the client wanted White killed, Paradox would kill him.

She peered through the scope at the rear floor-to-ceiling windows of Stevens' home. The ambassador was sitting on a sofa facing away from the sniper. Two DSS agents passed through the room from time to time. Paradox moved the rifle to aim at the back of Steven's head and slowly squeezed the trigger. The bullet made a soft clicking sound as it left the rifle with minimal recoil. The assassin saw the ambassador's head snap forward as the round hit the back of his head.

The two DSS men ran into the room and froze when they saw the ambassador slumped over with most of his face removed from the exit wound. One of them bent over the dead man, but the other pulled out a cell phone. Paradox put a round through his face then moved the sights to the agent kneeing next to Stevens. He didn't have time to take cover before a third round destroyed his head.

Paradox disassembled the rifle and stowed it in a black backpack. There was no hurry because no one would know Stevens was dead until morning when they came to take him to the embassy. When the rifle was secured, the assassin hoisted it over her shoulder and headed for the roof entrance that led to the ground. Paradox was out the door and walking away from the scene seconds later.

A rented Yamaha TMAX scooter was parked three blocks away. It was a popular model in Europe. In fact, since 2021, over 350,000 of them had been sold in the E.U. and its "blazing grey" color was nondescript enough to avoid drawing attention. It had a high-powered 530cc twin-cylinder engine and a lightweight aluminum chassis that allowed it to reach a top speed of 110 mph.

The assassin adjusted the backpack then hopped on the scooter and hit the keyless ignition. The motor sounded like a purring kitten as Paradox pulled out and left the neighborhood. The killer needed to ditch the rifle because Brexit meant passage between the U.K. and the E.U. required visitors to go through security. Once in the E.U., there were no worries because the Schengen agreement meant travelers didn't have to worry about border inspections.

Paradox took a quick detour through a seedy neighborhood and dropped the rifle in a dumpster. The assassin returned the scooter to the rental agency then took a train to Pancras International Station from which the Eurostar departed. After producing a ticket to Paris and going through security, the assassin boarded the train and took a window seat. The next stop was Paris and a date with Georges Toussaint. After a quick stop to kill him, it was off to the Hague to introduce the U.S. Chargé d'Affaires to a .308 bullet.

Chapter Sixteen

Saturday, March 25th; Basel, Switzerland; ViCafe Marktplatz

Brook sat in the ViCafe in Basel, sipping a *café crème* and watching the few people entering and leaving the shop. She'd changed a great deal over the years that she'd been with the SOG. All her senses were razor sharp. When she walked into a room, she registered faces, potential threats, and exits in a manner that didn't draw attention. Everything she did took strategic planning to an extreme level. She had to outthink her opponents because the stakes were life or death. Like a chess grandmaster, every move and variation had to be analyzed and the risks calculated and weighed against the options until she could zero in on the approach that accomplished her mission while keeping her alive.

She was wearing a brunette wig with the hair cut in a short bob and had switched to a Belgian passport in the name of Marie Peeters that matched her current appearance. She'd rented another car and made the forty-minute drive from Aarburg earlier this morning. It was time to check in with her handler, but even burner phones could be traced. Thus, the reason for being in Basel.

The café was empty on this rainy Saturday morning, so she took out the burner and dialed her handler. They input their numerical codes when he answered.

"What's new, Hector?" Brook asked.

"Well, the agency has revised its thoughts on the purpose of that list."

"How so?"

"As you said, we originally surmised that it was intended to draw our agents to locations where they could be killed. But yesterday's assassination of Jack Stevens and this morning's shooting of Georges Toussaint confirm it was also a ploy to cause CIA and MI6 agents to keep their distance so the targets could be assassinated.

"Shit, both ambassadors?"

"Yes. And several of our guys have had close calls with freelancers. Ajax managed to incapacitate one of them and interrogated her before he killed her. She said our favorite broker, Circe, put out a contract offering a hundred thousand Euros for any Western intelligence agent."

"That explains the two who came after me in Zurich," Brook said.

"Did you get any information from them?" Hector asked.

"Nope, I just put bullets in their heads. Do you have any idea who put out the contract on the agents?"

"Well, it gets quite complicated," Hector said.

"Of course it does. Nothing's simple about this."

"Elion Kastrati."

"Driton's brother?"

"Yes. Someone must have leaked information that either the CIA or MI6 was responsible for his brother's death, and like all mafia-like organizations, they have a general eye-for-an-eye rule. You killed his brother, but because all he knows is that either an American or British intelligence agency was responsible, he's casting a wider net for his revenge. And in case you're not familiar with him, Elion is a bonified psychopath. He's a bloodthirsty, skinny little wimp."

"Does he have any other siblings?"

"Not that we know of. No aunts, or uncles either."

"So, killing him should stop the family vendetta?"

"In theory. But there's one more thing."

"Fuckin A, Hector, you're killing me."

"Dasher hasn't checked in."

"What does his handler say?"

"His handler has also disappeared. We think they're working together to kill off CIA agents to build a nest egg and fall off the grid."

"Dasher's handler is a woman?"

"Yeah, they were childhood sweethearts."

"What the fuck, Hector, how did that happen?"

"Apparently it didn't show up in their interviews when they joined the agency and they're very good at keeping secrets."

"No shit, Sherlock. There's your leak. She's got all kinds of information on SOG field agents, what they look like, their locations, their various identities, and our protocols. I think it's also safe to assume Dasher's the one who leaked the information to Kastrati. Have you notified the other field personnel?"

"Yes, a general alert went out last night warning them. You should have the details in your email."

"Yeah, unfortunately, I've completely divorced myself from anything connected to the agency until this fiasco is finished. Where was Dasher's handler's base of operations?"

"Not clear, but then mine isn't either for obvious security reasons," Hector said.

"Damn!" Brook slumped back in her chair and stared out the window where the city was beginning to stir. "Okay, I'm going to call in some non-agency reinforcements. I can't go after Enigma and watch my back when a bunch of assassins and two rogue SOG operators hunting for me."

"Are you sure that's wise?" Hector asked.

"I don't have a choice. Who knows who else might be compromised? Besides, McGill knows the party I'm going to use." Andrew McGill was the Director of the Special Operations Group for the CIA.

"If you trust them, then I trust them," Hector said.

"Who's the next target?" Brook asked.

"Allison Barnard, the Chargé d'Affaires for the U.S. Mission to the Netherlands."

"And after her?"

"General David White, the commander of the U.S. European Command and NATO's Supreme Allied Commander Europe"

"All right. You'll have to send someone else to the Hague because at the rate Enigma is going, I'll never make it in time. I'll take my friends and set up in Brussels. Just out of curiosity, do you have any idea who contracted for the diplomats?"

"Sergei Lagunov."

"The Russian Foreign Minister?"

"Yes. We've intercepted a string of his emails that indicate he was hunting for non-Russian assassins for this job."

"And where is the Foreign Minister?"

"He's in Geneva, puttering around the U.N. offices, lobbying unsuccessfully to get several E.U. members to block the applications of Sweden and Finland to NATO."

"He's going to have to go, too," Brook said.

"Be very careful there, Zealot. Death from a bullet or knife will have repercussions that we don't want."

"There are plenty of other ways to kill someone. Men at his age often succumb to heart attacks due to poor eating and drinking habits as well as stress."

"Just be careful." Hector paused for a few seconds.

"One last thing," Brook said. "I assume Enigma is the one Circe contracted to go after the diplomats."

"Yes, that's what we think."

"All right, I need to find Circe first. She's the key to getting Enigma. Then there's the problem of Dasher and his sweetheart. Do you have a picture of his handler?" Brook asked.

"Yeah, I'll text it to you now."

Brook sipped her café crème and waited for the picture to come through. She opened the text and choked on her coffee. She coughed for several seconds trying to regain her composure. She took a deep breath.

"Son of a bitch, Hector."

"What is it, Zealot?"

"Dasher's handler. I've met her and I even know where she lives."

"What are you talking about? Handlers for one agent are never allowed to meet another agent."

"Well, it wasn't exactly a friendly meeting."

"What do you mean?"

"She has, or rather had a very nice apartment in the Marais in Paris."

"Shit, you mean—?

"His handler is Elise Garnier, the woman I shot in the foot. And she was scouting for Circe. It appears we have a murderous *ménage à quatre*."

Chapter Seventeen

Saturday, March 25th; Basel, Switzerland; ViCafe Marktplatz

Brook took out her Kerberos cellphone and sent a text to the one person she knew she could rely on for help—Cailan Bane.

She first met up with Bane in Afghanistan where he was the most proficient sniper in U.S. military history with over 200 confirmed kills. The Taliban coined a name for him, the Death Whisperer, because his shots were taken from a thousand yards or more, and you never heard the crack of the bullet because, by the time the sound reached you, you were dead.

Brook's mother and father were renowned scientists who developed a pan-coronavirus vaccine that saved millions of lives. But several anti-vaxx groups began harassing them and, in the process, murdered her father. When the harassment continued, Cailan and a group of his friends stepped in to protect her while Brook took out the leaders of the movement, known as the Disinformation Dozen. But there were two men she couldn't reach because they were on a militia compound surrounded by well-armed, fanatical men. Bane took out both with sniper shots from a thousand yards.

Their interests intersected again when Bane was hunting Driton Kastrati, the head of the Albanian mafia who was running an organ and sex trafficking ring. Because he was also a major arms dealer, the SOG had an interest in removing him from the living. The two had teamed up to kill him.

She knew he could and would help her, so she texted him and waited for a response. It took all of two minutes for him to answer.

"Hello, Brook, I won't ask you what you're up to because you'd have to kill me."

"Actually, I'm in a bit of hot water."

"Tell me where you are, and I'll leave today."

"Don't you want to hear what my problem is first?"

"Sure, but I'll start packing anyway."

She spent the next fifteen minutes detailing her agency assignment and the confusion about the contracts on U.S. intelligence agents and diplomatic staff. She told him about what she called a deadly *ménage à quatre* consisting of a top assassin called Enigma, Circe his broker, and a SOG agent and his handler.

"You found Dasher's handler and shot her?" he texted.

"Yeah, but at the time I thought she was just a go-fer for Circe. Turns out she's Dasher's high school sweetheart."

"How the hell did your agency miss that?"

"No idea, but I'm in the middle of a two-front war. I have to find and stop Enigma and keep Dasher and his babe from killing me."

"And I imagine both of those people are royally pissed off after you shot her."

"What can I say? The woman was a bitch and a stupid one at that."

"Did she know it was you who shot her?"

"I don't think so. I was wearing a balaclava when I met with her and later on when Dasher met up with me in Berlin, he didn't show any sign that he suspected it was me who shot his honey."

"I can be to you in twenty-four hours. I'd like to bring a friend if that's okay."

"Who's the friend?" Brook texted.

"Mirlinda Dzafer."

"The owner of the pub where I met your friends?"

"Yeah, but she has other skills, too."

"What kind of skills?" Brook asked.

"The kind that makes you and I look like amateurs."

"Geez, Bane, I'm not trying to be arrogant, but SOG operators are usually considered to be at the top of the food chain. Where'd Dzafer get her training?"

"She trained in a secret GRU program developed when Russia was still the Soviet Union. She's credited with killing twelve of the deadliest assassins."

Brook frowned, racking her brain as she tried to figure out what Cailan was saying about Dzafer. A chill ran up her back as it dawned on her what he was saying.

"Does her real name mean "defender" or "helper of mankind"?"

"Yes."

"Oh. My. God! And she owns a pub?"

"And she has a doctorate in business from Columbia University and is an Associate Professor of entrepreneurship at the University of Chicago."

"And you think she'll help me?"

"I know she will. Where do you want us to meet you?"

"Since my priority is finding Enigma, I need to locate Circe, her broker, and she's in Paris. I have a small apartment in the Latin quarter. Have you been to Paris before?"

"Yes."

"Do you know where Le Deux Magots is?"

"Yes."

"I'll meet the two of you there tomorrow at 3:00 for lunch and Cailan?"

"Yes?"

"Thanks for doing this."

"Life would otherwise be boring."

"See you tomorrow." Brook ended the call. She ordered a *pain au chocolate* and another *café crème* then slumped in her chair. Her thoughts raced at a mile per minute.

Sasha!

Mirlinda Dzafer was Sasha Nesti, the deadliest assassin to ever walk the planet. Bane once told her that he had some interesting friends.

No shit!

Never in her wildest dreams did she expect one of them to be the legendary Sasha. Brook finished her pastry and coffee then packed up her laptop. She had to pick up a few things from her home in Aachen then she had a six-hour drive to Paris. As she tossed her backpack on the passenger seat and slid behind the wheel of her rental, she felt safer than she had in a week. With Bane and Dzafer backing her, she was feeling far more confident about stopping Enigma and eliminating the murderous *ménage à quatre*.

Chapter Eighteen

Sunday, March 26th; Paris, France; Les Deux Magot

The day had been beautiful, and the sky was like a dome of cobalt blue. Earlier, the clouds had looked like airy cotton balls drifting under a gleaming sun. But then came the rain, at first like a whispering in the air, a gentle shower peppering the pavement and making it greasy. Gradually the drops grew bigger and heavier and the wind stronger and colder, until it became a message from winter saying it wasn't done yet. The drops beating on the awning of the café were like slugs fired from a shotgun and the deepening shadows made Paris a city of ghosts.

But Brook loved it.

She was the only one sitting outside the café. To her, the rain was like the white noise of nature, helping her block out distractions, and allowing her to think more clearly. She pulled the collar of the grey, Arc'teryx, all-weather jacket closed and flipped the hood up over her short blond hair.

Henri bolted out the door and hurried over to her. "*Mon Dieu,* Eliana, is that you?"

Brook laughed. "Yes, it's me, Henri. I decided to go for a different look. One that doesn't require any fussing."

"You are beautiful as always, but why are you sitting out here in the rain?"

Brook laughed. "Actually, I'm quite dry sitting here under the awning listening to the music of the skies."

"I know you are a poet, but you're going to be a very sick one if you don't come inside where it's warm and dry."

"Ah, Henri, don't you know that while the sun enables life, the rain grants it safe passage?"

The little man spun around waving his hands. "Please, Eliana, come inside."

"I'm waiting for a couple of friends who are visiting."

"And you think they will enjoy sitting out here, too?"

Brook nodded to two people approaching behind Henri. "We can ask them because here they are."

Cailan and Mirlinda stepped under the awning and threw back their hoods. Cailan hugged Brook while Mirlinda kissed her on each cheek."

"Nice weather," Mirlinda said.

"That is what I've been telling her," Henri said. "She needs to move inside before she catches pneumonia."

"Mirlinda, Cailan, this is Henri, an old friend who worries too much."

"Nice to meet you," Mirlinda said.

Henri turned to Cailan. "You must convince her to come inside."

Cailan smiled and signed his answer.

"He says it's a lost cause," Mirlinda translated.

Henri frowned. "You are mute?"

"Tragic accident when he was a child," Mirlinda said. "Three men broke into his home while his father was away and repeatedly raped his mother and twelve-year-old twin sister through the night. In the morning they cut their throats, killing the mom and sister, but botched the job on Cailan."

"*Mon Dieu,*" Henri whispered. "Monsters. So, you will not move inside?"

"I think we'll sit out here."

"*Sacré bleu,* all right, what would you like?"

"Do you mind if I order for us?" Brook asked.

"Not at all," Mirlinda said.

"Could we please have three salmon club sandwiches and a bottle of the *Chateau La Borie* Côtes du Rhône?"

"Of course." Henri laid a hand on Cailan's elbow. "And for you, I will bring something special to keep you from catching pneumonia-like these two." He disappeared into the café.

"Let's wait for our food before we dive into the situation," Brook said.

"I almost didn't recognize you with your hair like that," Cailan signed.

"I'm traveling under a different passport, one that the agency is unaware of, and this matches the photo."

"It's quite *au currant*," Mirlinda said.

Ten minutes later, Henri backed through the door carrying a large tray that he set on a neighboring table. He set place settings with napkins and silverware next to each of them and set wine glasses next to the place settings. He served them their sandwiches and uncorked the wine. He set the cork next to Brook and poured a small amount into her glass. She nosed it then sipped and nodded. He filled their glasses and set the bottle on the table, then set a snifter filled with an amber liquid next to Cailan.

"Frapin Cognac XO Chateau de Fontpinot for the gentleman. It will keep you warm," he said. *"Bon Appetit,"* He disappeared into the restaurant.

"Wow," Mirlinda said. "That's good stuff."

Cailan sipped his drink then nodded.

"So how do we proceed?" Cailan signed.

"The contract on the diplomats was placed by Sergei Lagunov," Brook said.

"The Russian Minister of Foreign Affairs?" Mirlinda asked.

"One and the same. I need to send a message to the Russians that killing U.S. diplomats is a game they don't want to play."

"You're not going into Russia, are you?" Mirlinda asked.

"No, Lagunov is in Geneva. I'll take him there."

"Cailan and I will contact Circe. And can you describe this Dasher guy for me?"

"He's a shade over six feet, medium-length gray hair, dark eyes, and wears black non-prescription glasses. His face is unremarkable, and he favors gray or navy suits without a tie.

"So, his overall appearance is forgettable and designed to blend in," Mirlinda said.

"Yes."

"All right, then as soon as we finish lunch, Cailan and I are going to find an internet café and contact Circe." She slid a card toward her with ten phone numbers. "The two numbers with U.S. area codes reach our Kerberos phones. The international ones are our current burners and are numbered one through four. We'll use them in the order they're listed and destroy them after one use."

"Try the Milk Montparnasse internet café. It's across town and in a spot popular with business travelers because there are a lot of hotels in the area."

"We're going to stop by my apartment and grab my MacBook then we'll head for the café," Mirlinda said.

"You have an apartment in Paris?" Brook asked.

"And several other European cities."

"So, you're going to be the bait?" Brook asked.

"Can you think of someone better?"

"No, no, I just wonder why you're doing this?"

"I don't like to see people set up and in case you didn't realize it, the bar klatch Cailan introduced you to when you visited included several tier-one assassins, a former member of the Russian Spetsnaz and mafia, and probably the most brilliant computer brain in the world. Osias will be helping on this one."

"Well, I appreciate your help."

"Not a problem. It keeps me in practice."

"This is very good," Cailan signed, pointing to his sandwich.

"The wine is excellent, too," Mirlinda said.

When they finished, Henri magically appeared and collected their plates. "Can I get you anything else?"

"I think we're good, Henri. Thanks." She handed him a credit card then signed the bill when he returned with it and left a twenty-five percent tip.

Cailan signed to Brook. *"Actually, I'd like a café crème to go."*

She told Henri to add it to the bill, but he said it was on the house.

Cailan touched both women's knees. *"You leave first, and I'll follow."* Cailan signed. *"When we arrived, I noticed a man inside the café sitting next to the window behind Brook reading the newspaper, but he's been watching us with an abnormal amount of interest since we sat down."* He nodded to Mirlinda. *"I'll meet you at the Hotel Millésime where I'm staying. I'm going to hang back for a minute."*

"Do you want me to circle back?" Mirlinda signed.

"No, I can handle this."

Cailan watched Brook and Mirlinda leave the café while he waited for his café crème. He glanced in the window and saw the suspicious man was still sitting at his table. Henri brought his coffee and Cailan thanked him. He pulled up his hood and made it a point to make eye contact with the stranger. He gave the guy a death stare then started walking. He saw the man get up and follow him. Cailan walked two blocks then turned down a walkway between two buildings. He turned and waited. The stranger came around the corner and stopped.

"Ah, are you waiting for me?" he said. He had a French accent.

Cailan cocked his head at him.

"You joined a lady at her table. Do you work with her?" the Frenchman asked.

Cailan just stared at him. He could see that his silence was making the stranger nervous.

"You know, she has a price on her head because she is CIA."

Cailan continued to give him a dead-eyed stare.

"You have nothing to say? Well, maybe I will help you." A switchblade appeared in his right hand. He waved it back and forth as he approached Cailan.

"You are very stupid, my friend. You have no idea what I am and what I can do."

The man was about four feet from Cailan pointing the blade at his face. But the stranger was overconfident. Cailan's hand darted out like a snake striking and slapped the back of man's knife hand, sending the blade bouncing off the wall. He shot a spear hand to the stranger's throat then grabbed him behind his head and pulled him forward into a powerful headbutt that shattered his nose. He reared back and butted him again, knocking out several of his teeth. Cailan moved his hand to either side of the man's head, twisted, and shoved it down sideways to meet a knee strike that crushed the Frenchman's temple. It fractured his skull but just to make sure, Cailan delivered a hammer strike to his other temple. The stranger melted to the ground like a deflating balloon.

As Cailan stepped over the body and headed toward his hotel, he signed. *"Guess I'll never know what you can do."*

Chapter Nineteen

Sunday, March 26th; Paris, France; Milk Montparnasse Internet Café

Cailan and Mirlinda got off the subway at Courcelles and exited the station. Mirlinda had her laptop in a crossbody bag and a Glock 19X compact 9mm pistol with a seventeen-round magazine in a Craft shoulder holster under her black water-resistant jacket that fell below her hips. She carried a suppressor in her left cargo pants pocket. Cailan let her get a block ahead of him and followed her as she executed a series of SDRs, looping through alleys and cross-streets to pick up anyone following her. She stopped at a coffee shop and bought a large black to go then crossed the street to the internet café. Cailan took a window seat in the coffee shop and kept up his surveillance.

Mirlinda paid for two hours of internet time and got a table in the back corner. She took out her laptop and placed a small piece of tape over the camera. She booted the TOR software then connected to the dark web through a military-grade VPN network just like Osias had instructed. She slipped into the dark web and went directly to the site that Osias had identified as the one Circe used. She opened the website and saw the same two questions Brook had described. The site operator wanted to know who the target was, and the timing required for the hit.

She ignored the questions and typed a message that said she was thinking of getting back into the business and was looking for representation. To bait her hook, she mentioned that she'd killed seven of the top assassins in Europe. Then to set the hook and draw the broker in, she listed Raven, Justice, Angel, the Gemini duo, Gort, and the Magician as the recipients of her contracts. She hit send and immediately got the same automated message that Brook had seen.

She leaned back in her chair and sipped her coffee, waiting to see if Circe responded. It didn't take long.

"I don't know who you're trying to fool, but you'll have to do a lot more than just claim responsibility for those deaths. Especially because I know the identity of the assassin who killed them. So here is my question and if you answer incorrectly, you'd better run."

"Fire away," Mirlinda typed.

"How did each one die?"

"Gee, I thought you were going to ask a hard one. So, here's the list: I broke the neck of one of the Gemini guys in the Whitehall hotel in Chicago. I shot his partner when he returned to the hotel room where they'd murdered a CIA agent. I killed Raven with a rifle round from a motorcycle while he ate dinner at the Alameda restaurant in Hondarribia, Spain. I took out Justice with a sniper round while he was on his way to Brussels. I poisoned Angel by gifting her an original copy of poetry by Tennyson that was coated with batrachotoxin. I cut up the Magician in a knife fight. And last but not least, Gort died after being injected with a syringe of botulinum toxin that he had in his hotel room. Satisfied?

The person on the other end of the connection went silent for several seconds.

"Sasha?"

"Very good. Now do we meet and discuss a partnership, or shall I look elsewhere?"

"I don't do face-to-face meetings with my clients," Circe replied.

"And I don't form partnerships without a face-to-face for the simple reason that if you try and betray me, I will kill you."

The person Mirlinda thought was Circe was quiet for several minutes. She sent a text to Osias asking if he was following their exchange. Her eyes widened when he said the person on the other line was located in a building in the Chaillot on the Avenue du President Wilson across from the Chamber of Commerce International building.

Mirlinda finished her coffee and was ready to pack up when a return text came.

"All right. I'll meet with you."

"Where and when?"

"L'Alsace Brasserie on the Champs Elyssee," Circe said. *"Seven o'clock. Lot's of people around so we both should feel safe."*

"Give me a phone number just in case," Mirlinda typed.

"In case of what?"

"In case I decide you're trying to set me up."

Circe sent her a phone number then logged off. Mirlinda quickly packed everything into her bag. She hurried out of the building to the coffee shop across the street where she ordered another coffee and joined Cailan watching the internet café.

"Success?"

"Yes. I think she was taken aback that I contacted her. She agreed to meet me at a brasserie on the Champs Elysée."

Cailan nodded toward the internet café. *"Looks like she sent someone to check up on you."*

A young woman in dark brown tights, light brown suede over-the-calf boots, a cream cotton turtleneck, and a beige hooded raincoat walked up to the windows of the café and peered inside. She checked the street then entered. A minute later, she left and crossed the street to the coffee shop where Cailan and Mirlinda sat. Mirlinda moved her chair next to Cailan and took his hand like they were lovers. The watcher entered, looked around, then ordered a coffee to go, completely ignoring Mirlinda and Cailan. She left as fast as she'd arrived.

"Looks like Circe doesn't trust you," Cailan signed.

"Nor do I trust her."

"Do you know where she lives?"

"Osias found her apartment building. He's working on the apartment number."

"So, how are you going to play this?"

"Well, I don't know what she looks like. So, I'm going to watch the brasserie then send her on a trek around Paris to a restaurant of my choosing."

"I'm at the Millésime Hotel in Saint-Germain des Prés. Do you want me to follow her?"

"No, but when Osias gets her apartment number, I want you to leave a little surprise for her."

"Just call me Surprises-Are-Us."

Chapter Twenty

Sunday, March 26th; Paris, France; Circe's Apartment

She went by the name Circe. It was just a moniker, but there was a certain significance to it. In Greek mythology, Circe was an enchantress and a minor goddess. It was a title she liked because of its symbolism and imagery. She viewed herself as a goddess who controlled some of the most dangerous people on earth, and the name threw enemies off her track. Plus, if any of those enemies harmed her, they would feel the wrath of a dozen murderous contractors because she was responsible for a major part of their yearly earnings.

No one had ever been successful at discovering her identity. That gave her an advantage and it was critical because like the assassins she supported with lucrative contracts, she was a criminal. Just because she didn't pull the trigger or twist the knife, she was a freelance broker of death. She had a law degree from Cambridge University in the U.K., but most of all, she knew how to read people and network. She was a premier schmoozer and was adept at making connections and putting the right people together for a job, even when the two parties didn't know the other existed.

And she was wildly successful.

She worked with politicians, private firms, and crime lords. She had contacts with arms dealers and government intelligence outfits who used her to find the customers of the arms dealers and then took them out. Private security organizations were always looking for work and she helped them locate jobs and brokered the contracts. Her Rolodex was full of professional killers and those that needed their services. With her true identity hidden behind the persona of Circe and a mutually supportive stable of professional assassins, she was ordinarily very secure in her life.

One of the contracts she was currently handling was the most lucrative she'd ever seen. The amount of money it offered was absurdly large: ten million Euros for the deaths of three U.S. diplomats and General David White, the commander of the U.S. European Command and NATO's Supreme Allied Commander Europe. The contract was placed by an anonymous party and the money was being held in an escrow account that she'd set up. But she liked to know who was behind something like this just in case they decided to ask for their money back and come after her. It didn't take much digging to learn the contractor was Sergei Lagunov, the Russian Minister of Foreign Affairs. That contract went to her best assassin and lover, namely the one called Paradox. It was an appropriate moniker because Circe credited Paradox's kills to the assassin Enigma to protect her significant other.

But a second job opportunity appeared in the form of a blanket offer of one hundred thousand Euros for the death of any CIA, SOG, or MI6 agent. It was an open-ended contract, meaning as long as her assassins were killing U.S. and British agents, they could collect the bounty. However, that agreement worried her because the person behind the contract was Elion Kastrati, a bonified psychopath. He was very impatient to see as many as possible killed.

Fortunately, she had access to a unique resource in the form of a SOG operator and his handler who were looking for a little extra cash and a way to disappear. The rogue's moniker was Dasher, and his handler went by Vixen. She chuckled at the use of the names of two of Santa Claus' reindeer. They were definitely a gift. Vixen had access to a treasure trove of information on other SOG and CIA agents and Dasher was her assassin bitch. They were critical because SOG operators were some of the best-trained and deadliest people walking the earth and possessing information on them through Vixen and Dasher gave Circe a lucrative advantage.

SOG operators guarded their identities judiciously and because their lives depend on secrecy, they were the ones that if you found out who they were, they would kill you. But with Vixen and Dasher working with her, the difficulty of identifying, finding, and killing them significantly decreased.

With the help of the rogue agents, the contract started like any other hit. But after the deaths of three of her assassin contractors, it was clear one of the targets was extraordinarily talented. Dasher speculated it was a woman whose call sign was Zealot. He'd met up with her in Berlin and tried to bait her into working with him, but she disappeared, most likely after contacting her handler and learning the truth about the man.

Ironically, Vixen or Elise Garnier had been moonlighting and working for Circe for several years. Usually, she screened potential job offers through a dark website. But When Circe saw the email from the person claiming to have killed some of the best in Europe, she bypassed Vixen and jumped in.

Sasha Nesti was legendary. Supposedly she and twenty-nine other children were raised in a secret GRU program during the last days of the Soviet Union. They were trained with every kind of weapon, explosive, and poison, and were unbeatable in hand-to-hand combat. When the program was about to be dissolved, five of the trainees killed twenty-four of the others but missed one—Sasha. She eventually killed the other five, and later was contracted to take out the top seven assassins in Europe to prevent them from participating in a contest to kill the U.S. president. She was a goddess in the assassin world but had dropped off the radar for several years.

And now she was back and looking for representation. But her refusal to go forward with Circe unless they met face to face was worrisome. While Circe had agreed to meet, she didn't feel good about it even though she'd set the place for the meet at the L'Alsace Brasserie on the Champs Elysée, a very public place.

The big questions were why was Sasha getting back in the business and why Circe? While it would be a major drawing card for business having her in her stable of assassins, she didn't need her. She had plenty of work and contractors looking for it.

But as she thought about it, she realized she could create a legend out of one of her own that would have the same effect on her business while raising the profile of one of her best. After all, who wouldn't want to have Sasha on their resume of kills?

Paradox was in the Hague on a job, so she grabbed her phone and sent a text to Dasher, explaining the situation and telling him she didn't trust Sasha. So, would he like the chance to kill her?

A return text appeared in minutes. *"Where will you be?"*

"At the L'Alsace Brasserie on the Champs Elyssee."

"It has tables for two next to the window. Get one and take the seat facing outside. When Sasha arrives, she'll ask you to switch because she won't want her back to the street. Be ready to move when I shoot her."

"Where will you be?"

"You don't need to know."

Dasher signed off.

Chapter Twenty-One

Sunday, March 26th; Le Marais, France; Le Colimaçon Restaurant
Mirlinda watched the area around the *L'Alsace Brasserie*, waiting for someone who looked like Circe to enter. The restaurant had large windows facing the Champs Elysée, which made anyone sitting at a window table easy prey for a sniper or a shooter walking by with a suppressed pistol. She scanned the rooftops but there was no sign of a sniper—no open windows or the tip of a suppressed rifle protruding over the edge of a rooftop.

She was sitting in a café across the street, sipping a glass of the house red wine when a woman who didn't so much walk as glide with an effortless gait approached and entered the restaurant. She was tall, maybe five-eleven, and her short blond hair was slicked back on her head. She was dressed in a white, V-neck, silk blouse under a burnt orange jacket, and loose brown pants. Her low pumps and clutch bag were a matching shade of burnt orange.

Although the clothes disguised the outline of her body, Mirlinda estimated that she was a trim 140 pounds with a low percentage of body fat. Her face was striking with high cheekbones and a straight nose. She looked to be in her early thirties and was Cosmopolitan-attractive.

Circe.

Mirlinda watched as the maitre'd seated her at a window table for two with her facing the street. Her body language said she was trying to portray a sense of nonchalance, but clearly, she was nervous. Mirlinda took out her phone and dialed the number for the hostess desk.

"*L'Alsace Brasserie,* how may I help you?"

"Yes, can you let me speak to your maitre'd, please?"

An hour ago, Mirlinda had slipped him fifty Euros and gave him an envelope that he was to give to the person she directed when she called.

Seconds later he came on. "Hallo?"

"Claude, give the envelope to the lady you just seated by the windows. She's wearing a burnt orange jacket."

"*Bien sûr.*" He hung up and Mirlinda watched him walk over to her table, bow, and hand her the envelope. Inside was a note that said despite her desire for a public place to meet, the brasserie was unacceptable, and she was to take the metro to La Grange Aux Canards in the Latin Quarter.

Mirlinda read the anger on her face as she gathered her purse and left the restaurant. Mirlinda followed her to the metro and hopped on the train two cars behind her. Twenty minutes later, they got off and she followed her to the restaurant. Mirlinda smiled as she watched the woman enter only to have the hostess hand her a note that directed her to go to Le Colimaçon in Le Marais. A table was reserved for them on the second floor of the restaurant.

Mirlinda grabbed a cab and reached the restaurant ten minutes before Circe. She watched her approach as she sat at the only window table overlooking the narrow cobblestone passageway that led to the restaurant's entrance. Mirlinda had positioned her chair so that she was out of sight to anyone outside. The woman called Circe clumped up the stairs, all pretenses of grace gone. She saw Mirlinda and stomped toward her.

"What the hell was this wild goose chase about?" she demanded.

"Security. Not that I don't trust you, but I don't."

"Whatever. Is the food good here?"

"I think you'll find it excellent, but that's not why we're meeting. Would you care for a glass of wine?"

"Definitely," she said as the waiter appeared. "I'd like a glass of the Pouilly Fuisse Château de la Chaise."

"And could I have a glass of the Corton Grand Cru Domaine Maillard, please," Mirlinda said.

"I have to say I was surprised to see your inquiry," Circe said.

"Why?"

"I mean, who you are and with your resume, I assumed you'd be working on your own."

"For the most part, I will, but every once and a while a broker can turn up a contract that interests me."

The waiter delivered their wine and asked if they wanted to order appetizers. He gave a short bow when Mirlinda asked him to give them a few minutes. The two women perused the menu for several minutes. When he returned, Mirlinda ordered the duck breast with honey cumin sauce and Circe asked for their bass with vegetable risotto.

Circe picked up her wine glass and tilted her head at Mirlinda. "So, why me?" She sipped the wine.

"My sources say you handle some very lucrative contracts."

Circe wiggled her head from side to side. "Most of them run in the range of a half million to a million Euros each."

"But I understand you're handling one that has placed a bounty on CIA and MI6 agents." She clucked her tongue. "Although at a hundred thousand per head, it hardly seems worth it."

Circe's lips curled in a smirk at the comment. "And just what does someone like yourself charge?"

Mirlinda's eyes bored into the broker. "I'd be more inclined to take a job that pays upwards of five million."

Circe laughed. "You must think a lot of yourself. I've never heard of a contract going for that amount."

Mirlinda lifted her wine glass. "Not even for removing U.S. diplomats?"

Circe blinked several times and tried to cover her surprise by sipping her wine.

"I don't know what you're talking about."

"How do you arrange payment between the client and the contractor?" Mirlinda asked, sipping her wine.

"I…I set up escrow accounts. The client wires me the money and I deposit it in an account that only I can access. When the job is finished to the client's satisfaction, I transfer the money to wherever the contractor specifies."

Mirlinda went to take another sip of her wine, but as she raised her glass, she noticed four people on the street below pointing at the roof of the building across the street. At the same time, Circe pushed her chair away from the window.

Mirlinda dove for the floor as bullets from a suppressed machine gun shattered the window. She commando-crawled across the floor as several patrons fell bleeding from bullet wounds. She glanced back and saw Circe huddled in the corner staring at her. Mirlinda continued crawling, bypassing the stairs, and aiming for a window at the back. She'd unlocked the catch earlier and had preplanned her escape route in case things went south and this definitely qualified.

Based on the length of time it was taking the shooter to empty a magazine, Mirlinda figured he or she had an FN P90 with a fifty-round mag. When the shooting stopped, she sprang up, threw open the window, and stepped out onto the roof of the neighboring building. While she had a Glock 19X in a shoulder holster, it was suicide to make a stand against someone with a gun that fired 850 to 1100 rounds per minute. Instead, she skipped across the roofs to an Israeli restaurant, Chez Hanna, and climbed down a trellis into their courtyard. She hopped the fence surrounding it and sprinted down the Rue des Rosiers. She cut right down Rue des Ecouffes and ran until she reached the Kuma Japanese restaurant. She stepped inside to catch her breath.

The place was a hole-in-the-wall with only seven tables. She grabbed a seat at the counter away from the door. She ordered the Katsu curry with rice and hot tea then closed her eyes and used a couple of relaxation techniques that staved off the effects of the adrenalin rush.

She took out her phone and sent a text to Osias. *"You got a location for me?"*

He sent back an address and apartment number. He told her he sent it to Cailan two hours ago and that he should be just about finished.

The waiter frowned as he set the bowl of curry in front of Mirlinda because she was wearing a wicked grin. She dug into the curry and finished her tea. Then it was time to finish her discussion with Circe.

Chapter Twenty-Two

Sunday, March 26th; Paris, France; Circe's Apartment
Circe opened the door to her apartment then closed and locked it. She tossed her keys in a bowl that sat on a cabinet in the hall. Her apartment was a third-floor three-bedroom modern affair with a beautiful view of the Eiffel Tower. Her living room was furnished in an ultra-modern style with a long, gray sectional that faced floor-to-ceiling windows. Off to one side, French doors opened onto a small balcony. The kitchen had white walls complimented by black cabinets and a gray, black, and white marble waterfall island with three leather-topped barstools.

She went to her liquor cabinet and poured herself a stiff shot of Frapin Château Fontpinot XO cognac.

"Putain de trou du cul! Je suis tellement baisé!" He missed her! He fucking missed her! Shit, shit, shit!

She took out her cell phone and sent a text to Dasher. *"You missed her. Do you know what this means for me?"*

Dasher answered a minute later. *"Does she know where you live?"*

"No, and neither do any of my clients, but you don't really think she can't find me, do you?"

"There's nothing I can do about it."

"Yes, there is," Circe sent. *"Find her and kill her."*

She disconnected. Circe tossed down the cognac and went into her master bathroom and poured herself a bath in her Jacuzzi bathtub. She went to her refrigerator and took out a bottle of Krug Grande Cuvée Champagne and a large burgundy glass. She opened the champagne and took it into the bathroom. She poured a glass and set the bottle on the ledge that ran around the tub. She sipped the drink as she returned to her bedroom and stripped off her clothes, leaving them in a pile next to her closet. She finished the first glass and returned to the bathroom. She slipped into the tub and poured herself another glass then turned on the tub jets, letting the swirling water ease the tensions of the evening.

Dasher's plan, whatever it was, went to hell in a handbasket. He missed the perfect opportunity to kill the number one assassin in the world. Instead, he pissed off the deadliest person to ever walk the earth and she was probably looking for both of them right now. Fortunately, her anonymity would hide her, but she'd have to stay in for several weeks and hope Sasha left town.

Circe soaked in the jacuzzi for half an hour and finished half the bottle of champagne when she decided it was time for bed. She stepped out of the tub and dried herself with a towel then slipped into a fluffy terrycloth robe. She poured another glass of champagne and with bottle and glass in hand she padded to the kitchen.

Sasha was sitting on a stool at her breakfast bar, sipping a snifter of Circe's cognac.

Circe didn't panic, because after Dasher missed, she felt this was inevitable. She kept her composure because she knew the importance of appearances and remaining dignified, although she felt like crying.

"How did you find me?"

"I have my ways."

She smiled, not knowing whether to feel excited or terrified. "Are you going to kill me?"

Sasha shrugged. "That depends on how you answer my questions."

Circe went to the bar and filled a snifter with cognac. She arched an eyebrow at the assassin. "Care for some more?"

Sasha shook her head. "No, I'm fine."

Circe took a seat at the breakfast bar and cocked her head at Sasha. "Sorry about tonight. I had no idea we were being followed."

"You were being followed, not me."

"But nobody knows who I am."

"Nor do they know me, which tells me you were communicating with someone so they could be at the restaurant before we were finished."

"I...I wasn't."

"Please don't lie to me. It really pisses me off. It's obvious you set me up otherwise why would you push your chair into a corner away from the windows just before the shooting started? But it doesn't matter. Who was the assassin?"

"I don't know."

Sasha was up in a flash and caught Circe by the throat then pushed her off her stool and rammed her head against the wall. She put her hands around the broker's throat and lifted her off the floor. Circe grabbed for her hands that were choking her, but the woman was much too strong.

"I'll only ask one more time, then I'll break your neck. Who. Was. It?"

Circe realized she was losing consciousness. She had no choice, so she rasped, "A man called Dasher."

Sasha set her down and eased the pressure on her throat, but her hands still encircled her neck. "Say again?"

"Dasher took the shots. He's a rogue—."

"I know who he is. What about Enigma?"

"What about her?"

"Where can I find Dasher and Enigma?"

"I don't know. We communicate via text."

"No phone calls or in-person meetings?"

"No, as I told you when you approached me about representing you, in-person meetings just aren't done. It protects both the contractors and me."

"Give me your phone."

"Why?"

Sasha drew a Garm fighting knife from a sheath on her left forearm and pressed the point against Circe's cheek. "Now."

"Okay, okay."

Circe turned to go to her bedroom with Sasha following. She took her phone from her nightstand and handed it to Sasha.

"Unlock it."

Circe unlocked the phone and handed it to the assassin.

Sasha took a short cord from her pocket and connected Circe's phone to her own. She tapped away on her phone's screen then watched the screen.

"What are you doing?"

"I'm cloning your phone and transferring everything to mine."

Circe felt her face flush as she realized the danger that could pose to her. Information on every client and contractor was in the phone, including their contact data.

Sasha unplugged the phones then dropped Circe's on the floor and stomped it to pieces.

Circe stared at her. "Why?"

"Can't have you contacting any of your friends before I kill them." She turned and left the bedroom.

Seconds later, Circe heard her apartment door open and close. She slumped down onto the bed and laid her hand over her heart. It was beating so fast, she thought she might be on the verge of a heart attack. All was not lost, however, because she had all the phone's information and more on a laptop sitting in her closet.

Her body felt drained like she was a wet rag being wrung out. Tomorrow she'd have to get a new phone and text her clients her new number, especially Dasher, Elise, and Paradox. But for now, sleep was calling.

Circe relocked the apartment door then went into her office and grabbed the novel she'd been reading. She carried it into the bedroom, knowing she'd probably only read a few pages before the tension of the evening caused her to fall asleep. She set it on the night table and took off her robe. She headed for the bathroom where she washed her face with ice-cold water. She brushed her teeth then switched off the main light and climbed into bed. She picked up the novel and opened to where she'd left off. But just as she expected, it only took a few pages before she was starting to doze off. She dog-eared the page and set it back on the nightstand then felt the urge to pee.

She slipped out of bed, turned on the lights, and headed for the bathroom. She was so tired she almost fell asleep while sitting on the toilet. She jerked from her stupor just before she fell off. She wiped herself off and then pushed the flush handle down.

It was the last thing she ever did.

Unknown to her, the action drove a firing pin taped to it into a detonator attached to the tank lid. The detonator set off a ribbon of C4 that ran around the inside of the tank and turned it into a porcelain Claymore mine. The explosion left the other units in the building untouched but left small pieces of Circe stuck to the walls and ceiling of the *en suite*.

Chapter Twenty-Three

Monday, March 27th; Paris, France; The Millésime Hotel

The Millésime was a boutique hotel located on the Rue Jacob. The entrance was formerly one of the gates of the Abby of Saint-Germain-des-Pres. The hotel itself was a restored mansion house. Cailan had a suite on the top floor. The ceilings were slanted because of the roof and large skylights brightened the living area. The living room had two sofas facing each other separated by a long wood and steel coffee table.

Cailan was wearing a long-sleeved gray Henley, black cargo pants, and Danner Striker Torrent Boots. He had his CZ-P10C in a shoulder holster. The television was on and although he didn't speak French, he had no trouble understanding the lead stories on the morning news. An explosion in the bathroom of an exclusive apartment complex had killed the owner who was identified as Marie Tremblay, a model with the d'Management group of Milan. The police said she'd been killed when a bomb placed in the toilet tank exploded. No motive for her death was given.

But the second story was labeled a terrorist attack on the Le Colimaçon restaurant. Someone had sprayed the second floor with automatic rifle fire. The shooting originated from a building across the street. Two people were dead and five were in critical condition. There was no mention of a woman who climbed out a back window and was followed by several more of the diners to escape the attack.

He'd ordered a double continental breakfast and two pots of coffee in anticipation of Mirlinda's arrival. He got a text on his cellphone informing him of his guest's arrival and a request for permission to send them up. He replied in the affirmative and opened his hotel room door waiting for her to get off the elevator. Mirlinda stepped off and looked left and right before she saw Cailan standing in the hall. When she entered his room, he took her raincoat and hung it in the bathroom.

"Another beautiful Paris day," Mirlinda said.

Cailan motioned to the coffee table where croissants and coffee awaited. They took one of the pastries and poured themselves mugs of coffee then settled in to discuss where they stood.

"So, based on the news, it looks like it went well with Circe," Cailan signed.

"Yeah, if you consider almost getting shot by someone with a P90 hosing the building doing well," Mirlinda said. "But I think we've made Brook's assignment a lot easier by killing her."

"How so?"

"Circe told me she puts the payout money in an escrow account that only she can access. That means that the assassins hunting CIA and MI6 agents no longer have a motive to continue because they won't get paid."

"It also means Enigma won't have access to the payout the Russians offered," Cailan signed. *"I'll tell Brook to have her handler put out a story that Marie Tremblay was the notorious assassin broker called Circe. That should call off the assassin dogs. Now we just have to find Dasher and Enigma."*

"I cloned Circe's phone before I left. It has all the information on her clients and assassins. She had numbers for Dasher and Vixen, whom I assume is Elise. I transferred the clone to my laptop because Mr. Computer Genius, Osias has remote access to my computer. According to Brook, Elise was not only Dasher's handler but also worked as a forward scout for Circe. There are a lot of calls to Circe from one number and if my hunch is correct, those were from Elise. According to Osias, the calls originated from two places. One was the apartment where Brook confronted her. He has the location of the second flat, but I don't know if she's there. What I'd like to suggest is you scope out the second location while I check out her old apartment.

"Why her and not Dasher? Can't Osias find his phone?"

"After he missed me last night, and with the news this morning about Circe's murder, I'm sure he realizes that whoever killed her, probably took her electronic devices, and now has access to all her contacts. If I were him, the first thing I'd do is ditch my phone and go to burners. But Elise may not know we've made the connection between her phone number and Circe and might still have her original phone."

"If she's at the second location, how do you want me to proceed?"

"I've got your favorite subsonic sniper rifle and scope in my arsenal at my apartment. It's in a fitted backpack so you can move around with it undetected. If you see Elise at the second location, position yourself on the roof of the building across the street. I'll set up a conference call with her so you can hear what's going on. I want her to set up a meeting with Dasher at the L'Alsace Brasserie. To motivate her to cooperate, I want you to put a bullet near her head."

"That should get her attention."

"I hope so, and I'll instruct her to tell Dasher that there's a rifle pointed at her head and if he doesn't meet with me, Elise is dead."

"I assume you're going to kill Dasher but how will you do it in such a public place?"

"Poison."

"And once he's on his way to hell, what do you want me to do with Elise?"

"Once we know where she is, tell Brook to alert a SOG team so they can take her in. I'm sure she's a treasure trove of information. Do we know what the next targets are?" Mirlinda asked.

"She said the next one on the list was the U.S. Charge d'affaires to the Netherlands followed by General David White, the supreme commander of NATO."

"Well, we don't have to worry about the Charge d'affaires because they recalled her to the U.S. to keep her safe. Even though you have Brook's people release information implicating Circe as a major assassin broker, I'll send out a group text to the people in Circe's contact list and let them know that she's dead, and with it, any payment on the contracts. It'll stop them from pursuing CIA and MI6 agents."

"That works," Cailan signed.

"But first we take out Dasher, so Brook won't have to watch her six."

"She's on her way to Geneva to pay a visit to Lagunov," Cailan signed. *"She didn't say how she was going to kill him, but she said she could get anything she needed from her handler."*

"The woman has some incredible resources."

"She said the agency is worried about her creating an international incident."

"Why? Do they think the only way to kill a man is with a gun or a knife?" Mirlinda asked.

"I think she knows that, but she said she also wanted to subtly send a message that will tell the folks back in the motherland to back the hell off. They do not want to get into a battle of reciprocal assassinations."

"I don't know," Mirlinda said. "Sounds like it could be fun."

Chapter Twenty-Four

Tuesday, March 28th; Paris, France; L'Alsace Brasserie

Mirlinda walked toward the apartment where Brook said Elise Garnier lived. She had a messenger bag over her shoulder that held a suppressed Glock19X and a plastic squeeze bottle containing a colorless liquid. She'd been watching the building since before dawn, but there was no sign of activity in the second-floor flat. As she was about to try to enter the building, her phone vibrated with a text.

"I'm sitting on the roof of a building across the street from the apartment Osias identified, watching Elise through my scope mounted on your McMillan sniper rifle. She's sitting in a wingback chair facing a floor-to-ceiling window while she works on her laptop."

Mirlinda smiled and answered. *"I'm going to check out her apartment then head for the restaurant and call her."*

She pocketed her phone and trotted up the stairs to the building. She caught the door as a young man exited and flashed him a dazzling smile as she entered. She threw back her hood as she climbed the stairs and pulled a black balaclava over her head. She took out a set of lockpicks and was inside in seconds. She drew her Glock19X and screwed on the suppressor then cleared both floors of the apartment. A bloody towel was in the master bathroom sink left over from when Brook shot Elise in the foot. No one had returned since then.

She left the apartment and took the metro to a stop that let her off across from the George V hotel and a quarter mile from the restaurant. She entered the hotel lobby and took a seat at a table in the atrium. She ordered a glass of chardonnay and when it was delivered, she sent Cailan a text, telling him she was setting up the conference call. She dialed his number and put him on hold while she called Elise. Her phone rang several times before she answered.

"Who is this?" she asked.

"Someone you never want to meet," Mirlinda answered as she conferenced Cailan in.

"Who are you?"

"My name is Sasha and if you want to live, don't move or hang up."

She heard a smack and Elise screamed.

"There's a very talented sniper watching you, so do exactly as I say, and you just might live. And believe me, his reflexes are faster than you and he will kill you before you can move an inch."

"What do you want?"

"I want to meet with your boyfriend."

"I don't have a boyfriend."

Mirlinda heard her scream as another bullet hit her chair.

"Do not lie to me, Elise, or should I call you Vixen? I want to meet with Dasher and you're going to set it up."

"Do you know what he'll do to you if you kill me?"

"Absolutely nothing. You do know who I am, don't you? I've killed twelve of the best and he's not in the top tier regardless of what he thinks. Now, I want you to have him call this number. You have five minutes and if he doesn't call, you die. Got it?"

"Yes, yes, I've got it."

"Good. Now I'm going to hang up and wait. Remember, five minutes."

Mirlinda hung up and texted Cailan. *"How does she look?"*

"Like she just shit in her pants."

"I'll get back to you as soon as Dasher calls. If she moves, just wound her." Mirlinda texted. *"I'll text Brook and tell her to have the SOG team take her captive once I've disposed of Dasher."*

Mirlinda raised her glass and admired the wine's color. She wafted under her nose and sipped. "Excellent.

Her phone vibrated. "Hello, Dasher."

"If you hurt her, I'll kill you."

"Your words exceed your skills, little man. You had the opportunity to kill me the other night, but you failed to realize I always have contingency plans in case things don't go as I hope. And now Circe is dead, cutting off your access to the funds she was holding in escrow, and I have her electronic devices that helped me find your girlfriend."

"What do you want?"

"I could answer that with a rhetorical statement, but I think we need to get down to business. I want you to meet me at your favorite bistro, L'Alsace Brasserie for lunch in one hour. No weapons. If I think you're armed, Elise dies."

"That's bullshit."

"This isn't a negotiation, Dasher. The only words I want to hear out of your mouth are 'yes, ma'am'. Got it?"

He paused but then replied, "Yes ma'am."

"Good boy. I assume you have several suits?"

"Yes, ma'am."

"Good. Wear a gray one, preferably with a pinstripe, and place a blue pocket handkerchief in the breast pocket."

"I don't have one of those."

"Then you'd better buy one. When you get to the restaurant, ask for Claude, the Maitre'd, and ask for the table reserved for Margarite Arnaud. It'll be a corner two-person number. Take the seat with your back to the windows. Before you sit, remove your jacket, and turn 360 degrees before draping it over the back of your chair. Roll up your sleeves, turn your pants pockets inside out, and sit. Cross one of your legs American style with your ankle on your knee and raise your pant leg. Then do the same with the other leg. When you're finished, place your hands on the tabletop. And wait. Did you get all that?"

"Yes, ma'am."

"Then I'll see you in an hour and whatever you do, don't try to contact or visit Elise because my friend will kill her before she can move a muscle and, in all probability, he'll kill you too."

Mirlinda disconnected. She texted Cailan. *"The meet is on. I'm heading for the restaurant. I don't know if he'll try to get to her first, but if he does, take them both down. Otherwise, I'll let you know when Dasher is dead."*

She left the hotel and entered the brasserie. She told the host she was waiting for someone and would sit at the bar until they arrived. She took a seat at the end that let her see the entire room and asked for a wine menu. A bottle of Gevrey-Chambertin *Les Evocelles* Philippe Rossignol 2016 jumped out at her. It was an outstanding year in Burgundy's *Côte d'Or* that produced some hauntingly beautiful reds. The €150.00 price tag was high, but for what she had planned it was perfect. She ordered a bottle and two glasses. As the bartender set two glasses in front of her, she told him to uncork the wine and let her taste it then let it breathe.

He opened the wine and set the cork on the bar next to one of the glasses. The wine had a dark, saturated blue-purple color, almost black at the center, which shaded to bright fuchsia at the edge. It had aromas of fresh black and red fruit, including ripe griotte cherries, wild strawberry preserves, and black raspberries, along with crushed peonies, and a faint suggestion of freshly cracked black peppercorns. She sipped and found it to be super concentrated and supple, with a core of mineral-saturated black fruit flavors that echoed the nose. It was perfect.

She reached into her pocket and took out a small squeeze vial. After checking to see that no one was watching, she carefully dripped three drops into the empty glass and then rolled it around the lower edges. The liquid was a cocktail of batrachotoxin dissolved in ethanol. With a fifty percent lethal dose of around five micrograms per kilogram body weight, an amount the size of two grains of table salt was enough to kill a grown man. When the liquid dried, Mirlinda repeated the process until she'd made three applications. She checked the glass to make sure there was no sign of a residue then poured some of the wine into her glass and settled back to wait for Dasher.

Mirrors over the bar let her observe the brasserie without turning around. She sipped her wine and watched as the Maitre'd escorted a man in a gray pinstriped suit with a blue pocket square to the corner table she'd reserved. He shrugged out of his jacket and turned in a circle. After draping the coat over the back of the chair, he rolled up his sleeves and turned his pockets inside out like she'd instructed. Last, of all, he pulled up his pant legs, showing he wasn't carrying a backup gun in an ankle holster.

He put his hands flat on the table and scanned the bistro. The SOG rogue looked nervous and probably scared. After all, a world-class sniper had his girlfriend pinned down and he was about to meet a legendary assassin. She took a deep breath then picked up the bottle and glasses and started for his table.

She never made it.

Chapter Twenty-Five

Tuesday, March 28th; Paris, France; L'Alsace Brasserie

She's dead. Paradox's emotions were roiling in a maelstrom, rushing between grief to anger to thoughts of stone-cold revenge. Had she not been in the Hague getting ready to assassinate the U.S. Charge d'affaires, she might have been able to prevent her death. She warned Circe to break off communications with the woman acknowledged as the assassin of assassins. Even so, she could've taken the meeting at face value rather than try to set the killer up.

But while Circe was a brilliant businessperson, she was ignorant of the ways of death and had no idea of the capabilities of someone like Sasha. If you were going to take out Sasha, you'd better not miss. Otherwise, you'd end up looking like a Rorschach test on the wall of your bathroom like Circe. Paradox had no idea what had motivated Circe to send Dasher after the assassin. The guy and his little bitch could teach a class on how to fuck up an operation. The only reason Circe worked with them was that it gave her access to U.S. intelligence. But Paradox had her own information channels and had never seen the need for them.

But karma came after everyone eventually. Paradox didn't care who you were. What goes around comes around. That's how it worked. Sooner or later the universe gave you the revenge you desired, and

Paradox was getting ready to deliver the first part of it. There was no way someone could've left the site of the shooting, beaten Circe to her apartment, and planted the bomb. Sasha wasn't working alone, and Paradox intended to find and kill all of those involved.

She'd been watching Dasher's apartment where both he and his bitch were staying then followed the SOG operator as he left earlier this morning. He was wearing a gray mid-thigh length raincoat with the hood pulled up. She was wearing a black reversible rain jacket with a black leather Dyna purse looped over her left shoulder. The purse held a suppressed HK VP9 pistol loaded with 15 rounds of Hornaday Critical Defense rounds.

She followed him onto the Metro to the Latin Quarter then up the stairs to the Strada Café. While Paradox knew what he looked like, neither he nor his bitch had a clue as to who she was, but she hung back and waited until he'd ordered a coffee and had taken a table at the back of the room before she stepped up to the counter. She ordered a café crème as she watched him in her peripheral vision. He grabbed a newspaper and draped his raincoat over the back of one of the chairs at his table. Under it, he was wearing a gray suit with a white shirt and a navy and maroon rep-striped tie. She took her drink to a table in the front corner of the café where she could watch her quarry.

She took out her phone and opened a news application while she observed Dasher. He picked up his phone and smiled as he answered it. But it only lasted a moment. Something was wrong. His face flashed from expressions of anger to one of worry. He took a pen from his shirt pocket and wrote something on a napkin then hung up. He checked his watch and then sat there staring at whatever he'd written on the napkin. He kept checking his watch, but after three minutes, he made a call. Again, his facial expression registered anger but within seconds it changed to something that surprised Paradox.

It was fear. Heart-stopping, blood-chilling fear.

Dasher slumped forward with his face in his hands. Paradox could see his breathing was considerably faster than normal. He leaned back, crossed his arms, and chewed his lip while he stared at his phone. He checked his watch and swore as he left the table and started for the door. Paradox watched him head for the entrance to the Metro then followed. When she reached the stairs, she took off her black jacket and reversed it so that it was now gray and flipped up the hood. When the train came, she got in using the door at the opposite end of the car from Dasher and took a seat in the corner with her hands in her pockets. She kept her head down, watching Dasher out of the corner of her eye.

After several stops, Dasher got up and examined the Metro map over the door. He seemed to find what he wanted and stared straight ahead. At the next stop, he got off and walked to the stairs that led to another train line. Before Paradox got off the train, she pulled on a plain ballcap that she took from her pocket then proceeded to follow Dasher.

At first, she thought he was performing a surveillance detection run, but he wasn't taking any precautions like stopping to tie his shoe or using reflections in the plastic-covered billboards to pick up a tail. Instead, he paced back and forth and kept looking at his watch. He had to get somewhere and there was a time limit for his arrival.

When the train came, she repeated her previous entry into the opposite end of the same car. They rode for another fifteen minutes when Dasher got off at the George V stop and trotted to the stairs to street level. Paradox let him get three-quarters of the way up before following him. He dashed across the street and ducked into the George V hotel. She followed and saw him enter a men's clothing boutique where he bought a blue pocket square. He paid and tucked it in the breast pocket of his suit as he hurried out of the hotel and recrossed the street.

He was walking fast and checking his watch as he ducked into a restaurant called the L'Alsace Brasserie. Paradox slowed and read the menu posted outside another restaurant. She assumed he was meeting someone, although who was unknown. It occurred to her that perhaps the SOG found his apartment and were holding Elise hostage under penalty of death if he didn't surrender. She knew the organization didn't suffer traitors, so perhaps they were offering him a deal, namely him for Elise.

Paradox put her hands in her pockets and strolled past the restaurant. She had to force herself not to gape at what Dasher was doing. He was standing with his back to the windows. His jacket and suit coat were hung over his chair, and he was rolling up his shirt sleeves.

What the hell? No assassin worth their salt ever put their back to a window—willingly.

Dasher was definitely meeting someone, and if it was the SOG, they'd take him away and bury him in a dungeon so deep, Paradox would never be able to find him and exact her revenge for the clusterfuck that cost Circe her life.

She walked another fifty yards past the restaurant then unzipped the side compartment of her purse. She shifted it to her right shoulder and pulled up her hood then turned and walked back toward where Dasher sat. He was staring straight ahead with his hands flat on the table. She aimed the purse across her body and paused behind him. She fired four shots at his head then kept walking toward the Metro. The traffic noise covered the residual sound of the suppressed bullets, but as she reached the metro entrance, she broke into a sprint and dashed down the stairs. She slipped between the doors of a waiting train as they were closing and took a seat as it pulled out of the station.

Paradox knew Circe was well aware of the dangers, but she didn't deserve to die because of the stupidity of others. Paradox was a fan of forgiveness as long as she was allowed to get even first. The assassin knew Dasher wasn't the one who killed her. That was probably Sasha, but it gave her a measure of satisfaction, knowing she'd taken out a man who should've known better than to go after the queen of assassins, which resulted in Sasha taking out her revenge on Paradox's lover. And as for going after Sasha, she recalled a saying she'd heard that was very applicable.

"Mama didn't raise no fool," she whispered.

Chapter Twenty-Six

Tuesday, March 28th; Paris, France; La Traboule

Mirlinda froze as Dasher's head exploded and rocked forward, landing face down on the table. The restaurant went from quiet to pandemonium in seconds. She saw a tall woman in a gray jacket wearing a baseball cap walk away. She had a purse over her right shoulder and Mirlinda was certain she'd fired a suppressed gun through it.

She set the wine and one of the glasses on the bar but dropped the one with the poison on the floor and crushed it. She joined the stampede out the door and walked away from the restaurant toward the Metro. She took out her cell phone and sent a text to Cailan.

"All set. It's a go for the SOG team."

"Dasher's dead?"

"Yes, but not by my hand. A woman whom I think was Enigma stopped outside the restaurant and shot him through the window then disappeared."

"Did you get a look at her?"

"Not really. She had the hood of her jacket pulled up and a ball cap pulled down over her face."

"The SOG team just arrested Elise. I'm packing up."

"Why don't you meet me at Un Amour de Bistro in the eighth arrondissement? It's a casual place that serves good tapas."

"I'm going to drop my backpack in my hotel room first. Not a good idea to be walking around Paris carrying a sniper rifle."

"Good point. Just cab it to the bistro. The Metro will take too much time and I'm hungry and thirsty."

"See you soon." He disconnected.

Mirlinda reached the bistro twenty minutes later and got a table for two in a quiet corner. She ordered four different tapas and a bottle of Menetou-Salon Domaine de Loye 2020. The waiter uncorked the bottle and poured a small amount into her glass. She tasted it and nodded. He filled her glass a third full and placed the bottle in a stone cooler on the table.

Dasher's murder was bold for even the best assassins. But Mirlinda had to admire her style. The woman used her body to shield her suppressed gun as she fired it through her purse such that none of the pedestrians had any idea what happened. If that was indeed Enigma, it was impressive work. She stood opposite Dasher, checked his position once, and never looked at him again as she shot him. Then she casually walked away.

The way she did it indicated to Mirlinda that it was personal. Dasher's reckless attempt to kill Sasha led to Circe's death, although she would have died even if he hadn't tried for her. A chill ran down her spine as she realized if she'd joined Dasher at his table seconds earlier, she might have been another of Enigma's victims.

"Dang, I think I'm rusty," she whispered.

While she had an innate ability to pick up people tailing her, she'd missed the fact that someone might want Dasher out of the way. She sipped her wine. Of course, it didn't matter because she'd been about to kill him herself. Still, she told herself to be more cautious in the future.

Cailan arrived as the tapas were delivered.

"And what are we eating?" he signed.

"I ordered the casserole of scallops, pan-fried marinated salmon, crispy prawns, and home fries. And the wine is a very nice Sauvignon Blanc."

Cailan nodded his approval as he sampled the food and wine. *"I'm not normally a wine drinker, but this is very good."*

"I offer it in my bar," Mirlinda said. "It's a go-to of mine."

"So, why don't you expand on what happened to Dasher."

Mirlinda switched to sign. *"I ordered a very expensive bottle of wine, which turned out to be a waste. But I did manage to drink a little of it before all hell broke out. I dried enough batrachotoxin in his glass to kill him several times over and saw him enter. When he did everything I asked him to do in our phone conversation, I grabbed the glasses and the wine and took one step toward his table when I saw the woman as her purse rose slightly and she shot him."*

"She didn't take the gun out of her purse?"

"No, she shot through the leather. The gun was suppressed and with all the traffic noise on the Champs Elysée, no one noticed, and she was able to walk away."

"Rather bold, don't you think?"

"Very. I couldn't see her face, but she was tall, maybe five-ten, and slender."

"Why do you think it was Enigma?" Cailan signed.

"From what we know, she fit the description, but just the way this went down tells me this was personal for her."

"I don't understand."

"I think Enigma and Circe were lovers and she thinks Dasher's rash move trying to kill me is what got Circe killed."

"Geez, I'm glad she doesn't know the truth," Cailan signed.

"Yeah, well we're going to have to step up our game because this woman isn't afraid to take chances."

"Brook should be in Geneva by now. I'll contact her and tell her what happened so she can be extra vigilant."

"After she takes down Lagunov, we're left with eliminating Enigma and your buddy Elion Kastrati," Mirlinda said.

Mirlinda popped a prawn in her mouth. Her face wore a smirk as she chewed.

"What's so amusing?" Cailan asked.

"As the Keith Urban song says, he's a stupid boy."

Chapter Twenty-Seven

Tuesday, March 28th; Geneva, Switzerland; The Geneva Train Station

The TGV Lyria was the best that a high-speed train could offer. Although the distance between Paris and Geneva was a little over 300 miles, it covered the distance in three hours. The seats were comfortable, the food was excellent, and the scenery was breathtaking. They were thirty minutes out of Geneva when Brook got a text from Cailan, saying he had Elise Garnier, alias Vixen pinned down and Mirlinda had arranged a meeting with Dasher where she would kill him.

Earlier, Brook had spoken with her handler and told him Circe was dead, and with it, any payments for CIA and MI6 agents were nullified. To make sure Enigma wouldn't go after General David White, Hector said he'd drop a story with the Associated Press and the BBC that Marie Tremblay was a notorious recruiter for assassins and was a party to several dozen deaths. Enigma and the other assassins in her stable would know that the bounty money had dried up and would scatter.

She gave Hector a list of equipment she needed and was instructed to purchase a black Victorinox rollaboard suitcase and pack it with clothing. When she arrived in Geneva, she was to browse books in the station's Payot Libraire and go to the history section and look through a book entitled, "A Concise History of Switzerland." A woman wearing red shoes would exchange suitcases with her. Brook's new suitcase would contain all the requested equipment. Hector also got her a reservation for a tour of the Palais des Nations that housed the headquarters of the United Nations offices. Normally reservations had to be made months in advance, but Hector being who he was got her one for tomorrow.

The train slowed as it pulled into the station and came to a stop. Brook packed the novel she'd been reading and grabbed her suitcase off the overhead rack then followed the other passengers off the train. She took the stairs down to the main station and checked a directory for the location of the bookstore. She found it and walked toward it, constantly scanning the area for anyone or anything out of the ordinary. She was wearing a brunette wig cut in a bob and her eyes hid behind oversized aviator sunglasses. Neither Hector nor anyone else in her organization knew what she currently looked like.

She moved leisurely through the book racks, stopping to peruse a magazine then strolled over to the section on Switzerland. She stepped away from her suitcase as she pulled a copy of the designated book off the shelf and flipped through the pages. A woman wearing a white ruffled blouse tucked into a navy pleated pencil skirt and a structured jacket nipped at the waist left an identical suitcase next to Brook's. But the identifying feature of her outfit was her red shoes.

Brook replaced the book and grabbed the contact's rollaboard as she left the store. Before she left the station, she swung by a Lady's room and removed her wig, reverting to her blond, crewcut Dylan Payne identity. Her hotel, the Eastwest was located in the city center in the residential area of Les Pâquis, a stone's throw from Lake Geneva and a seven-minute walk from the train station. She had a room with a king bed, a small desk, and a Nespresso machine.

Geneva lay at the southern tip of the expansive Lac Léman, more commonly known as Lake Geneva. Surrounded by the Alps and Jura mountains, the city had dramatic views of Mont Blanc. Home to the headquarters of Europe's United Nations and the Red Cross, it was a global hub for diplomacy and banking. French influence was widespread, from the language to gastronomy.

She checked in and then proceeded to her third-floor room. She dropped her backpack on a chair. She performed her usual examination looking for surveillance devices. When she cleared the room, she placed her suitcase on a luggage stand to examine its contents.

A black case the size of a hardback book held an FN509, a suppressor, and two extra seventeen-round magazines. Two Craft holsters, one shoulder, and one back-of-the-waist style were packed between an assortment of clothes in her size. A second case held a Sig Sauer P365 SAS. She liked it for its 10+1 capacity, more than any other subcompact pistol. Heck, that was more than a full-size 1911. It came with a Comfort Tac ankle holster.

A third small case contained the means by which Brook planned to kill Sergei Lagunov. Hector had learned the Russian foreign minister had two serious health issues. The first was congestive heart failure, a chronic condition in which the heart doesn't pump blood as well as it should. The second was Type 2 diabetes and the two were interrelated. There are two classes of beta-adrenergic receptors: beta1, which is more abundant and is responsible for regulating the strength of the heartbeat, and beta2, which is believed to be a minor, less important receptor. Targeting beta receptors with beta-blocker drugs is a mainstay treatment for heart failure.

However, recent studies showed that high levels of insulin were a key factor in heart failure associated with the illness. When the insulin receptor was activated by elevated levels of insulin, it sent a message to the beta2 receptor, which disrupted signaling through the beta1-adrenergic pathway and reduced the heart's ability to pump, leading to heart failure.

Lagunov used an insulin pump to regulate the delivery of the hormone into his blood. The third case contained insulin pods that on the surface looked like his normal brand. However, they were a specially formulated version. Lagunov used cartridges that had a concentration of 100 units of insulin per milliliter of fluid. However, the insulin in the pods that Brook planned to substitute contained 5000 units of insulin per milliliter of fluid. The combination of a fifty-fold higher dose flooding

Lagunov's system would cause his heart to fail before anyone could rescue him.

Lagunov had the fifth-floor Lakeview Heritage suite at the Beau-Rivage on the Quai du Mont-Blanc. The hotel was founded in 1865 by the Mayer family and was still a family-owned business. It was located facing Geneva's jet d'eau and was one of the city's landmark establishments.

Brook's hotel was conveniently located only a block away. She changed into faded blue jeans, a burgundy tee shirt, and a bulky cream-colored fisherman's knit sweater that hung below her butt. She threaded her belt through the back-of-the-waist holster and checked to see her gun had a full seventeen rounds in the magazine. She holstered it and adjusted the sweater to hide it. She shrugged into her gray Arc'teryx jacket and left the hotel to begin her reconnaissance of the Beau-Rivage.

She grabbed a cup of coffee from the hotel bar then went to her right as she exited the hotel. She turned right again on the Rue Doctor-Alfred Vincent. Just before she reached the lake, she stepped into a short alley that led behind the hotel. A loading dock and an employee entrance were possible access points to the hotel that would allow her to avoid the scrutiny of the front desk and hotel security. The age of the hotel meant there were no security cameras in the hallways.

She left the alley and circled to the main entrance. With its celebrated chef, Dominique Gauthier, the hotel restaurant Le Chat Botté boasted a Michelin star. According to her intel, Lagunov dined there every night. She thought about having Hector get her a dinner reservation for tomorrow, but she decided it might compromise her if she was seen in the hotel too often.

She left the hotel and crossed the street to the Rotonde du Mont-Blanc and sat on one of the benches. The park had a perfect view of the Jet d'Eau and Mont Blanc in the distance. But it also allowed her to watch for Lagunov's return to his hotel for the evening.

An hour later, her watching was rewarded as a black Mercedes Maybach bearing two small Russian flags on the front grille pulled up in front of the hotel. She checked the time. Four-thirty. One man exited the front passenger seat and scanned the area while another held the rear door as an overweight man with a receding hairline stepped out of the car.

Lagunov.

He nodded to the two men who followed him into the hotel. Fifteen minutes later one of the men reappeared and got back in the car and the limousine pulled away.

So, one bodyguard with the Foreign Minister. Not a lot of security for a guy with such a big mouth. It wouldn't matter. She was planning on entering when no one was home. After she finished switching the insulin cartridges, she just had to wait for nature to take its course, namely the death of the asshole who was responsible for the deaths of several of her colleagues.

Chapter Twenty-Eight

Wednesday, March 29th; Geneva, Switzerland; The Palais des Nations

The historic Palais des Nations, originally built for the League of Nations in the 1930s, housed the United Nations Office in Geneva or UNOG. Located in a beautiful art deco building overlooking Lake Geneva, it's the largest center for conference diplomacy in the world. Staffed by more than 1,300 employees, it's also the busiest conference center, holding over 5,000 meetings per year.

Brook took a cab to the facility and arrived an hour early for her 10:00 tour. The guard at the entrance checked her passport and made sure she had a reservation. Once he confirmed it, he directed her to a lounge area where several other people were waiting for the tour to start. A blond woman in a gray fitted suit appeared at exactly 10:00. She introduced herself and then led them through the expansive front hall to one of the main conference halls. She informed them about the UNOG and its activities to maintain world peace and foster international relations and development. Several of the tourists snickered at her statement for good reason. The war between Russia and Ukraine and the fighting among the former Soviet satellite countries didn't speak well of their efforts. The organization recently removed the Russian woman who formerly served as the Director-General of the9 UN Geneva and replaced her with a Danish delegate.

As they continued the tour, the guide pointed out the impressive paintings covering the walls and ceilings of various areas of the building, but what Brook noticed most was the presence of heavily armed soldiers wearing the blue berets of U.N. forces. The tour continued for another uninformative forty-five minutes before the guests were deposited back at the entrance. She had hoped to find the location of the Russian diplomatic mission, but those offices were off-limits to tourists, and with the U.N. soldiers patrolling the halls, she couldn't risk detouring from the group.

She didn't bother to examine the grounds with the others, instead opting to head for the cab stand and catch a ride back to her hotel. She tossed her black sling bag on the bed and changed into loose-fitting blue jeans, a light blue tee shirt, and a black hoodie. She threaded her back-of-the-waist holster through her belt, positioning it behind her right hip then pulled on a pair of Ryder sneakers. She clipped a Benchmade Gold Class Infidel auto OTF knife to the right pocket of her jeans then headed out to grab a late lunch and watch the Beau-Rivage to determine if Lagunov returned to the hotel at approximately the same time each day.

Brook crossed the river and walked to the Cottage Café located in Brunswick Park, just a stone's throw from the Beau-Rivage. The café was a little brick house opposite the Brunswick Monument. It served as a temporary accommodation for construction workers between 1876 and 1879 then became a gardener's pavilion before eventually becoming a café in 1930. In 2007, it was purchased by chef Nicole Boder. She was born in Morocco but grew up in Israel. When she was twenty, she moved to Neuchâtel where she worked as a waitress for fifteen years before working for three years as a chef at the Maison des Arts du Grütli in Geneva. She opened her restaurant, the Cottage Cafe in October 2008.

Inside, the single room had old gold stuccos, a black tile floor in the bar section, and furniture and oddities obtained from flea markets. The veranda had a brown parquet floor and awnings over the outdoor tables that provided a cozy shelter on a rainy day.

The café faced the Brunswick Monument, an eerie neo-gothic structure of pink marble. Built in 1879, it was the resting place of Charles Frederic Auguste Guillaume, the Duke of Brunswick. He was a rich, eccentric philanderer who was dispossessed of his throne by his brother and spent the rest of his life traveling across Europe where he was involved in numerous political and moral intrigues before retreating at last to a suite in the Beau-Rivage Hotel where he finally died.

Brook took a table on the outdoor veranda that gave her a clear view of the front entrance to the Beau-Rivage and scanned the menu. She ordered dried plums wrapped in smoked bacon and spinach and feta cakes. Since she expected to be there awhile, she also ordered a half bottle of a 2021 Corail Chateau Roquefort Rosé from Provence.

Her phone vibrated with a text from Cailan. He told her Elise was in SOG custody and Dasher was dead. But Mirlinda wasn't the one who killed him. He said Mirlinda watched a tall, slender woman in a hooded raincoat and ballcap walk by on the street and pause outside where he was sitting with his back to the windows of the L'Alsace Brasserie. She shot him and casually walked away. She couldn't see the woman's face, but she thought it might have been Enigma. She also said that Dasher's murder looked to be personal. If so, it meant that although the cadre of assassins hunting CIA and MI6 agents were no longer motivated to hunt them nor were the U.S. diplomats in danger, Enigma might be looking for the ones involved in killing Circe, whom Mirlinda suspected was her lover. He closed his text by telling her to watch her back.

Well, that sucked.

Enigma might not be hunting diplomats but, as Circe's lover, she certainly would know that Lagunov was the one who offered the contract. And if she was pissed off because someone had killed her lover, she would also know there was a possibility that an assassin would try to kill the Russian. It was the same dilemma they faced with the flash drive. What better bait than either Sergei Lagunov or Elion Kastrati, the originators of the contracts, to draw the ones responsible for Circe's death into a killing field? There was no question in her mind that Enigma would watch those targets, waiting for one or more assassins to show up.

"Shit, as if this wasn't tough enough," Brook muttered. She took a paperback novel by Jack Higgins entitled "Dark Justice" from her back pocket and settled in to read. She'd become enamored with Higgins' writing and especially his Sean Dillon character who was an assassin like herself. By the time Lagunov's car appeared, she'd just finished the book. She checked the time and nodded. Again, four-thirty.

She shoved the novel into her pocket and took the last sip of her wine. She took a leisurely roundabout walk back to her hotel, stopping to do some window shopping. It was a way for her to check for anyone tailing her. When she reached the hotel and stepped into the elevator, she took out her phone and checked the recording for the surveillance camera that she'd left in her room. She fast-forwarded through the last five hours and when she was sure no one had visited her room, she proceeded down the hall and unlocked her door. She took a rubber wedge and shoved it under the door then slipped out of her hoodie and decided to catch a couple of hours of sleep before she grabbed dinner.

She took her gun and lay on her back on the bed. She set the gun on her stomach and closed her eyes. Her internal clock woke her two hours later. She checked to make sure the rubber wedge hadn't moved then took her gun to the bathroom. She set it on the sink within easy reach of the shower then stripped off her clothes and stood under the hot water for ten minutes. She dried off then pulled on a pair of black Duluth Women's Dry-on-the-Fly bootcut cargo pants and a gray cotton Henley. She strapped the Sig Sauer P365 to her ankle, pulled on her sneakers, and clipped her Infidel knife to the right pocket of her pants. She slipped into a gray tweed jacket then removed the rubber wedge and activated her surveillance camera before she headed for the hotel bar.

The black lacquer bar seated sixteen in matching black leather chairs. The mustard-colored walls glowed with light from contemporary wall sconces. The two bartenders wore white shirts with burnt orange ties and were busy making cocktails for the few people in the place. She took a seat at the far end where she could observe the others. She ordered smoked salmon on toast with crème fraiche and a glass of Xavier Vignon Côtes du Rhône Blanc then checked out the guests. There were four couples occupying tables, and one gentleman in a navy suit with his tie loosened sitting at the opposite end of the bar, scrolling through his phone. When her food and wine were delivered, she realized she was very hungry and downed the salmon in minutes.

She was debating whether or not to order dessert when a woman entered who didn't so much as walk as stalk into the bar. Her stride was like a panther, looking for prey. At approximately six feet, she swung her arms and used her hips to sashay across the floor and ensure all eyes were on her. Her power gaze exuded confidence and authority. Her face was striking with high cheekbones and a straight nose. Her short black hair was slicked back on her head. She was dressed in a white, V-neck, silk blouse under a black jacket and loose gray pants. She wore low black pumps and carried a black leather clutch bag. Although the clothes disguised the outline of her body, Brook estimated that she was a trim 140 pounds with a low percentage of body fat.

She took a seat in the middle of the bar, midway between Brook and the lone man, and ordered a champagne cocktail. Brook watched her in the mirror over the bar and noticed the glances she cast her way. She looked like either a corporate executive or a professional model. After fifteen minutes, the woman picked up her drink and walked over to Brook.

"Mind if I join you?" she asked.

Brook turned to size her up, trying to decide what the woman's play was. "Why would you want to join me?"

"Because I'm bored and looking for some intelligent conversation."

Brook nodded to the bar stool next to her. "Please, have a seat."

The stranger offered her hand. "Cecille Allard."

"Dylan Payne," Brook said.

Allard's handshake was firm and although her nails were polished and manicured, Brook felt callouses on her palms and fingers.

"You share your name with one of my favorite songwriters, Bob Dylan," Allard said.

"Are you a folk music fan?" Brook asked.

"Sort of, if you consider artists like Joni Mitchell and Judy Collins folk," she said. "How about you?"

"I'm more of a rock aficionado," Brook said.

"Who are your favorites?"

"I like groups like AC/DC, Pink Floyd, and ZZ Top."

"Are you a musician?" Allard asked.

"No, I'm a corporate troubleshooter."

"And what exactly does that entail?"

"When my clients have an issue, I go in, analyze the problem, and present several potential solutions. If they like one of them, I facilitate the problem's resolution." She sipped her drink. "How about you?"

Allard's lips curled in a coy smile. "I'm a professional model. I work with the Elite Model Agency out of Paris."

"Isn't Elite one of the most famous international modeling agencies?

"Yes, it's ranked eighth on Forbes' Most Influential Modeling Agencies list."

"Hmm, impressive." Brook's phone buzzed with a text. She took it out of her pocket and read the message.

"Ms. Allard, the woman sitting next to you is not what she claims to be. She is an assassin. Be careful."

Brook frowned and shook her head as she pocketed her phone.

"Something wrong?" Allard asked.

"No, one of my corporate clients in Zurich wants to discuss a marketing issue tomorrow." She finished her wine and slid off her seat. "I've got to get up early to make it to Zurich in time for this meeting. Nice meeting you."

Allard nodded and motioned to the bartender for another cocktail. Brook felt her eyes on her as she left the bar. Her mind was racing as she headed for the elevators. She paused to scan the area for anyone who might have been the source of the mysterious text but didn't see anyone suspicious. She took the elevator to the third floor and checked the app that connected her phone to the camera in her room. It was clear, so she swiped her card and immediately began packing her clothes, guns, insulin cartridges, and her surveillance clock radio into her rollaboard.

She shrugged into her jacket then used the TV remote to check out online. She slipped the straps of her backpack over her shoulders and cracked the door to make sure the hall was empty.

She took the stairs to the ground floor but went out a rear door and walked south toward the Rhone River. She paused when she was three blocks away and made a reservation at the CitizenM Hotel which was a short walk over the Pont de la Machine bridge. It was an ultra-modern hotel with small, but comfortable rooms and an excellent lounge and bar area. She did a complex series of SDRs before heading to the hotel.

An hour later, she double-locked the door to her second-floor room. She dropped her backpack on the floor next to the small desk and hung her coat over the chair. She left her rollaboard in a corner and removed her gun and holster. She kicked off her shoes and flopped on the bed with her gun on her stomach.

Her mind was flying close to the speed of light with unanswered questions. Who sent the message? Was the woman at the bar Enigma? Did the female assassin know who Brook was? And how the hell did the one sending the text know who she was?

"Son of a bitch," she whispered. "This is truly devious."

Chapter Twenty-Nine

Thursday, March 30th; Geneva, Switzerland; The Beau-Rivage Hotel

Brook left her hotel with her backpack across one shoulder and crossed the Rue de la Machine. She stopped off at a Starbucks just past the bridge and ordered a grande Americano and a cheese Danish then took a seat at a corner table. The previous night's text message spooked her. She still had no answer to her questions, and the warning to be careful was disturbing. Was there another leak in the SOG? Otherwise, how could anyone know who she was and that she was here?

The mysterious texter said the woman she met last night was an assassin, which led Brook to conclude she was Enigma. It was a bold and arrogant move by the woman. It caused Brook to switch hotels, but it didn't affect her plan. Her agenda for the day called for her to scout the Beau-Rivage and find the employee dressing areas. She planned to steal one of the housekeeping uniforms that would allow her to move through the hotel unnoticed. His recon from two days ago indicated there was a fair amount of worker traffic going in and out of the employee entrance around the loading dock. But she had to be extra careful after the warning last night.

She finished her Danish and coffee and left the Starbucks, heading northeast on Rue François-Bonivard. She went left on Rue des Alpes for four blocks before turning right on Rue de Berne and proceeded to Rue de Zurich. Her route was designed to allow her to pick up a tail as well as bypass the Eastwest Hotel. She headed southeast on Rue de Zurich and entered the Novotel and took a seat in their coffee shop. She ordered a café crème and watched the hotel's entrance for a half hour. When no one suspicious appeared, she left the hotel and wove her way through back streets to the alley behind the Beau-Rivage.

It looked like controlled pandemonium as vans unloaded linens and produce. She joined a group of people entering through the employee door. One of the men headed for the basement, so she followed him and found the locker rooms. She slipped through the door marked *"Femmes"* and paused to listen. The room was empty as the staff would've arrived two hours ago to begin their work for the day.

Brook moved down a row of lockers to a table and rack where freshly washed and pressed uniforms were stacked. She chose a white blouse with a Peter Pan collar, a pair of black wool slacks, and a black jacket, and checked to make sure they were the correct size. She carefully folded clothes and placed them in her backpack. She went through a row of lockers, jimmying the locks until she found one with a uniform hanging inside, indicating that the owner wasn't on duty. She pocketed the name badge and turned to leave.

She checked the hall outside the room then slipped out and went back to the employee entrance. She took a step out the door and turned toward the street when her phone vibrated with a text.

"Duck!"

She lurched to her right as a bullet tore through her left arm. She dropped to her hands and knees as chips of asphalt exploded next to where she'd been standing. She shuffled back into the hotel and rolled to sit with her back to the wall. Although her arm hadn't started to ache yet, it was bleeding badly. The bullet tore through her triceps muscle. She pushed herself off the floor and headed downstairs to the locker room. Thankfully, it was still unoccupied. She grabbed a bunch of hand towels from the table with the uniforms and stepped into one of the bathroom stalls. She sat on the toilet and gritted her teeth as she wriggled out of her sweatshirt so she could inspect the wound. Just as she hoped, it was a through-and-through in her triceps. She wrapped a towel around her arm and tied it off using her teeth and right hand. She wrapped a second towel around it then pulled on her hoodie and used a third towel to soak up as much blood as possible. When she was satisfied that the wound wasn't obvious, she paused and took a couple of deep breaths.

"What the fuck?" she whispered. If the mystery texter hadn't warned her, the bullet would've taken her through the chest. A dozen more questions ran through her mind, but they would have to wait. Right now, she had to get away from the hotel. She knew from her previous recon of the area that the only building with a view of the alley was the Library-in-English building across the street. But it had a steeply slanted roof, which meant the shooter was inside it. So, whoever it was wouldn't be able to change their position easily. Brook picked herself off the toilet and brushed off her pants. She threaded her way through the hotel and went out the front entrance. She headed south past the Cottage Café and returned to the CitizenM. The lobby was deserted so she was able to make it to the elevator without drawing attention.

When she reached her room, she kicked the rubber wedge under the door then slipped off her backpack. She stifled a scream as she shed her hoodie. She managed to strip off her clothes then stepped into the shower and carefully cleaned the wound. She wrapped a towel around her arm and took a trauma kit that she carried on every assignment from the rollaboard. She patted the wound dry and took a packet of Bleed Stop powder from the kit. She sprinkled it into the entry and exit wounds. The bleeding stopped in seconds. Next, she took a pair of plastic gloves and a tube of triple antibiotic ointment from the kit and placed a washcloth in her mouth. She bit down hard, using the washcloth to muffle her scream as she squeezed the ointment into the wounds. Finally, she opened a container of Gorilla glue, took a deep breath, and applied it to the edges of the entry wound. She squeezed the edges together and held it closed for five minutes. When she finished, she stood in front of the mirror and repeated the procedure for the exit wound.

By the time she was done, her body glistened with a sheen of sweat. She felt exhausted. The adrenaline hangover was peaking, and she could barely keep her eyes open. Rather than fight it, she took two 500mg Tylenol tablets and curled up on the bed to clear her mind and think. The shooter had to be Enigma seeking vengeance for the death of her lover. And if she was indeed the woman from the bar last night then she knew what Brook looked like. It was unnerving the way whoever it was had anticipated how she'd try to gain access to Lagunov.

Brook fluffed her pillows and sighed as she pulled the covers over her. The prudent thing to do was get out of Geneva and leave Lagunov to the rest of her organization. The question was, was she the prudent type?

Chapter Thirty

Friday, March 31st; Geneva, Switzerland, Jardin Anglais

Brook slept for sixteen hours and while her mind felt alert, her arm hurt like hell. She pushed back the covers and grabbed the bottle of Tylenol. She washed down two of the extra strength tablets with water and then checked her wounds. There was no sign of redness that would indicate an infection and no further bleeding. She did some light stretching until her stomach reminded her that she hadn't eaten in twenty-four hours.

She pulled on her underwear and covered her wounds with sterile gauze pads from the trauma kit and used Eco-Flex self-sticking flex tape to secure them in place. She struggled to dress in black cargo pants, a gray long-sleeved cotton Henley shirt, and Doc Martin combat boots. She grit her teeth to keep from screaming as she threaded her holster through her belt and positioned her gun behind her right hip. She gingerly shrugged into her Arc'teryx jacket. Brook took out the clock radio that was a motion-activated camera and set it on the desk then grabbed her keycard and headed for the lobby to grab breakfast.

She grabbed a ham and cheese croissant and a tall coffee and took a table outside in the central courtyard. She took a bite of the croissant and sipped the coffee then took out her cell phone to check in with Hector.

"What news?" Brook texted.

"No more information on Enigma," he sent back. *"Do you have everything you need for Lagunov?"*

"I'm not sure I'll be able to take him."

"The only reason you'd say that is if something was terribly wrong."

"Two nights ago, I was sitting in the bar of my hotel when a woman who said she was a professional model sat next to me and struck up a conversation. While we were talking, I got a text warning me she was an assassin."

"Who texted you?"

"I don't know."

"How can that be?" Hector asked. *"Could it have been one of the friends you enlisted to help you?"*

"No, they're still in France."

"Damn."

Brook imagined the worried look on her handler's face.

"Do you think the woman was Enigma?" Hector asked.

"I presume so, but there's more. I went to the Beau-Rivage to see about stealing a uniform so I could get to Lagunov's room. I picked one up but as I stepped out the door to the back alley, I got another mysterious text."

"What did this one say?"

"Duck."

"Shit! What happened? Were you hurt?"

"I caught a bullet through my left triceps. I've taken care of it, but if I hadn't thrown myself into the alley wall, that bullet would have taken me center mass."

"Okay, I'm going to talk to Andrew McGill. I think we should pull you out of there."

"Why?"

"Are you serious, Zealot? You've been shot and the assassin knows your face. You've been compromised and you need to get to safety now!"

"See what McGill says," Brook texted. *"I've got the uniform for the Beau-Rivage and I can be in and out tomorrow."*

"Are you listening, Zealot? You've been blown. Get out of there. Don't try to go after Lagunov."

"Take care and stay in touch, Hector." Brook disconnected. She took another bite of her sandwich and sipped the coffee. She loved European brew. It was richer and stronger without tasting burnt. She finished her sandwich and was about to go back for seconds when she got another text from her mystery angel.

"Go to the Jardin Anglaise and bring binoculars. Watch the Beau-Rivage."

"What the hell?" she whispered. Was this a trap to lure her out in the open where she'd be vulnerable to another sniper shot? She had no idea who the person texting her could be, but whoever it was, if they'd wanted her dead, they wouldn't have warned her yesterday. No, the mystery person had saved her life, so she decided to do what was asked.

She went back to her room and retrieved a pair of ZEISS Terra ED compact binoculars. She left the hotel and walked north toward the lake and the Jardin Anglaise. Located on the lake shore opposite the Jet d'eau, the Jardin Anglaise, or English garden with its famous flower clock, monumental fountain, and hundred-year-old trees, was one of the most spectacular parks in Geneva. It was created in 1854 and designed following the model for English landscape gardens. Idyllic paths wound through the flowers and trees that made up more than 25,000 square meters of the urban grounds. The L'horloge Fleurie or flower clock stood in its center and was created in 1955 to commemorate Geneva being the mother of high-end watchmaking. The clock looked different depending on the time of year as it was made of various flowers that bloomed in different seasons. The park was also the location of the Four Seasons fountain and was home to several statues of Swiss artists.

Brook strolled through the park, luxuriating in the tranquil atmosphere. She kept her gaze moving, searching for threats, but found none as she approached a walkway that looked out on the lake and the Jet d'eau. She turned and faced the city, scanning the rooftops and windows for any sign of a sniper. Fortunately, the trees interfered with a clear line of sight to where she was standing.

She turned back to the Beau-Rivage and watched a sleek red Skater 28 flat-deck speedboat cruise leisurely toward the river. She recognized it because it was considered the Porsche of the waters. Its twin 400R outboards could send it flying over the water at better than 110 mph. The person behind the wheel was wearing a full wet suit and hood. She couldn't identify the driver because whoever it was kept their back to her.

The boat made a slow turn and headed away from the river then slowed and drifted until it was parallel with the Beau-Rivage. A black Mercedes Maybach pulled up in front of the hotel. Brook checked it out with the binoculars. At first, she thought it was Lagunov's ride but the flags on the front grill of the limo weren't Russian.

They were American.

Lagunov and a tall slender man with close-cropped silver hair in a black suit came down the steps and slipped into the backseat as a bodyguard held the door. As soon as the bodyguard got into the front passenger seat, Brook saw a flash from the speedboat. Almost simultaneously, the limousine exploded in a ball of fire. Brook's mouth hung open at the fiery scene before her. She heard a motor revving and saw the Skater increase its speed and power away up the lake. It continued to pick up speed as Brook watched it quickly disappear in the distance.

She lowered her binoculars. "What the hell?" she whispered.

As Brook thought about it, it seemed as if the mystery assassin wanted to send a message to somebody. She smirked as she walked back to her hotel.

"Yeah, and that was a pretty clear 'Don't fuck with me' message."

Chapter Thirty-One

Saturday, April 1ˢᵗ; Geneva, Switzerland; The TGV Lyria

Brook headed toward the platform where the TGV Lyria train waited to take her to Paris. She'd packed her trauma kit, a few clothes, and her gun in her backpack and ditched the rollaboard next to a dumpster on her walk to the train station. There was no way she would've been able to get it into the train's overhead storage rack with her arm feeling the way it did. As it was, carrying the backpack over her right shoulder was awkward because it limited her access to her weapons.

She showed her ticket then boarded the first-class section and plopped into her seat. She'd purchased both seats in her row so she had some privacy and could keep her backpack on the seat next to her. She put her head back and closed her eyes as the train started out of the station. In the last three weeks, she'd killed five people: two men on an assignment, three assassins who tried to kill her, and narrowly escape an assassin's attack that left her wounded and hurting.

And people who worked nine-to-five thought they had it tough.

However, she knew she had little justification to complain. No one had forced her into her current life. She'd willingly taken all the steps that led to where she was today, even if she didn't know at the time where those steps would eventually lead her. She was an assassin. It wasn't just what she did. It was who she was, and she was good at it. She remembered her mother's advice that if she didn't like it, stop doing it. But as Brook had explained to her, quitting would be easy if she didn't like her work. But she loved it.

A steward came by with his cart, so she asked for two cups of coffee, cranberry juice, and the cold breakfast that consisted of an assortment of croissants and Danishes. Her mind was still roiling over the mystery person texting her about the female assassin at the hotel bar; the warning that saved her from dying from a sniper's bullet; and the destruction of the limousine and its passengers. Whoever it was seemed to be following her for the sole purpose of watching over her. That thought made her scan the train car for anyone showing an interest in her.

The car was only a quarter full. A man and a woman sitting together had their laptops out and appeared to be business associates. Another man had a stack of files on the table in front of him. The screen of his laptop was open to an Excel spreadsheet. A grandmotherly woman sitting with a young girl who appeared to be her granddaughter was explaining the TGV and how fast it would travel. No one stuck out as a threat, so she took out one of Gregg Hurwitz's Orphan X novels and settled back to read while she ate her breakfast.

She polished off a cheese Danish and half of the juice when her phone vibrated.

"How is your arm?"

What the heck? It was the mystery person.

"I assume you're the one who warned me about the sniper?" Brook sent back.

"Yes. Sorry, I should have sent it earlier, but I found her just before you came out of the hotel."

"Well, thanks for saving my life. You said 'her.' Was this the woman at the bar?" Brook asked.

"Yes."

Brook thought about her next question. She wasn't sure who was who anymore. "Screw it," she said.

"Is she Enigma?"

"No. Her moniker is Paradox. She was Circe's lover."

"I don't think I've heard of her."

"That's why they call her Paradox. Circe led her clients to believe she was Enigma to protect her. But no one suspects a top model to pull a gun from underneath her skirt and put two rounds through the back of your head."

"From what I've seen, she's quite good."

"Better than good. In my opinion, only two are better."

"And who would those be?"

"Enigma is the second best, but no one touches Sasha."

"Do you know Sasha?"

"Only by reputation, but how you say, "ça suffit?"

"You're French?"

"Non."

"But you speak French?"

"Oui, but I speak several languages."

"How many?"

"Eight."

A thought struck Brook. Her guardian angel knew an awful lot about the assassin business. Whoever this was had to be either an assassin or possibly affiliated with an agency like MI6 or the CIA.

"Do you work for a government agency?"

"No."

"Have you ever worked independently for an agency like the CIA or MI6 in the past?"

"As a contractor."

Another thought occurred to her that the mystery person might know something about the list on the flash drive and Enigma's killing of the U.S. diplomats.

"That was you who blew up the car, correct?"

"Yes."

"Lagunov was one of the men but who was the other?" Brook asked.

"David Harms."

Oh my God, Brook thought. *"The CIA director?"*

"Yes."

"Why?"

"The list on the flash drive that set off these killings."

"Why is that a problem?"

"Lagunov offered the contract for the diplomats and Harms caused false accusations to be leveled at someone and in this business, when that that happens, the remedy is to remove the cause of the falsehoods before he can do any more damage."

"I don't understand. Who was falsely accused?"

"Who is being credited with the assassinations of your diplomats?"

A chill ran down Brooks. *"Enigma. So, you're saying Enigma isn't the one who killed the U.S. ambassadors?"*

"Yes."

"Then who did?"

"Paradox. As I said, she hides behind Enigma's name."

"But my agency seemed sure the murders were carried out by Enigma. One of the first CIA agents killed was taken out by a crossbow bolt which is a signature method used by her."

"No, Paradox is mimicking Enigma."

"Why would she do that?" Brook asked.

"By hiding behind Enigma's name, she can hunt her prey, knowing your agency is looking for the wrong person.

"But what's David Harms role in this? It can't be just making false accusations."

"Ask yourself the question, 'Why was the CIA director staying at the same hotel as the Russian Foreign Minister?'"

Brook's mind went into a tailspin. Was the mystery person implying that the CIA director was working with the Russians?

"Are you implying that David Harms was working with the Russians?" she asked.

"Not working with them. He was one of them."

Holy shit! Brook had never met the man. The SOG kept its agents out of the limelight to protect their identities. She reported to Andrew

McGill, but she wondered if he knew about this…or was he a part of it, too?

"So, where does Enigma come into the picture?" Brook asked.

"Enigma is an easy scapegoat to blame for the deaths of the U.S. ambassadors and CIA and MI6 agents. Russia isn't happy with the sanctions and with the war going poorly for Putin, the Russians have resorted to more subtle means of counterattack."

"But I have a directive from my agency to hunt Enigma. Why is that?" Brook asked.

"What do you know about Enigma?"

"According to my agency, she's a woman of Balkan or Central European descent. No one knows anything else about her other than she's reputed to be one of the deadliest in the business."

"You said Enigma is a woman?"

"Yes. I was told SOG and MI6 have been hunting her for several years. She's taken out over two dozen high-value targets, but one of her hits got a little sloppy. She was wounded and an analysis of the blood left behind indicates Enigma is a female."

The mystery person went silent for a minute.

"Are you still there?" Brook asked.

"Yes, yes, I'm here. I was busy trying to control my laughter."

"What's so funny?" she asked.

"That information is correct, but the conclusions are wrong."

"How so?"

"The men Enigma killed were leaders in the fields of weapons, drugs, and human trafficking. And when I say weapons, it was not limited to rifles and pistols. Tanks, fighter jets, bombs, and missiles were also trafficked."

"So, they were bad people who deserved to die," Brook said.

"Yes."

"Then why are the SOG and MI6 hunting for Enigma?"

"That's an interesting question since they were the ones who contracted for Enigma's services."

Holy double shit, Brook thought. *"So, the wrong conclusion is that Enigma only killed at the behest of the CIA and MI6, and the hits were on people that I would've killed myself?"*

"Partially."

"What do you mean? What other conclusions are wrong?"

"I'll give you a riddle and if you can solve it, you'll have the answer."

"I'm not very good at riddles," she said.

"Regardless. You said blood found at the scene of one of Enigma's hits indicated a female, correct?"

"Yes."

"That's true but is the conclusion true?"

"I have no idea?"

"Solve it and you'll know more about me than anyone."

"Wait, what do you mean? Who are you?"

"Why Ms. Payne, I thought you'd have figured it out by now. I am Enigma."

Chapter Thirty-Two

Saturday, April 1st; Paris, France; The Ritz

The Hemingway bar was one of the most famous yet smallest bars in the world. Every evening patrons strove to get one of the twenty-five seats in the iconic bar to enjoy the cocktail craft of Colin Field, twice voted the best bartender in the world. The bar had the aura of a members-only club with tufted leather armchairs, a library, photos of famous past visitors, and the absence of music to encourage conversation.

But Paradox wasn't interested in conversation. She was ensconced in a leather armchair at a corner table, stewing over the events in Geneva while sipping the bar's signature cocktail, a Serendipity made with Calvados, fresh mint, white sugar, crystal clear apple juice, and topped off with Brut champagne. The cocktail's name was appropriate because, through an act of serendipity, she happened to meet one of the people she was sure played a role in Circe's death.

Dylan Payne was the name the assassin was using. Paradox had been watching Sergei Lagunov because she was sure the CIA had figured out that Lagunov was the one who'd placed the contract on the U.S. diplomats. She also surmised they'd send someone to watch him, if not kill him. That Dylan Payne showed up confirmed her theory.

She thought she had the American assassin dead to rights when she came out of the hotel, but she ducked just as Paradox took her shot. Payne's timing was uncanny. It was almost as if someone warned her moments before Paradox fired. If so, it meant it mean Payne had an invisible associate watching her back and that person knew what Paradox looked like. And despite Paradox's surveillance, someone had blown Lagunov to hell, destroying one of her traps.

Now that she was back in Paris, she'd had to find an apartment. She and Circe had shared the one where the broker was killed and returning there was out of the question. Earlier today, she'd signed a contract to purchase an apartment in Village Royal in the 8th Arrondissement. It was located on the top two floors of a magnificently renovated old building. The entrance on the 4th floor opened onto a bright reception area, a separate kitchen, and a guest bathroom. The second level was accessed by an internal spiral staircase and led to two bedrooms and a bathroom. Paradox planned to use the second bedroom as an office and library. The purchase price also included a parking space in the underground garage.

She still planned to keep her arsenal in a storage unit along with hiking and skiing equipment to disguise its contents. The only weapon she was currently carrying was an OTF knife with a four-inch blade.

But she wasn't worried because she was an expert in the Russian Systema Spetsnaz. It was one of the most complete knife fighting styles and was said to have originated in the 10th century. The entire system was built on four pillars to assemble a fearless, precise warrior: breathing, relaxation, body position, and movement. These pillars ensured an assassin like herself could adapt and conquer any opponent in her path. The combat knife was sacred to her. She was trained to execute the opposition in the shortest amount of time possible, stripping away any fancy movements to get to the point. Once she approached a striking distance with a piece of cold steel the whole goal was to eradicate the threat in a few movements. There was no room to ponder any action, which is why she drilled appropriate reactions to perfection.

Of course, when facing another assassin with a knife, the best bet was to run, and she could run like the wind. In the face of uncertain odds, she felt it was better to live to fight another day when those odds were more favorable to her.

Her thoughts returned to Dylan Payne and how she might still be able to kill her. She was shocked to hear that the CIA's director was killed along with Lagunov by the RPG. She had no idea why they would be riding together, but whatever the reason, she felt with Lagunov dead, Payne would leave the country, especially since she was wounded. But there was a second Judas goat that could lead CIA operators to their slaughter—Elion Kastrati. He was a pompous, narcissistic, little shit who put out the broad contract on any CIA or MI6 agent in retaliation for the murder of his brother.

Paradox could watch him, but Dylan Payne was still stuck in her mind. She recalled Dasher said he'd approached a SOG agent in Berlin with the intent of either getting her to join him and his girlfriend in hunting CIA agents or if that didn't work, kill her and collect the reward. But Dasher's girlfriend also worked for Circe, screening those inquiring about assassinations. Her follow-up on one of those inquiries ended up getting her shot in the ankle by an intruder who thought Elise was Circe. While the intruder's face was covered by a balaclava, her height and build suggested it might have been Dylan Payne, meaning she might be based out of Paris.

Paradox couldn't scour Paris and watch Kastrati at the same time and if she waited until someone showed up to kill Kastrati, Payne might be gone. But Paradox had several contacts who might be interested in making some money in return for killing Payne.

She finished her drink and hurried back to her room. She checked to see that the camera monitoring her room showed there'd been no intruders. She went in and double-locked the door then opened her laptop. She took out her cell phone and dialed a number she hadn't used in over a year. A man answered after the fifth ring.

"Eleanor, this is a surprise."

"I'm sure it is, Elliot." Elliot Rampoule was a former member of the Belgian Special forces. He left the military five years ago to found the Rampoule Group, an organization of mercenaries for hire. All his employees were former members of either the Belgian Spec Ops Group or the German Kommando SpezialKräfte or KSK.

"To what do I own the honor?" he asked.

"I want to offer you a contract."

"A contract? Hmm, what kind of contract?"

"The kind you can do blindfolded, but it's worth €250,000."

"You have that kind of money?" he asked.

"What do you think, Elliot?"

"I assume you want us to kill someone?"

"That's correct." She explained the situation regarding Payne.

"And you suspect she may have a backup?"

"Possibly, but you'll have numbers on your side, so you may be able to identify her support person."

"Do you have a picture of her?" Elliot asked.

"I can send it to you in a second."

"All right, half the money upfront. You know where to send it. As soon as I see it in our account, we'll find her, and I'll personally lead my team to kill her."

Paradox tapped away on her laptop. "The money should be in your account. Her picture's on its way. Let me know when it's done."

"We'll be in touch, Eleanor."

Chapter Thirty-Three

Sunday, April 2nd; Paris, France; Brook's Latin Quarter Apartment

The first thing Brook did upon arrival in Paris was see a physician that the agency used in emergencies. The doctor cleaned the glue off the wounds and stitched them closed after applying more antibiotic cream. She gave Brook a ten-day supply of a combination antibiotic to ward off infection then rebandaged her arm. She offered to give her a pain reliever, but the only thing Brook would take was acetaminophen. She couldn't risk dulling her reflexes with Paradox lurking about.

Once she arrived in her Latin Quarter apartment, Brook collapsed into bed and slept for twelve hours. She rolled out of bed and padded to the bathroom where she dropped two 500 mg tablets of Tylenol then drew a hot bath. Ordinarily, she liked showers but with her head under a full stream of water, it would be easy for someone to break into her apartment without her knowing. Besides, she had to keep her wound dry. When the tub was nearly full, she climbed in, resting her left arm on the edge of the tub. She soaked in the water for a half hour, which wasn't shrewd tactically, but she needed the time to relax her mind.

When she felt better, she extricated herself from the tub, dried herself, and struggled into khaki cargo pants, and a black short-sleeved cotton tee shirt. Dressing wasn't easy with her wounds and bending over to pull on and tie her Ryder sneakers was even more of a problem. She didn't have much strength in her arm, which was worrisome with a top-tier assassin hunting her. She had to contact Hector her handler and find out what the real story was behind Enigma.

She sent him a text on her Kerberos phone. *"We need to talk. Now!"*

Five minutes later, he called. "Zealot, what happened in Geneva? My God, David Harms and Sergei Lagunov were killed."

"I know. I saw it happen."

"Did you do it?"

"Uh, I can't fit an RPG in by backpack."

"Thank God! With both of them dying in the attack it won't look like we were responsible. But couldn't you have stopped it?"

"No, I was across the lake watching through a set of binoculars."

"I…I don't understand. You just watched it happen and did nothing?"

"Let's back up for a minute and recap my recent adventures. First of all, I'm recovering from a bullet wound in my left arm, so I don't have the physical ability to do much of anything right now."

"Did you see a doctor?"

"Yeah, and she stitched the wounds and bandaged them. Gave me some antibiotics to fight off any infection, so I'm recovering."

"Have you figured out who sent the message that warned you before you were shot?"

"The same person who warned me that the woman sitting next to me in the bar at the Eastwest hotel was an assassin."

"What did the woman at the bar look like?"

"Tall, maybe six feet, trim and fit with a fair complexion and short black hair slicked back. She said she was a professional model for the Elite Modeling Agency out of Paris."

"That's Enigma," Hector said.

"No, Hector, it's not. The woman sitting at the bar goes by the moniker Paradox. However, the person sending the texts and watching over me was Enigma."

"What? How do you know it's Enigma?"

"Because she told me who she was. She said Circe led everyone to believe Paradox was Enigma to deflect the blame for the hits."

"That's crazy."

"Yeah, and here's something else that's crazy. She said the CIA and MI6 contracted her to carry out the 'high value' hits that were drug dealers, gun runners, and human traffickers. Just the kind of people the agency sends me after."

"Enigma said she was a contractor for the CIA?"

"She said she's being set up to take the fall for the hits on our ambassadors and CIA agents."

"That's interesting because just before he left for Europe, Harms put out a directive broadening the hunt for Enigma to include several other operators."

"It came from Harms, not Andrew McGill?"

"No, and he's pissed off about him going around him."

"That's reassuring."

"How so?"

"I'll ask you the same question Enigma posed to me. Why was the Director of the CIA staying in the same hotel as the Russian Foreign Minister? And why were the two of them leaving in Harms' limousine?"

Hector didn't answer right away. "Zealot, are you implying—?

"That the CIA director was a Russian agent? You bet your ass."

Hector went silent, but Brook could hear him breathing.

"Cat got your tongue, Hector?"

"I…I don't know what to say. This is the first I've heard of this."

"I want to talk to Andrew but let him know that I'm inactivating my Kerberos and going dark. I'll check in with him at midnight tonight using a burner. Make sure he knows and Hector?"

"Yes?"

"McGill knows one of the people I'm working with and if that person isn't deadly enough, the other one will make agency personnel shit their pants."

"Why are you telling me this?"

"I just want you and the others to know not to fuck with me. If the agency is compromised, I'll stay dark until you work it out. But if you're setting me up, my friends and I will cloud up and rain all over the agency."

She disconnected then turned off the phone and took out the SIMS card. She went to her desk and took out a box of burners with prepaid minutes. She placed two of them in her pants pockets then threaded the holster with her FN 509 through her belt.

She didn't tell Hector the other half of Enigma's disclosure about the facts being accurate but the conclusions being wrong. Enigma intimated that the blood found at the site of the killing attributed to Enigma was female, but the conclusion was wrong. After thinking about it long and hard, Brook concluded Enigma must be male, but how was that possible if the blood indicated the assassin was female? She'd have to research that later but first she needed food and coffee and since she hadn't had time to shop, she left her apartment and headed for Les Deux Magots. It was her favorite place to while away an afternoon and sort through the facts whirling around in her head.

A chocolate croissant wouldn't hurt either.

Chapter Thirty-Four

Sunday, April 2nd; Paris, France; Les Deux Magots

The sun was hiding somewhere behind a featureless grey blanket of low clouds as Brook eased herself into one of the green and yellow wicker chairs at a table tucked in a corner near the door of the café. She was far enough under the green and white awning that she'd stay dry if it decided to rain. Brook found Sundays to be far more peaceful than during the week when the sounds of cars, buses, and honking horns turned the Parisian mornings into a cacophonic symphony.

Henri stopped by on his way to place an order. "Eliana, I will be with you in a minute." He disappeared into the café.

Brook shifted in the chair, trying to find a position that was comfortable for her arm. Once she found just the right one, she leaned her head against the window behind her and closed her eyes. She did some deep breathing which helped her control the pain. She heard the door open and felt Henri looking at her. She opened her eyes as he slid a chair out and took a seat.

"You are hurt," he said.

Brook smiled. "And what gave it away?"

He waved his hand in a circle. "The look on your face and the way you are holding your left arm. What happened?"

"I tripped and fell on my shoulder. Nothing's broken, but it hurts quite a bit."

"Do you need a painkiller?"

"I just take Tylenol. That other stuff makes me loopy."

"You also need food. May I suggest you skip the pain au chocolate and crème café and let me bring you eggs on toast and a pot of black filtered coffee?"

"That would be wonderful, Henri. Thank you."

"You rest. I'll be back with your coffee and food."

Brook closed her eyes again. There was no sign of infection this morning when she'd checked, but she thought she might be running a fever.

Henri returned with her coffee and filled her cup. He pushed it toward her.

"Drink. It'll warm you up."

He disappeared as she reached for the cup and sipped. It was strong and black. Les Deux Magots had some of the best coffee in town.

Henri returned with her eggs and set them in front of her. He frowned and put his hand on her forehead.

"*Mon Dieu*, you are running a fever. Eat your food and I'll take you home."

"That's not necessary, Henri."

"Hush. Eat and do as I say."

Brook picked up a fork and cut off a piece of the toast and egg. She chewed it slowly. It was just what she needed but she was worried. She'd never been shot before, and her body didn't like it. She felt weak as a kitten and there was no way she could fight off an attack from Paradox if the assassin found her. She had to get off the street as soon as she finished her breakfast, but she was suddenly so tired, she wasn't sure she could walk back to her apartment.

Henri appeared, but he wasn't wearing his apron. Instead, he was wearing a waist-length black leather jacket over his white shirt and jeans. He held out his hand.

"Come. I've called a cab."

"Henri, it's okay. I'll just walk back to my apartment."

"You won't make it. You're burning up. Now come. I will take you."

She let him lead her to the cab and helped her in. Her vision was blurring, and she felt like she could sleep for a month. He gave the cab driver an address, but it wasn't hers. He was taking her to his place.

Henri's apartment was located in the heart of the historical Saint Germain des Prés on Rue des Canettes, a historical street known for its 17th Century buildings and charming restaurants. The building was near several farmer's markets, theaters, cafes, and bars and was also only a mile from Les Deux Magots.

Henri herded her up a cobblestone walkway to an elevator. He took out a set of keys as they got off and led her down the hall. He opened the door and helped her inside.

His apartment was a completely renovated unit with 18th-century stone walls and beams in all the rooms. It overlooked a large courtyard with lots of sun coming in through the floor-to-ceiling windows. The fully equipped kitchen was opposite a small dining table. A queen-sized bed was behind a divider that separated it from the living area where matching sofas in gray tweed formed an "L" facing a television and stereo system mounted on the wall.

"You lay down on the bed. I'm going to make some tea."

Brook was too tired to argue, so she kicked off her shoes and laid back on the bed. She was asleep in seconds. She woke up sometime later to the sound of a guitarist playing a jazz song. Soft light came from the next room, and someone was humming along to the song. She noticed someone had removed her coat and rebandaged her arm. She panicked momentarily when she realized her gun and holster weren't on her hip. She winced as she swung her legs over the edge of the bed and tried to stand up.

"No, no, no, no," Henri said, emerging from the other room. "You must rest. I'm fixing food and we will eat in a few minutes."

Brook blinked as she focused on the dwarf. He was wearing a tank top and blue jeans, but what stood out was how buff the little man was.

"Well, it looks like you work out, Henri," Brook said.

He held his hand out and wiggled his palm. "I use a local gym."

"Well, whatever you're doing, it's working."

He blushed. "Stay there while I finish dinner. I'll help you to the table."

'That's okay. I need to get up and move around." She stood up slowly and waited a minute until she was sure she had her balance then followed Henri to the dining room table and a chair he'd pulled out. He seated her then went to the stove and finished whatever he was making. He brought two plates to the table and set one in front of her.

"Nothing fancy. A croque-monsieur and a fruit salad. I have wine, but I think it best if you stick with water."

"I agree. Thank you. This looks delicious." She took a bite of the sandwich. "Mmm, this is heavenly, Henri."

"Thank you. I cleaned and bandaged your arm. No sign of infection, but your body is still recovering from the shock of the bullet."

Brook stared at the little man.

He took a bite of his sandwich and stared back. "Yes, Eliana, I know a bullet wound when I see one and before you do something rash, your weapons are sitting on my coffee table."

Brook took another bite of her sandwich then ate a spoonful of the fruit. "So, I guess you've figured out that I'm not a writer."

He shrugged. "*Sauf si tu as vraiment énervé quelqu'un, non.*"

"There's no book, but I can't deny I may have pissed off someone."

Henri stood and went to one of his kitchen cabinets and took out two snifters and a bottle of Castarède Réserve de la Famille Twenty-Year-Old Armagnac and poured two fingers into each glass. He set one of the snifters in front of Brook.

"No wine, but Armagnac is good for the soul. This one has rich, harmonious flavors, with ripe fruits, coffee, and butterscotch notes followed by a long, sweet finish."

Brook waved the glass under her nose then sipped. "It's excellent."

Henri nodded. "You are a friend, Eliana, and I won't ask you who you work for, but are you in danger?"

Brook debated what to tell the little man. He'd shown himself to be truly concerned about her by bringing her to his home and nursing her back to health. She knew it violated every protocol in the book to talk openly to him about her work, but she was extremely vulnerable right now and if Paradox tracked her to her apartment, Brook probably wouldn't be able to defend herself, not that Henri could protect her from someone like Paradox.

She leaned back in the chair, cradling the snifter in her right hand, and cocked her head at Henri.

"I work for the Special Operations Group of the United States CIA…and I am an assassin."

Henri stared at his Armagnac and nodded his head slowly. "So, the answer to my question is yes, you are in danger."

"I am, and with this wound, I'm not sure I can defend myself against the one looking for me."

"Does this person know where you live?" he asked.

"I'm not sure."

"Then you must stay here. Whoever this is will not suspect you are with me. Do you have associates who can help you?"

"I do, but they're not with the agency. I can't trust the SOG right now. I was given information that the CIA director was a Russian agent."

"Wasn't he killed in Geneva the other day?" Henri asked.

"Yes, but that doesn't mean there aren't others who are Russians. Another SOG agent and his handler went rogue and were helping a group of assassins take down my colleagues."

"Are they the ones after you?"

"No, my two non-agency associates eliminated them."

"Can they protect you?"

"They could, but they're following up and eliminating another threat, so they're not in the country right now."

"So, you are alone?"

"Yes." She checked her watch. "Oh, my gosh, I didn't realize it was this late. I have to make a phone call in fifteen minutes."

"Don't get up. Finish your food and make your call." He grinned. "I have a case of selective memory loss. But you must stay here until the threat to your life has been eliminated."

"You're sure it's not a burden?"

"*Non*, I have two days off, so I can care for you until you're well enough to go out on your own."

"I feel strange confiding in you like this. It's not something I've ever done before."

Henri stood and gave her a crooked smile as he put a hand on her right shoulder. "We little people are often taken for granted. I've always wanted to rescue a damsel in distress, so this is my chance. Now, I'll leave you to your phone call while I move to the living room and do some work on my laptop."

Chapter Thirty-Five

Monday, April 3ʳᵈ; Paris France; Henri's Apartment

Brook grabbed one of her burner phones from her daypack and sat at the kitchen table. She dialed Andrew McGill's number and waited. He answered on the fourth ring.

"Input?"

"Charlie, Echo, Foxtrot, Sierra, Victor, X-ray. Counter?"

"Golf, India, Romeo, Victor, Yankee, Papa. Zealot, what's going on?"

"That's what I want to know."

"Hector said you saw the person who blew up David Harms' car, killing him and Sergei Lagunov."

"Not exactly. The person who did it was in a speedboat and too far away for me to see, but that's not the problem. Who gave me the assignment to hunt down Enigma?"

Andrew didn't answer for several seconds. "No one. Until Harms put out the blanket order, no one was tasked with hunting Enigma."

"You mean you didn't send through the sanction?"

"No."

"Then why did Hector give me the sanction?"

"David Harms."

"Let me ask you a couple of very important questions. Has Enigma worked for SOG before?"

"Who told you that?"

"Enigma."

"You've spoken to her?"

"She saved my life and seems to have become my guardian angel."

Brook heard him take a deep breath. "This is between you and me. No one else is to know, but yes, Enigma is a contractor for the SOG."

"That's two points in your favor."

"What do you mean?"

"I'm trying to parse out who I can trust and the fact that you were pissed off about Harms going around you to sanction Enigma is one point. That you admitted to her being a SOG contractor is another point. Now, let's see if you can earn a third. Why was Harms hanging out with Sergei Lagunov?"

"I think you've figured it out."

"Explain it to me in your own words," Brook said.

McGill sighed. "I've had one of our best analysts monitoring Harms' emails, texts, and phone conversations. As soon as I heard he was killed, the analyst remotely downloaded the contents of his hard drive."

"Shit, is that possible?"

"For him, it is, but it's completely illegal. We discovered that David Harms was a deep-cover Russian agent. The reason he stayed in the same hotel as Lagunov was to give him a status report on the assassinations of our diplomats. He was pissed off at Circe's death and the release of information indicating she was a major contractor for assassins. Especially because it was accompanied by all the assassin's names as well as the names of the victims whose deaths were previously thought to be either accidents or due to natural causes. So those guys are probably scattering to the wind right now."

"Not all of them have scattered," Brook said. "Enigma said Circe was covering for an assassin called Paradox by implying her work was that of Enigma's."

"Why would she do that?"

"Because the two of them were lovers."

"Crap, and speaking of lovers, at least we don't have Dasher and his honey Vixen to worry about."

"True, but Paradox is a problem. She knows what I look like, and she probably thinks I was partly responsible for Circe's death, so I'd bet money she's hunting me." Brook related the events of her Geneva trip.

"Shit, are you okay?" McGill asked.

"Well, let's just say I'm going into hiding until my arm heals a bit more. Right now, I'm pretty much worthless."

"What about Bane? Isn't he with you?"

"He was going to take out Elion Kastrati, the guy who put the blanket contract out on all CIA and MI6 agents."

"Call him back. Kastrati can wait," McGill said.

"I will, but it doesn't solve the problem of traitors in our midst."

"After we realized Harms was a Russian agent, my analyst wizard did a blitzkrieg on the CIA and SAC and identified four more of them. None of them are SOG. I've tasked a team to pick them up and take them to one of our special offshore facilities. We'll be having a question-and-answer session with them shortly."

"Good, so my priorities are to get Cailan back here and hunker down until we can find Paradox."

"I know it's probably a ridiculous request but watch over Enigma. I put out an order canceling the sanction on her, but I don't want some maverick going after her anyway."

"I'll do what I can." Brook disconnected. Again, she didn't bring up Enigma's riddle about the information being correct, but the conclusions drawn by the agency were wrong. Nor did she tell him she was working with Sasha.

She sent a text to Cailan recapping the situation and asked him to postpone going after Kastrati. She needed help and protection. His return text said he and Mirlinda would be there in eight hours and would meet her at the Millésime Hotel later today at about 1:00 PM.

When she finished her communications, she dropped the burner phone on the floor and smashed it. Henri appeared frowning.

"I trust you did that for security purposes and not out of anger."

Brook laughed. "Yes, I'm not angry, just worried. My job has become much more complicated than usual, not that it's ever routine."

"Anything you want to talk about?" He smiled. "Or that you can talk about?"

"My boss said David Harms was a deep cover Russian agent and they've identified four other agents buried in the CIA. He's having them picked up by a SOG team for questioning."

Henri arched an eyebrow. "Really?"

"Well, it's a bit more extreme than asking them questions over a cup of coffee."

"*J'imagine bien.*"

Brook sighed. "I don't know, Henri. This assignment has become so topsy turvy."

"I…I don't pretend to know what your job entails, but topsy turvy doesn't sound good."

"I shouldn't be telling you this, but we've been friends for what? Five years?"

"*Oui.*"

"I guess I think of you as my older brother." She frowned. "You are older, aren't you?"

"I am forty-two," he said.

"I'm thirty-eight."

Henri grinned. "Two new experiences for me. Before today, I've never rescued a damsel in distress, nor have I had a little sister."

"Yeah, well your little sister is going to be short-lived if I don't get some serious protection soon."

"Ah, what about your non-agency friends? Can you call them back to help you?"

"I just did. They'll meet me at the Millésime Hotel tomorrow at 1:00."

"Do you think you're up to it?"

"I need to discuss some things with them."

"Will you go back to your apartment then?"

"Well, I don't want to impose on you, but I was thinking to have them stay at my place while I stay here with you."

"Your friends are assassins too?" Henri asked.

"Let's just say, they can handle themselves."

"So, they will be bait for this person who is hunting you?"

"Something like that. They're very good at setting traps."

"Then I think it is a plan. While you are at the hotel, I will go shopping for food."

"You're sure it's no trouble?"

"*Bien sûr que non.* You are my sister. *Ma maison est votre maison.*" He checked his watch. "But now you need sleep." He pointed to the bed. "I will take the couch."

"But you shouldn't have to give up your bed."

"Nonsense. It folds out into a bed. I will wake you for breakfast in the morning. Then, I will drop you off at the hotel. I'll give you my cellphone number and you can call me for the return trip."

Brook stood then leaned over and kissed Henri on the top of his head. "You're a good big brother, Henri."

Chapter Thirty-Six

Monday, April 3; Paris France; The Millesime Hotel

The smell of bacon frying woke Brook. She checked her watch and saw it was 10:30. She rolled out of bed and stretched. She'd slept in her tee shirt and panties so she grabbed her pants and pulled them on before checking out what Henri was cooking. He was leaning over peering into his oven as she stepped into the kitchen. He turned toward her holding a pie pan with a pair of oven mitts and set it on a hot pad.

"Ah, you are just in time," he said.

"What did you make?"

"Quiche Lorraine accompanied by a pot of black pour-over coffee."

"My goodness, you didn't have to fuss for me."

"Pah, as your doctor I say you need protein to build up your strength. How is your arm?"

"It's still sore, but I feel much better than yesterday."

"Good. You eat then shower. I put out fresh towels. While you are with your friends, I will pick up some clothes for you. You can't go back to your apartment until your friends have rid you of these vermin infesting your life. Once you've showered, I will see to your arm and change the bandage then I will drive you to the hotel."

Brook cocked her head at him, but he anticipated her question.

"I have a Mercedes-AMG GLA 250 with an automatic transmission that has pedal extensions so I can drive."

"Nice car."

"*Les voitures françaises c'est de la merde.*"

Brook laughed. "I agree. French cars are shit."

"Now, no more talking. Sit and eat."

Brook sat down as Henri served her an enormous piece of the quiche. He set an oversized mug of coffee next to her plate. He cut a piece of the quiche for himself and joined her. They ate quietly. Brook was ravenous and polished off her breakfast in minutes. When she looked up, Henri wore a mischievous grin.

"Nothing like a bullet wound to spark an appetite," he said.

"It was so good."

He cradled his coffee mug in both hands and watched her. "Are these people you're meeting the ones I met at the café?"

"Yes, Cailan Bane and Mirlinda Dzafer."

"What do they do when they're not assisting you?"

"Cailan owns a video game design company called Imaginarium."

"*Mon Dieu*, I have their Streetfighter games. I love them"

"They're very popular. Mirlinda is a professor of business at the University of Chicago, but she also owns a gastropub that has one of the finest selections of affordable wines in the city. She's quite the expert."

"Does she offer French wines?" Henri asked.

"Yes, she makes an annual trip in the spring to meet with her suppliers and taste new wines."

"Ah, I must speak with her so I can…how you say…pick her brain?"

"I'm sure she'd love to talk with you after…you know."

"Of course, of course. First, they kill the vermin then we talk wine."

"I'm going to shower then you can change my bandage and take me to see my friends."

He reached into his pocket and withdrew her remaining burner phone. "I entered my contact information into the phone so you can call me when you're ready for me to take you back here."

"Wow, I don't think there has ever been a better big brother."

"Stop. You make me blush."

Brook left the kitchen and headed for the bathroom. Henri had left fresh towels on the toilet. The bathroom was quite modern with a waterfall shower and a granite counter and sink. But the most spectacular feature was a mosaic on the shower wall depicting a tiger fighting a multi-colored dragon. She took off her clothes and tried to shower without getting her bandaged wound wet. When she was finished, she dried herself and dressed in her same clothes. She hung her towel on a rack and then found Henri at the kitchen table with first aid supplies laid out on the table. He pointed to her chair.

"Sit."

He gently removed the bandage and checked the wound. "No sign of infection, so that's good."

He applied an antibiotic cream then placed a sterile gauze pad over each wound and secured them with Eco-Flex tape. He slid a glass of water toward her and placed four capsules in front of her.

"The red and white capsules are Extra Strength Tylenol. The yellow and white one is cefazolin while the blue one is doxycycline. Both of those are antibiotics."

"How did you get ahold of those?" Brook asked.

"While you were sleeping, I went to the pharmacy around the corner. The druggist knows me and gave me the antibiotics after I told him my sister had stepped on a nail. I told him you were vaccinated against tetanus, but we wanted to avoid an infection."

She downed all four pills at once. "Well, I think I'm ready."

"Then let's go."

He led her out of the apartment and down the hall to the elevator. They went out the back of the building to a cul-de-sac where his denim blue Mercedes was parked. He opened the passenger side door for her and when she was in, closed the door and went around to the driver's side. He slid behind the wheel and started the car. He wove through the streets until he turned left onto Rue de l'Université and pulled into the semi-circle drive of the hotel. He touched her hand before she got out.

"Do not, under any circumstances leave the hotel alone. Wait for me and I will pick you up. *Comprendre?*"

"I understand, big brother." She stepped out of the car and entered the hotel. Cailan was sitting in a chair in the lounge area watching. His face wore a look of concern when he saw her approach.

"Your arm?" he signed.

"It's better than it was yesterday."

"Who was that who dropped you off?"

"Henri Aubert, the man who waited on us at Les Deux Magots. He probably saved my life. I thought I was strong enough to walk to the café, but I almost passed out when I reached it. Henri took off work and took me to his apartment where I slept for, I don't know how long. He fed me and changed my bandages. Did the same this morning and dropped me here."

"So, he knows you were shot?"

"Where's Mirlinda?"

"She's got a suite where we can talk privately."

"Why don't we continue this conversation there."

He nodded and led her to the elevators. When they reached her floor, he led her down the hall and knocked. Mirlinda opened the door and motioned them inside. She was holding a suppressed Glock 19X behind her back. She took one look at Brook and clucked her tongue.

"So, I'm guessing greeting you with a hug isn't a good idea."

"Yeah, probably not."

"Would you like some coffee?" Mirlinda asked.

"Yes, please."

Brook and Cailan took seats on the sofa while Mirlinda served coffee and then sat in a wingback chair opposite them.

"So, why don't you start by filling us in on everything," Mirlinda said.

Brook started by recounting the events in Switzerland including the appearance of the mystery texter whom she learned was Enigma.

"The person texting you identified themselves as Enigma?" Mirlinda asked.

"Yes."

"And she's the one who took out Lagunov and the CIA director?"

"Yes, Enigma said he was a deep-cover Russian operator and my boss, Andrew McGill confirmed it."

"How?"

Brook explained how McGill had one of his analysts hack into and download the contents of Harms' hard drive. "They've identified four other Russians in the CIA."

"Which makes it very hard for you to trust them," Mirlinda said.

"And which is why I told Andrew I was going dark until they worked it out. The funny thing is, I was originally tasked with finding and eliminating Enigma, but Andrew said the sanction order didn't come from SOG. It came from Harms. He's canceled the sanction, but he's now tasked me with protecting Enigma."

"Nothing like a 180-degree turnabout to confuse things," Mirlinda said. "My next question is why?"

"Because Enigma is a freelance contractor for SOG."

"Holy shit, I've dealt with the CIA before and I knew they were screwed up, but this takes the cake," Mirlinda said.

"But there's one thing I haven't told McGill," Brook said. "Enigma asked me what I knew about her. When I mentioned that blood left at one of the scenes of an assassination attributed to her indicated Enigma was a female of Slavic origin, the assassin said the facts were correct, but the conclusions were wrong."

"What does that mean?" Cailan signed.

"I'm not sure. It could mean she's not of Slavic origin or…"

"Enigma is not female," Mirlinda said.

"But how can the blood evidence indicate a female when the assassin is male?" Brook asked.

"One way to find out." Mirlinda took out her Kerberos and called Osias.

"Hey Mirlinda, I'm just starting breakfast. How's it going in Paris?" he asked.

"Interesting. We have a riddle for you."

"Oh, I just love riddles. That was sarcasm in case you didn't pick it up. Fire away."

"How can DNA analysis of a blood sample indicate a person is female, but in fact, that person is male?"

"That's a good one. Is this a trick question?" he asked.

"No, but it's critical for our work here."

"Give me a half hour or so and I'll get back to you." He disconnected.

"If anyone can figure out this riddle, it's Osias," Cailan signed.

"Paradox seeing you is a big problem," Mirlinda said. "Regardless of how you change your hair, I'd be able to recognize you and I'm sure she can too. And if, as we suspect, she's hunting those who might have had a role in the death of her lover, the fact that she tried to kill you at the Beau-Rivage says you're a prime target."

"That's a given," Brook said. "The problem is if she comes for me the way I am right now, I don't think I can defend myself at the level needed."

"Do you think she knows where you live?" Mirlinda asked.

"I don't know, but I'm sure she can eventually figure it out."

"Do you have someplace to stay other than your apartment?"

"I'm staying with Henri Aubert right now."

"The waiter at the café?" Mirlinda asked.

"Yes. He really came through for me these last two days."

"Does he know what you are?"

Brook took a deep breath. "Yes, I told him who I work for and what I do for them. He said I need to stay at his place because the assassin won't suspect that."

"He's right, but can you trust him?" Mirlinda asked.

"He and I have been friends for five years and I think his concern is genuine."

"But he won't be able to protect you if this Paradox woman comes after you."

"True, the only thing he can offer me is a place to stay out of sight. But that brings up something I want to bounce off you guys. What would you say to one of you staying in my place while the other watches for Paradox?"

Mirlinda looked at Cailan and arched her eyebrows. He pursed his lips.

"Might be a good way to catch her. You stay in the apartment, and I could provide overwatch."

"What about Kastrati?" Mirlinda asked.

"We give it a couple of days and if Paradox doesn't show, I'll split off and go after the Albanian. By that time, Brook should be well enough, and you can provide overwatch. I brought a couple of the masks Henrik made for me, so I won't draw attention as I circle the neighborhood."

Mirlinda thought for a minute then nodded. "Sounds like a plan. Let's do it."

Her cell phone vibrated with an incoming call. The caller ID said it was Osias.

"That was fast," Mirlinda said. "I'm putting you on speaker."

"A bone marrow transplant," he said.

"Explain," Mirlinda said

"A bone marrow transplant turns the patient into a chimera. What I mean is that the DNA in their blood is different than the DNA in the rest of their cells. Bone marrow transplants are used to treat several diseases, particularly cancers like leukemia."

"Why would that affect a DNA test?" Brook asked.

"The way it works is a doctor first destroys a patient's blood cells or bone marrow. This is usually done with chemotherapy or radiation. The doctor then puts in new bone marrow from a matched donor. Bone marrow contains blood stem cells. These blood stem cells are responsible for making our blood. Our blood cells need to be replaced constantly. What this means in a bone marrow transplant patient is that his or her blood comes from the donor's stem cells and has the donor's DNA.

"So, if Enigma is a male who received a bone marrow transplant from a female donor, his blood would appear to be that of the donor female's but if you took a cheek swab, it would appear to be the male recipient."

"So, all this time people have been looking for a female assassin when in fact Enigma is a man?" Brook said.

"It's just a possibility," Osias said. "I don't know if it explains your riddle."

"It does," Cailan signed. *"In addition to the riddle, the moniker fits. Enigma means something that baffles understanding and cannot be explained. It's like a conundrum."*

"I'll be damned," Brook said.

"Me too," Mirlinda said.

"And me three," Cailan signed.

Chapter Thirty-Seven

Monday, April 3rd; Paris France; Le Balzar

When Brook stepped out of the hotel to wait for Henri, the rain had given way to an expanse of sapphire blue sky dotted with puffy clouds. The aroma of spring rose from the street as the sun dried the pavement. She took a seat on a metal bench under the hotel's portico. Mirlinda had the key to her apartment and she and Cailan were on their way to pick up clothes and weapons from Mirlinda's place. She would take up residence in Brook's place later today with Cailan cruising the neighborhood, watching for Paradox.

Her arm hurt and even though her activities today were limited to conversation, the act of intense planning left her tired. For the first time in her career as a SOG operator, she was scared. She was frustrated at her inability to walk a city block without succumbing to mind-numbing fatigue. Of course, this was the first time she'd been shot. Mirlinda said she'd experienced the same feelings of helplessness when she'd been shot. She said only through the help of Cailan and his late partner Dan was she able to pull through and survive.

Her thoughts were interrupted as a yellow and black Yamaha TMAX scooter pulled into the hotel's driveway. The rider was a small man wearing black riding leathers and a black Shoei GT-Air II helmet. He parked the bike and approached her as he removed his helmet.

"Hello, Eliana, how was your meeting?" Henri asked.

"Gosh, I was looking for your Mercedes," Brook said.

Henri waved his hand to the sky. "The weather has cleared, so I thought you might want some fresh air and a light lunch."

"I'm very tired, but that sounds good."

Henri produced a second helmet and handed it to her. "Put this on and I'll help you onto the back."

She wrapped her right arm around his waist as he hit the electronic ignition and merged into traffic. Ten minutes later, they found themselves at Le Balzar in the heart of the Montparnasse district.

"Welcome to Le Balzar," Henri said. "In the past, it was a haunt of many famous artists and writers, from Picasso to Modigliani; from Cocteau and Gershwin to F. Scott Fitzgerald."

He helped Brook off the scooter, and they took a table outside but tucked against the windows where they sat side by side facing the street.

"You look tired, Eliana."

"I am. Too much thinking."

"But your friends agreed with your plan?"

"Yes. One of them will stay in my apartment while the other provides overwatch."

"How will he do that?"

She smiled. "He's a master of disguise and has several that he can use as he circulates through my neighborhood."

"And he can provide this overwatch you mention?"

"Trust me. He's one of the deadliest men walking the planet."

A waiter appeared and handed them menus.

"Ah, if you don't mind, I will order for us. Something light, *non?*"

"That would be great," Brook said.

"S'il vous plaît, pourrions-nous avoir deux Saumon fumé de la maison Nordique, blinis à la crème et une bouteille de Côtes de Provence Rose?"

The waiter nodded. *"Bien sur."* He brought the wine and two glasses and uncorked it. He splashed a sample in Henri's glass and set it in front of him. Henri nosed the wine, sipped, and nodded.

"Excellent."

The waiter filled their glasses and then disappeared.

"I went shopping and bought clothes for you, so you don't have to live in what you're wearing."

Brook arched an eyebrow. "What exactly did you buy?"

"You favor cargo pants, so I bought three pairs in black, gray, and khaki. You also like cotton mock turtlenecks, so I have four of them in muted colors. Five sets of underwear and last but not least, two pairs of sweatpants and tee shirts."

"Where in the world did you develop your observation skills to the point where you can look at me and know my size and what I like?"

"Eliana, you forget I have worked at Les Deux for twelve years. I am a confidant to my customers as well as a waiter. I make suggestions for food and wine that I know will fit their tastes because I observe them closely and I have a memory that will put an elephant to shame. So, recognizing your preferences is just another aspect of my life.

The waiter brought their food and Brook suddenly realized she was ravenous. She finished off the salmon in no time then leaned back to enjoy the wine.

"I see you liked my choice for lunch," Henri said.

"It was delicious."

"When you are ready, we'll go back to my apartment, and you can take a nap."

"I'm just very tired right now," she said.

"I have never been shot, but the body reacts to any major trauma with a need for rest."

"I think I'm ready to go," she said.

Henri called for the bill and paid then they mounted the scooter and took off. Henri wove in and out of traffic, but Brook noticed him checking his mirrors constantly.

"What's wrong, Henri," she asked.

"I don't know how they found us, but there is a car following us. It pulled out when we left the café and has been on us since."

She leaned forward and looked in one of his mirrors. "The bronze minivan?"

"Yes."

"Can you lose them?"

"I could if you weren't on the back with only one arm to hang on, so perhaps it's better to see what they want."

"What? Are you crazy? Henri, I'm in no condition to fight off whoever these guys are. Go! Lose them."

Henri zipped around a corner, but the van picked up speed and stayed with them. He made a hard left at the next block and accelerated, but the van was keeping up.

"*Oh merde avec ça,*" he whispered. He took a hard right into an alley and stopped halfway down it.

"What are you doing?" Brook hissed. "If these guys are assassins, we're dead."

Henri hopped off the scooter and removed his helmet. The look on his face was something Brook had never seen before. It was the face of death staring back at her.

"No, we're not." He pointed to a dumpster. "Stay behind the trash can and wait for me."

"Are you crazy?"

"You have your gun?"

"Yes, but—."

"Stay out of site. This won't take long."

She drew her gun as she backed away from the scooter and ducked behind the dumpster. Henri turned and faced back the way they came as the van pulled into the alley. It stopped and five men got out.

"Well, well, well, a midget. What's up, little man? You gonna try and stop us from taking the woman?"

Henri smiled. "As Master Yoda would say, 'There is no try.'"

"Ooo, did you hear that boys?" They laughed.

"Well, you ain't no Yoda," he said as all five drew pistols.

Henri spread his arms and bowed. "For you who are about to die, I salute you."

Out of nowhere, two knives appeared in his hands. He lunged and gutted the first man with one of his knives, ripping the blade upward and spilling his intestines over his belt. The gun fell from his hand, but Henri snatched it before it hit the ground. He fired once, hitting the second man in the right eye. With his other hand, he threw the second knife, burying it in the third man's chest.

The other two men were momentarily stunned but raised their guns to fire. However, Henri grabbed the first man and spun him around, using him as a shield to absorb the bullets. He pushed the man forward into the other two, dropped low, slid across the pavement, and kicked the legs of the fourth man out from under him. As he went to the ground, Henri pulled the knife out of the first man and raked it across the fourth man's throat. Arterial blood fountained across the alley.

Henri kipped to his feet, launched himself at the alley wall then pushed off, flipping completely over the last man. As he went over him, a thin razor wire garotte appeared in his hands. He slipped the wire around the man's neck while he was in midair and hit the ground behind him on both feet. He pressed one foot against the man's back, crossed his arms, and pulled with all his strength. The man's mouth opened, and his tongue shot out spewing blood. His eyes bulged out of their sockets, as he dropped to the ground, bleeding out from his nearly decapitated head.

Henri straightened and dropped the wire as he surveyed the damage he'd wrought. Five men dead by his hand in less than thirty seconds. A wide-eyed Brook stepped out of the shadows and stared at Henri. He gave her a crooked smile.

"So, now you know that just as you are not only a writer, I am also not only a waiter."

"No shit!" Brook said, surveying the carnage.

He bowed with a flourish. "Allow me to introduce myself. In your circles, I am known as Enigma."

Chapter Thirty-Eight

Monday, April 3ʳᵈ; Paris France; Henri's Apartment

It was dark when Brook woke up. She checked her watch and saw it was 9:30. She and Henri hadn't talked after he killed the five men and announced that he was Enigma. She was too tired, so she fell onto the bed and was asleep in seconds. She noticed her shoes were off and Henri had covered her with a blanket while she slept.

She was shaken by what she'd seen him do. He moved so fast and with such precision, it was like some kind of staged movie scene. He truly was an enigma. That thought made her laugh.

Henri appeared, holding a glass of Armagnac, and cocked his head at her. "What's so funny, Eliana?"

Brook sat up and swung her feet over the edge of the bed. She was laughing so hard, she could barely catch her breath. "Do…do you know… what my current…assignment is?"

He frowned, pursed his lips, and shook his head.

"I…oh God, it's so funny. I'm supposed to protect you."

Henri's eyebrows arched. "Really?"

"Yes. While he knew it might be difficult due to my injury, one of the last things my boss Andrew McGill said was he wanted me to watch over you. And here you are watching over me."

"A bit of serendipity, wouldn't you say?"

"Definitely. My God, Henri, I've never seen anyone move like you did nor did I ever suspect you were Enigma."

"As to the latter, no one ever suspects one of the little people. As to the first, growing up, I was picked on quite a bit. I had to learn to defend myself against much larger opponents, so I started practicing parkour and blended it with Krav Maga, Silat, and Paranza Corte. And although I am also an expert with a pistol or rifle, I think if you ask Andrew McGill, he'll tell you most of my kills were performed with a knife."

"How long have you been at this profession?" Brook asked.

"I've been studying the arts since I was ten and I killed my first man when I was fourteen. He was being abusive to my mother. I stabbed him in the back with a stiletto."

"I think I know the answer to your riddle," she said.

"Before you answer, take a seat at the kitchen table. You're a chocolate aficionado, so you'll love what I have."

She stood and steadied herself before taking a step. She sat at the table and sniffed the air. "What is that heavenly smell?"

Henri took two small plates with chocolate Bundt cakes lightly dusted with powdered sugar and set one in front of her and the other at his place. He took a bowl and spooned a dollop of cream on each.

"Crème fraiche. Would you like an Armagnac?"

"Please."

He set a snifter next to her and sat. "*Bon appetit.*"

As Brook cut a piece of the cake, liquid dark chocolate oozed out of the center.

"This is what Americans call a chocolate lava cake," Henri said.

"Did you make this?"

"*Non*, I went to a bakery while you were sleeping. I just reheated them."

"It's delicious."

"I thought you'd like it. Now tell me the answer to my riddle."

She sipped the Armagnac and held the snifter in both hands as she smiled at him over the rim. "First of all, when I was showering in your bathroom, I noticed you have quite an assortment of drugs in your medicine cabinet. Some of the drugs are immunosuppressants and you have an assortment of antibiotics. Then I checked with a friend who told me that people who've had leukemia and were treated with successful bone marrow transplants were chimeras. While their tissue was still their original type, their blood was now the same type as the donor's. You must've had leukemia or some other hematological cancer and received a bone marrow transplant from a female donor."

He nodded. "My sister."

"So, your blood makes it seem that you're female, when in fact, your male."

"Very good, Eliana."

"Since we're being honest, my name is not Eliana. It's Brook Nathan."

He held out his hand. "Nice to meet you, Brook Nathan."

Brook's expression changed to one of concern. "How are you feeling, Henri?"

"I'm fine. I've been cancer-free for twelve years, but I still keep the drugs around. I seem to be susceptible to respiratory infections, so I keep a stock of several types of antibiotics just in case. Pneumonia could kill me."

"How did you come to work for McGill and the SOG?"

He shrugged. "Word gets around. Circe used to be my agent and gave me a job that was contracted by the SOG."

"What was the job?"

"They wanted the leader of a particularly bloodthirsty rogue group that had broken away from the Odessan mafia killed. I ended his life and collected a quarter of a million Euros for it."

"Was she always your broker?"

"*Non*. Six years ago, I realized she was contracting the murders of people who in my book of ethics didn't deserve to die. So, I inactivated the email account she used to reach me and told her the day that I heard from her again would be the day I'd kill her."

"I assume that motivated her to stay away?"

"*Oui*, but she found Paradox and they became lovers and by crediting Paradox's kills to me, she protected her."

"That's kind of unusual, isn't it?"

"What do you mean?"

"For a broker to be lovers with her main assassin."

"It is more common than you might think, but if whoever killed Circe hadn't reached her first, I would've gone after her."

"Because she was blaming Paradox's kills on you?"

"*Oui. C'était une fille très stupide.*"

"I agree. She was a very stupid girl."

He took a bite of the lava cake then sipped his Armagnac. He leaned back in his chair staring at the amber liquid. "May I ask you a question?"

"Of course, big brother."

He grinned. "I could get used to being called that."

"C'mon, bro, what's the question?"

He took a deep breath. "Did you kill her?"

"Who? Circe?"

"Yes."

"Nope, can't take credit for that one. That honor belongs to my two friends."

He shot forward in his chair. "The video game designer and the wine expert?"

"Well, yes. Like you and I, they are more than they appear to be. I met Cailan in Afghanistan where he was the deadliest sniper the military had ever seen. They called him the Death Whisper because his shots were taken from a thousand yards or more, so his targets were dead before the sound of the bullet arrived. In his spare time, he roams the streets of Chicago with a friend, ridding them of the vermin that prey on helpless people."

"*Un passe-temps tres honorable.*"

"Yes, it's a very honorable pastime. But also, a very dangerous one."

"And what about the lady? I have to tell you when I first saw her, she reminded me of a lioness."

"Why?"

"Because while the males are lazy, the females do the hunting and she struck me as someone who might be a deadly enemy."

Brook grinned. "Once again, your observational skills and intuition come through with flying colors."

"Is she a good friend?"

"She is now, but she's a very good friend of Cailan's. He and I have worked jobs before, and he thought she could be a big help."

"So, what is it she does besides teach at a university and run a gastropub?"

"From what I understand, she kills people the police and federal authorities can't touch."

"Like you?"

Brook choked on her Armagnac. When she got over her coughing fit, she laughed. "Oh no, I'm not in the same league as her."

"Then who does she kill?"

Brook thought for a minute. "I believe she's killed twelve of the top assassins in the world."

Henri's face scrunched in a frown "Who…?"

Brook watched his eyes widen as the realization hit him.

"*Mon Dieu*!" he whispered.

Chapter Thirty-Nine

Tuesday, April 4th; Paris, France; Brook's Apartment

Brook's apartment was located on the Rue Dupin near Le Bon Marche in the Cherche-Midi neighborhood. Her place was on the top floor of a five-story building that had a glass-enclosed elevator, a charming courtyard, and a caretaker. The entrance hall led to a living room that connected to a separate dining room. The flat had two bedrooms, one of which she used as an office, and had floor-to-ceiling bookshelves that hid a long narrow closet where she kept her arsenal of weapons. The apartment featured period elements like decorative moldings and parquet floors, and there was a balcony that ran the length of the living-dining rooms and overlooked the courtyard garden.

Mirlinda went through the place, adjusting the curtains and lamps so they wouldn't backlight her after dark. The apartment had a heavy solid oak door and frame equipped with state-of-the-art deadbolts. She had placed suppressed guns and fighting knives at strategic spots in the apartment, so she was never more than six feet from a weapon. That was in addition to the two Garm fighting knives strapped to her forearms in sheaths under a loose-fitting long-sleeved tee shirt. Over it, she wore a down vest lined with Kevlar and rated at level III protection.

After Brook told them a five-man team had tried to kill her, she and Cailan were on high alert. The funny thing was, Brook didn't say how they escaped. Yet the news reported five men were brutally killed in an alley the previous night. One was shot, two had knife wounds, one had his throat cut, and the fifth man was almost decapitated with a wire garrote. While Brook might've accounted for the one who was shot, she was in no shape to kill three with a knife and it took two hands to wield a garrote, yet Brook only had one good arm. She and Cailan discussed it and concluded that Henri was more than he appeared to be. Whatever happened, if Henri was responsible for one or more of the deaths, it meant Brook was in good hands.

She removed the light bulbs in the entry hall, bedrooms, and kitchen leaving the only functional lamp next to a wingback chair tucked in a shadowed corner. She carried a full-length mirror into the living room and set it up so she could see the door's reflection from her chair. She moved next to the door and smiled. In the darkness, the mirror misled anyone entering the apartment to think Mirlinda's chair was where the mirror stood when she was really across the room.

Not surprising for someone in Brook's profession, she also owned a four by six foot free-standing, moveable panel made of mil-spec ballistic glass mounted on four heavy-duty lockable caster wheels. She said it was rated to be able to stop 7.62mm FMJ bullets fired from an automatic rifle. Mirlinda had the shield positioned between her and the hallway. She set a suppressed Glock 19X and a Pneu-dart X-2 tranquilizer gun next to her on a side table. The dart gun's cartridges contained enough batrachotoxin to kill a man in under a minute.

She picked up her copy of "Entrepreneurship: The Practice and Mindset" by Christopher P. Neck and Emma L. Murray. She was planning on using it in her university course and settled in to read while she waited for any potential visitors to arrive.

****

188

An old man in a tan trench coat shuffled along the sidewalk in the Latin quarter. A black herringbone Thompson Baker Boy hat covered his bald head that was ringed with white hair. He used a blackthorn walking cane to aid him as he walked. He looked like a harmless aged Frenchman out for an evening walk. But his looks were deceiving.

Under his coat, Cailan had a Brugger and Thomet SPC9 PDW SD, a permanently suppressed, eighteen-inch machine gun in a sling under his right arm. Under his left, a suppressed CZ P-10C was snugged in a custom shoulder holster and a USMC KA-BAR knife was strapped to his right hip.

This was the second disguise he'd used tonight, and he had two more to lessen the chances that someone would find his presence suspicious. A man stepped out of the Dupin Restaurant and pressed his right index finger to his ear as he walked toward Brook's building across the street. He stopped just before the Dynamo Cycling Sévres and turned down an alley. Cailan heard him talking to someone, describing his view of Brook's apartment.

When the stranger ended his conversation, Cailan drew his CZ, holding it near his right leg, and turned into the alley. The man was standing ten feet from him when he raised the gun and shot him twice in the face.

He knelt next to the assassin and transferred his earbud and radio to himself. He took out his cell phone and texted Mirlinda.

"Company's on the way. One down, unknown how many others. I'm moving to your building."

As he crossed the street, he saw four men walking toward the building. Two split off and headed to the rear while the remaining two entered the courtyard and approached the front door. Cailan texted Mirlinda as he circled to the back.

"Four guys. Two coming in the front. Two heading to the back. I'll take the ones in back then head to your floor and provide overwatch."

He drew the SPC9 and extended the buttstock. One of the two potential intruders was in the process of picking the lock on the rear door while the other watched the alley. Cailan fired a three-round burst to his head and the same to the head of the lockpicker. He collapsed the buttstock and shoved the gun under his coat. He grabbed the first guy under the arms and dragged his body to a dumpster. He faced him to the edge then hoisted him into the bin. He repeated the process with the second guy.

He texted Mirlinda. *"Two more down. On my way to you."*

****

Elliot Rampoule led his associate, Jacob Claes, up the stairs to the fifth floor where their target lived. They held suppressed HK VP9 pistols in two-handed grips and aimed at the floor. The watcher out front signaled that a shadow moved across the window just before the lights went out, signifying someone was home.

This was no longer just a job for Elliot. The five men killed the previous evening were a part of his unit. They weren't just killed; they were slaughtered like farm animals even though the news report said all five had drawn guns. Rampoule had never heard of a single person with the ability to kill five armed men so viciously. Whoever it was must have taken them by surprise because all his men were ex-members of either the Belgian Spec Ops Group or the German KSK. They were highly trained and Rampoule couldn't imagine them dying while facing down a single assassin. Nevertheless, they were dead and the one he suspected was responsible for the massacre was about to meet an equally grisly fate.

They reached the apartment and Rampoule motioned for Jacob to stand to one side of the door while he checked the locks. Whoever the resident was didn't kid around in terms of security. The door was solid oak and Rampoule figured both it and the frame were steel reinforced, so trying to kick it down would only result in a broken ankle. There were three deadbolts positioned up and down the door in addition to the lock in the doorknob. Rampoule ran his hand over each deadbolt the checked the door handle.

"Fils de pute!" he whispered.

"What?" Jacob asked.

190

"The door. It's unlocked."

"That means we're expected," Jacob said. "What do you want to do?"

Rampoule leaned his back against the wall and closed his eyes. Whoever was in there was deadly and he had no desire to end up like his compatriots last night. But a quarter million Euros for this job wasn't chump change. He motioned for Jacob to follow him to the stairway door.

"Okay, we go in low and fast. You go left, I'll go right. I don't know the layout of the apartment, but you'll be heading to the front of the building, which will probably take you to the living room. Clear it and wait for me. I'll try to herd the killer to you."

Jacob nodded and they returned to the door. Rampoule put his hand on the doorknob and counted down.

"Three, two, one."

On one, they entered the room as silently as possible. Rampoule peeled off right down a short hallway that led to a back room. He dove through the doorway, coming up to a knee, and swept his gun around the room. Streetlights from a window revealed a floor-to-ceiling bookshelf that stretched the length of the room. There was a desk opposite it, but the footwell was open so there was no place to hide.

He heard a thump like something heavy hit the floor…like a body. Rampoule was a former elite soldier. One of the best, but as he felt a bead of sweat run down his back, he realized that for the first time in his life, he was scared. He turkey-peeked into the hall, but it was dark. He held his gun two-handed and crouched low as he crept down the hallway. He started toward the apartment door and was just about to step into the hall and run when a voice cautioned him.

"I wouldn't go out there if I was you. There's a friend of mine holding a Brugger and Thomet SPC9 PDW SD and I believe he has twenty-four rounds left. He's already killed your associates in the alley and the guy across the street. So why don't you put down your gun, come into the living room, and have a seat?"

Rampoule strained his eyes, staring into the darkened room ahead. He thought he saw the woman sitting in a corner chair, so he raised his gun and fired five times. The image disappeared in a shower of shattered glass. Before he could react, he felt a sharp pain in the back of his neck. He grabbed for the source and pulled out a tranquilizer dart. He whirled around, looking for his attacker, but the hallway was empty.

His limbs suddenly felt very heavy, and his gun slipped to the floor. When he didn't hear it hit, he turned and came face to face with an old man in a scally cap holding a small machine gun. Rampoule took a staggering step backward, leaned against the wall, and slid to the floor. His throat felt tight, and he had trouble swallowing but he managed to focus on the face of a dark-haired woman watching him.

"Who…"

That was the only word he could get out because his mouth wouldn't work properly.

The woman knelt next to him a frowned. "I wish you hadn't fired at the mirror. We're going to have to patch up the holes in the plaster wall after we clean up the broken glass. I'd ask you to help, but you won't be able to." She checked her watch. "Because you're going to be dead in about another half minute."

She stood and snapped her fingers. "Oh yeah, you wanted to know who I am? My name is Sasha Nesti."

Rampoule managed a groan. That bitch Paradox had sent them after the legendary Sasha?

"*Merde tout*," he whispered just before he died.

Chapter Forty

Friday, April 7th; Monte Carlo, Monaco; the Hôtel de Paris

Mirlinda arrived at Cote d'Azur Airport in Nice. A limousine awaited her arrival to take her to the Hôtel de Paris in Monte Carlo. Situated on a prominent escarpment at the base of the Maritime Alps along the French border, Monte Carlo was the home of the world-famous Place du Casino that made Monte Carlo an international byword for the extravagant display and reckless dispersal of wealth. It was also the playground of Elion Kastrati, the man who'd placed a sanction on any CIA or MI6 agent in retaliation for the assassination of his bloodthirsty brother.

The Hôtel de Paris where she was staying, was established in 1864 by Charles III of Monaco and was located on the west side of the Place du Casino in the heart of Monte Carlo. It belonged to the *Société des Bains de Mer de Monaco*, meaning it was very exclusive and very expensive. But expense didn't matter because proximity to the casino was paramount. It was where Kastrati spent eighty percent of his evenings.

Mirlinda checked in and one of the bellhops took her suitcase and escorted her to her third-floor room. He set her suitcase on a luggage rack and opened the French doors to a small balcony that overlooked the bay. He bowed when she tipped him and backed out of the room.

She examined her room to make sure there was nothing out of the ordinary then opened her suitcase. She pulled off a Velcro strip, holding part of the lining in place, and took out Boker Anti-Grav ceramic knife with a carbon fiber handle and set it on a side table. Next, she removed a small hair dryer and a curling iron and took them into the bathroom where she took them apart and set the pieces on the countertop. The parts were to a Glock 26 Gen5 and because they were disassembled and in the hairdryer, they were invisible to x-ray machines. The gun barrel was inside the curling iron. Five minutes later, she'd assembled the gun.

She took a bottle of water from the minibar and set it on the small desk. She set her laptop next to it and opened an electronic file on Elion Kastrati. Osias had given them considerable information on him. She cracked open the water bottle as she went through the file. Elion was twenty-eight years old and the brother of Driton, the late head of the Odessa mafia. He was described by Interpol as being hot-headed and had been involved in several assaults. However, they were always blamed on his security personnel because Elion was a five-eight, 135-pound wimpy little shit.

"Definitely has a Napoleon complex," Mirlinda said.

He'd rented Villa La Vigie, one of the most prestigious villas on the French Riviera thanks to its history, architecture, and unique location. It sat on a hill overlooking the sea and was visible from anywhere along the shoreline. Karl Lagerfeld, the famous designer had used it as his summer home for years. Because of its location, Cailan had reserved a top-floor suite at the Monte-Carlo Bay Hotel that was directly across the bay and gave him a clean shot at the little shit as he sat on his balcony.

She put away her laptop and laid out her clothes for the evening. She showered then dressed in a black collarless silk blouse under a gray pinstriped Hugo Boss suit. Her shoes were gray suede ankle boots with a pointed toe and a two-inch heel. She slipped her credit cards into holders in a small, black, Willow wallet on a gold chain and slid her knife into its lining.

She set up her digital clock surveillance camera and checked it was connected to her phone then left her room and headed for the casino across the street.

The casino Monte-Carlo differed from those in Los Vegas. There were no smells of all-you-can-eat buffet shrimp, and it lacked the gaudy neon and strobing lights. The high rollers here were billionaire Russian oligarchs, movie stars, and beautiful people. No men in cheap off-the-rack suits gliding around the floor like circling sharks.

Its beating heart was the Salle Europe. More than one James Bond movie had been filmed inside its walls that echoed with the calls of croupiers and the muffled sounds of chips falling on felt-topped tables. The walls and ceilings were decorated with a plethora of gilding, paintings, sculptures, and bas-reliefs. The bar was just off the gaming floor where guests could sit in a relaxed atmosphere, sipping cocktails and champagne while they quietly watched the gaming action. If you were a casino aficionado, it was the place to be.

Mirlinda took a table at the edge of the bar where she could see the entire gaming floor. A waitress in a black suit and white shirt with a Peter Pan collar took her order for a half bottle of Domaine Deliance Cremant de Bourgogne. Minutes later she returned to uncork the bottle and fill a flute with the bubbly. Mirlinda sipped and nodded her approval. Cremant had everything she loved about champagne—the brioche and bread dough bouquet, full body, and tiny bubbles—without breaking the bank. Cremant was the general term for French sparkling wines that didn't come from the Champagne region, but they were made and aged by the same process. It was one of the wines she most often recommended in her Chicago pub.

The casino had a dress code after seven, meaning no shorts, polo shirts, or sandals. Many of the men wore tuxedos while the women were in glitzy long dresses and heels with their hair in elaborate styles. But as an assassin, Mirlinda had to be able to move if necessary. Her shoes, while stylish, fit snuggly to allow her to run and the two-inch heel was a weapon. Stomping on the instep of an attacker or pistoning a kick to a knee was guaranteed to do serious damage.

Mirlinda groaned inwardly as she watched a tall man with short brown hair, graying at the temples in a black suit and a white shirt unbuttoned to the middle of his chest, threading his way toward her table. The guy had to be at least six-five. Her earlier thought about no circling sharks would need revising. He was carrying a glass of clear liquid in a tumbler.

"Shit, a fucking Russian," she whispered.

"Hello, pretty lady. Mind it if I join you?" He didn't wait for an answer, pulling out the chair opposite her and sitting.

"Let me ask you a question, Ivan."

He frowned. "My name is not Ivan."

"Maybe not, but you're Russian, so it's close enough."

"How do you know I'm Russian?"

"First, you look like someone who thinks he's God's gift to women. Second, you're drinking vodka straight up. And third." She scrunched her nose. "Russian men don't wear deodorant. They just keep splashing on the most obnoxious cologne they can find and assume it hides their odor." She sipped her Cremant. "Hot tip, Ivan. It doesn't work."

His eyes narrowed and he tossed back his drink then motioned for a refill. "Do you know who I am?"

The waitress came with a new tumbler of vodka, but before she could leave, Mirlinda touched her arm.

"Excuse me, could you call a doctor? This man has lost his memory and can't remember who he is."

When the waitress looked puzzled, Mirlinda smiled. "Never mind. I'm sure he'll remember eventually."

The Russian spoke through gritted teeth. "I am Mikhail Prokhorov."

"Ah, the former part-owner of the pathetic Brooklyn Nets. And, as I recall, you gained international notoriety when you were arrested at the French ski resort Courchevel in January 2007 and were held in connection with a prostitution investigation."

"I was cleared of the charges."

"Billionaires can afford good lawyers. Let's get back to the initial question I wanted you to answer. Why is it that when someone like you sees a woman sitting by herself, enjoying a drink and watching the crowd, you think she wants company?"

"Are you gay?"

Mirlinda grinned. "I'm straighter than the pole your mother dances on."

"Yobanaya suka!"

"Fucking bitch? How original."

"You speak Russian?"

"And seven other languages, so as they say in France, '*S'en aller. Tu m'agraces.*'"

"What does that mean?"

"Leave. You annoy me."

He swept his gaze around the floor then stood and left. Mirlinda sighed in relief. She didn't want to cause a scene that would draw attention to herself. The waitress appeared and refilled her glass then winked as she moved away.

A commotion started up near the entrance as two very large men tried to enter but were stopped at the scanners that spanned the entrance. The four casino guards in body armor, carrying Six Sauer MPX rifles made it easy for the security personnel to relieve the two men of their guns. The first guy pressed his left ear, nodded, then stepped through into the casino. His buddy followed him.

They swept their gazes over the casino floor then the first guy again communicated with someone outside and seconds later, Elion Kastrati appeared with a girl who couldn't have been more than fifteen on his arm. He scowled at the security personnel as if this was an unexpected inconvenience, yet Mirlinda knew from talking with Osias that he was here every night. The man must like to tweak the noses of the house security and broadcast the fact that he was a big man. Actually, in his tight leather pants, silk shirt open to his belt, and black velour jacket, he looked like an escapee from a pimp school.

She watched him pass through security followed by two more gorillas then head for the blackjack tables. One of the players got up and offered Elion his seat. Kastrati sat while his female escort stood behind him. One of his men brought him several stacks of chips, which meant this was going to be a high-stakes game. A waitress brought him a bottle of Krug Champagne but no glass. Elion just swilled it down straight from the bottle.

Mirlinda watched him play. He was reckless but lucky. As the game progressed, she estimated he'd made close to 10,000 Euros. She heard him say one last hand and watched as his first two cards were a nine and an ace totaling twenty. She watched him go all in as the dealer's hand showed a four and a five. The dealer drew a card, a five. He drew a fourth card, a deuce. The dealer's total was now sixteen with one draw remaining. Time seemed to stand still, and the lavish surroundings, bas-reliefs, and Bohemian crystal chandeliers faded into the background as the people around the table held their breath. The dealer drew his last card—the five of spades. Twenty-one. Elion lost everything.

He sat there staring at the table for several seconds then rose, grabbed the girl, and motioned for his bodyguards to follow him as he exited the casino. Mirlinda finished her bottle and followed him out just in time to see him climb behind the wheel of a white Ferrari F8 Tributo. His escort got in on her own and she'd barely shut the door when he roared off into the night with a black Range Rover following him.

She checked her watch—11:30. She forwarded the information regarding Elion's timetable to Cailan who would be arriving by car tomorrow. Then she'd visit the casino one more time. A third visit would not be necessary because by then Elion would be dead.

Chapter Forty-One

Saturday, April 8th; Monte-Carlo, Monaco; Monte-Carlo Bay Hotel

Cailan followed the directions on his GPS as he drove through the streets of Monte-Carlo to the Monte-Carlo Bay hotel where he had a top-floor suite reserved. He rented a VW GTI in Paris and took off at about seven this morning. The drive had taken him ten hours, which included stops for lunch and gas, and he was looking forward to getting out and stretching his legs. He pulled up to the hotel and exchanged his keys for a tag with the valet. He unloaded a gray twenty-five-inch Travelpro suitcase and a teal blue Osprey Farpoint 40 backpack. He slung the backpack over his shoulder and grabbed the handle of his suitcase then headed for the front desk to check-in.

"Good afternoon, sir. Welcome to the Monte-Carlo Bay," the clerk said. "Checking in?"

Cailan handed him a note that explained he was mute and gave all the particulars of his reservation. He slid his passport and credit card toward the clerk and smiled. The clerk nodded and typed Cailan's information into his computer.

"I have you with us for one night, Mr. Bane. Is that correct?"

Cailan nodded.

"And how many keys would you like?"

Cailan held up one finger. The clerk handed him his key card.

"Will you need help with your luggage?"

Cailan smiled and shook his head.

"Enjoy your stay. If you need any assistance, just call the front desk."

Cailan smiled. Apparently, the clerk missed the part about him being mute. He took his keycard and went to the elevators. He pressed the button for the top floor then checked the room numbers as he got off. He opened his door and locked it behind him. He rolled the suitcase to a corner and shrugged out of the backpack and set it on the floor. He opened the French doors that led to his balcony and checked out the view. Villa La Vigie where Elion lived was directly across the bay. He lifted the suitcase onto a luggage stand and entered the combination to its lock. He took out a titanium briefcase and set it on the living room desk.

He entered a second combination and opened it, revealing a disassembled Desert Tactical Arms Stealth Recon Scout or SRS sniper rifle with a 5-round box and chambered for .300 Win Mag snugged in fitted foam compartments. The case also held a SilencerCo Omega 300 suppressor, a Nightforce NXS 8-22x56 telescopic sight mated to a BORS optical ranging system, and a box of VOR-TX copper-tipped triple shock 180-grain bullets. The TTSX projectiles traveled at just under 3200 feet per second and were designed for rapid expansion, high weight retention, and deep penetration.

He took a pair of Nikon Laserforce Rangefinder binoculars from his backpack and stepped in front of the open French doors. He could've stayed at Mirlinda's hotel since it was right across the street from the casino where Elion hung out every evening. It would've been an easy shot to take him as he either entered or exited the building. But it would have made getting away safely difficult. He ranged the distance from his hotel room to the wide balcony and table where Elion played cards every evening after leaving the casino. It was a 580-yard shot across the bay. Cailan would be long gone before anyone could determine the origin of the shot.

While he had a picture of the Odessan, he felt it would be better to get a look at the man close up, so he locked up his gun case and placed it in the suitcase. He changed into black wool pants, a burgundy cotton turtleneck, and a gray wrinkle-resistant Palazzo sport coat. His steel-toed Kevlar Ryder sneakers were fine with his outfit. He didn't bother with a weapon since he knew he'd have to pass through metal detectors, and this was purely a reconnaissance trip.

He caught a cab in front of the hotel and sent a text to Mirlinda telling her he was on his way to the casino and the first thing he was going to do was get something to eat. Her return text said she had a table for two where they could watch the gaming floor.

Cailan arrived at the casino ten minutes later and found Mirlinda after he passed through security. Tonight, she was wearing a Claret-colored velvet suit with a black turtleneck and black Rockport Tristina boots. She poured him a glass of the same crémant she'd ordered the previous night and slid a menu in front of him.

"How was the drive?"

"Long, but uneventful," he signed.

"Those are the best kind."

A waitress arrived and Cailan placed an order for a fried calamari appetizer to share and spaghetti alla carbonara for his dinner.

"How's Elion's entourage look?" he signed.

"Four moose-size bodyguards. He bets big and wins for a while then gets cocky and loses it all," Mirlinda signed.

"How does he take losing?"

"Not great. He usually leaves after a big loss."

Cailan nodded toward the entrance. *"Is that him?"*

A short, skinny guy with long black hair parted in the middle wearing snug-fitting navy wool pants, an unbuttoned white shirt that showed off a hairless, white chest devoid of muscle, and a blue velvet blazer entered the casino flanked by four large men.

"Bingo," she whispered.

The waitress delivered the food and Cailan ate while they watched Elion play roulette for a while before moving to the blackjack table. Once again, he began betting big. As he finished his dinner, Cailan nudged Mirlinda's foot.

"There's a big guy with short brown hair, graying at the temples in a navy blazer and a white shirt unbuttoned to the middle of his chest, sitting at the bar watching us."

Mirlinda raised her champagne flute and checked the bar. *"Mikhail Prokhorov."*

"The Russian oligarch?"

Mirlinda nodded.

"What's his interest in us, or more likely, you?"

"We had a little verbal sparring match last night. He seems to think any woman sitting alone is an invitation for him to join her. If he wants to continue our discussion, I'll put the fear of God in him."

"Stupid man." Cailan signaled for the check. *"Are you leaving tomorrow?"*

"Yes. I have a 10:00 flight to Paris. How about you? When are you taking him?"

"Later tonight. I'll do the deed then check out and drive back to Paris. I'll see you and Brook Monday."

Mirlinda stood and pecked Cailan on the cheek.

"Drive carefully." She headed for the ladies' room.

****

Just before she reached the ladies' room, Mirlinda saw Prokhorov lay some money on the bar then follow her. The washrooms were down a short hall on her left. The women's was on the left with the men's on the right, but there was a janitor's closet just before the men's room. She checked its door and found it open. She took the ceramic knife out of her purse and stepped into the closet. Heavy steps approached and stopped in front of the closet. Mirlinda grinned because Prokhorov was planning to use the closet to hide in and then grab her as she left the washroom. She moved to the rear and crouched next to a group of mops and buckets. The Russian opened the door and slipped inside, leaving it slightly open so he could watch for his prey.

202

Mirlinda rose and grabbed his collar, twisting it tight. She pulled him backward and kicked him behind his knee, driving him to the floor. She placed the blade against his throat.

"Looking for me, Mr. Playboy?" she whispered.

"What do you want?" He croaked.

"A better question would be what do you want? I mean, why are you in a janitor's closet watching the lady's restroom?"

"I...I—"

"Don't bother trying to lie, Mr. Prokhorov. I know you fancy yourself a ladies' man, but here's a bit of advice. *Nyet* means *Nyet*. But apparently, you can't take the hints I gave you yesterday. So, here's the deal. I can cut your throat and leave your body in this closet and by the time they find your body, I'll be long gone."

"Please, don't. I'm sorry."

"You're right on that point. You're a sorry excuse for a human and by eliminating you I would be removing scum from the gene pool. But I'm feeling benevolent tonight."

She set her knife on a shelf and put the Russian in a rear naked choke hold while she dragged him backward. The move surprised him, and he was out before he could resist. She lowered him to the floor then placed her knife in her purse. As she was about to leave, she glanced down at him sprawled on the floor.

"Ah what the hell." She kicked him several times in his groin.

"That should do it."

She checked the hall then slipped out the door and headed for her hotel.

"That's one oligarch asshole who won't be contributing to the gene pool anymore."

Forty-Two

Saturday, April 8th; Monte-Carlo, Monaco; Villa La Vigie

Cailan stayed at the casino for two more hours, watching Kastrati lose money. The little wimp had a temper. He went on a rant and threatened the croupier after his final loss at the blackjack table, the Casino management intervened and politely informed him that if he couldn't act like a gentleman, he would no longer be welcome. One of Kastrati's men took his arm and said something to him that convinced him it was in his best interests to leave.

Cailan paid his bill and left before Kastrati. He waited outside and watched the Odessan pick up where he left off inside as he waited for the valet to bring his car. He jumped behind the wheel of the white Ferrari and took off, leaving his bodyguards and a very young girl behind. A black Range Rover pulled up and one of the bodyguards helped the girl into the backseat. The driver took off at a much more leisurely pace. Cailan figured they were accustomed to Kastrati's temper tantrums and knew there was nothing they could do. Their vehicle certainly couldn't keep up with the Ferrari.

Cailan grabbed a cab and took it back to his hotel. When he got back to his room, he took a bottle of water from the minibar. He kept the lights off in his room as he stepped out onto his balcony, admiring the way the stars reflected off the dark water. He looked across the bay where the Villa La Vigie was lit up like a beacon. Osias' information indicated Kastrati rarely went to bed before dawn and liked to play cards with his guards at a table for six on the wide balcony that ran around two sides of the building. Cailan doubted the stakes were as high as they'd been in the casino. He opened his backpack and took out the binoculars. A servant was lighting two tall outdoor propane patio heaters. Cailan took that to mean it was almost showtime.

He took the titanium case out of his suitcase and set it on the coffee table. He unlocked it and pulled on a pair of thin black leather gloves then began assembling his weapon. The Stealth Recon Scout or SRS sniper rifle was a manually operated, rotary bolt action rifle in a bullpup configuration with an aluminum alloy receiver and a proprietary injection-molded polymer stock. It had Precision-made, free-floating barrels in .338, .300 win mag, and .308 that could be quickly replaced by the user. Its single-stack box magazines held five rounds of ammunition in each caliber.

Cailan had it set up for .300 win mag because they carried significantly more energy downrange and the heavier bullets were better suited for large animals like humans. At the same time, it would not be as loud as a .338. The .300 Win Mag was rated out to a maximum effective range of 1,300 yards and Cailan shot 0.5 MOA using the combination of the SRS and VOR-TX ammunition. At a distance of 580 yards, the weapon system was more than sufficient to take down Kastrati.

He assembled the rifle and attached the Nightforce NXS 8-22x56 telescopic sight and BORS optical ranging system. The BORS was an integrated ballistics computer that mounted directly on the riflescope and coupled to the elevation knob. It instantly took care of most of the calculations required for a shot so Cailan could focus on the task of achieving first-round hits. After determining the range to the target, Cailan simply turned the elevation knob until the BORS screen matched his target's distance. Internal sensors automatically calculated the ballistic solution and eliminated the need for a spotter.

He set the rifle on the floor then moved an end table in front of the French doors. He placed the desk chair behind it and set the rifle on the table and dropped the bipod. He sat in the chair and position himself behind the gun. Once he'd dialed in the range and adjusted his sights based on information from the BORS, he scanned the villa. Wide French doors that led from the living room to the balcony deck were open and the four bodyguards were talking with a man who appeared to be in charge. One of the men wheeled a portable bar onto the balcony while another pushed an identical cart loaded with food and parked it next to the bar.

Two young girls wearing skintight leather pants and sheer, white, form-fitting tops appeared. Neither girl looked to be over sixteen and Cailan assumed they were responsible for serving the players. The guy who appeared to be acting as the host steered two men in sports jackets, loose-fitting black pants, and open-collared shirts to the table. Neither looked like a bodyguard. Both were considerably older than Elion, so Cailan thought they were either business associates or senior members of the Odessa mafia. The host escorted three more players to the table where the girls served them food and drinks. Elion finally appeared and shook hands and kissed each of the five men then took a seat at the table facing Cailan's window.

Cailan thought about taking out all six of the men at the table. In all likelihood, they were either members of the Odessa organization or involved with them in some capacity. But he recalled that the point of only taking out Elion was because he was the last in his family line, meaning no one had to swear an oath of vengeance on the killer. That was how he got into this situation in the first place.

No, by killing Elion, he'd remove the source of the blanket contract to kill CIA and MI6 agents. The others wouldn't care, especially after seeing Elion die. They would know there was someone out there who might decide to come after them if they continued the vendetta.

Cailan folded his left hand under the rifle and rested his right hand on the trigger and grip. He peered through the scope and saw Kastrati motion to the girl manning the bar. She set champagne flutes in front of each player then opened a bottle and poured a measure into each glass. Kastrati grinned and raised his glass in a toast. His eyes seem to look right at Cailan as he squeezed the trigger. While the sound of the shot in the hotel was no louder than someone snapping their fingers, the boom as the supersonic bullet rocketed across the bay was quite loud. But with the cacophony of traffic sounds, it went unnoticed.

But Kastrati noticed.

The bullet blew through his heart, rocking him back in his chair as his champagne glass bounced off the table onto the balcony floor. The two girls were the first to react and dropped to their knees. Kastrati's five guests were frozen for several seconds before each scrambled out of their chairs and crawled toward the French Doors.

Immediately, Cailan shut the balcony doors and picked up the expended cartridge then started disassembling the rifle. He placed the parts in the foam cutouts of the titanium case. He snapped the lid shut and spun the combination then placed it in his full-size suitcase. He tucked his binoculars in his backpack then put the chair and table in their original places. He scanned the room to make sure nothing was out of place then took the TV remote and turned on the television. He checked out online, shut off the TV, and headed for the elevator.

He gave the valet his claim ticket and ten minutes later he was weaving his way through the city. He had booked a room at a hotel in Avignon that was a three-hour drive. He planned to leave around noon tomorrow and make the six-hour trip to Paris where he'd drop his equipment off at Mirlinda's apartment and then return to the Millésime Hotel. As he drove away, a rhyme popped into Cailan's head regarding Kastrati's death.

Roses are red, violets are blue. God made me a sniper, so I could kill you.

Chapter Forty-Three

Monday, April 10th; Paris France; The Millesime Hotel

Brook followed a hotel employee wheeling a tray with an urn of coffee and a platter of croissants to Cailan's room. Cailan opened the door and motioned for him to park the cart next to the windows then signed the check and carefully hugged Brook.

"Welcome back," she said. "I hope you didn't lose too much money in the casino."

"The only person who lost anything was Elion Kastrati and he lost his life."

"I saw that on the news yesterday. Pardon the pun, but his death made quite a splash."

Cailan winced. *"Ouch."* He motioned to the cart. *"Help yourself to coffee and croissants."*

As Brook poured herself a cup of coffee and helped herself to a *pain au chocolate*, someone knocked on the door.

Cailan drew his CZ P-10C from under his zip-up hoodie and checked through the peephole. He let Mirlinda in. She hugged Cailan and then kissed Brook on each cheek.

"How's the arm?"

"Much better. It still hurts, but I've almost got full range of motion back and my strength is about seventy percent."

"Are you still staying with Henri?"

"No, I'm at the Relais Christine hotel. I don't want to compromise him and until Paradox is out of the way, it's not safe to go back to my apartment."

"Nice hotel. I've stayed there before," Cailan signed.

"We had a little altercation with five guys at your apartment before we left for Monaco," Mirlinda said. You have a couple of bullet holes in your front wall, but other than that, we left it as we found it."

"Five?" Brook said. "Geez, she really wants my ass badly. Henri and I were followed after we left you at the Hotel Millésime. Henri pulled his scooter down an alley and faced off with another five."

"Wait, Henri killed the five guys?" Mirlinda asked.

"Yeah, he has some hidden skills that I wasn't aware of."

There was another knock on the door. Cailan drew his gun but didn't see anyone through the peephole. He shook his head and shrugged.

"It's okay, I invited him," Brook said.

"Invited who?" Mirlinda asked.

Brook opened the door, and she swept her hand to the person waiting outside.

"Cailan, Mirlinda, I'd like you to meet Henri Aubert, better known in our world as Enigma."

Mirlinda's jaw dropped. Cailan holstered his gun and extended his hand. Henri shook it as Cailan motioned him toward the breakfast cart.

"Now I understand the meaning of the name."

"It fits, don't you think?" Henri said as he poured himself a cup of coffee and helped himself to a croissant. He took a seat in a wingback chair and bit into the pastry.

"Good, but not as good as those we have at Les Deux," he said.

"Do you speak sign?" Cailan asked.

Henri set his plate on the small table next to his chair. *"I speak sign and seven other languages."*

"You had a bone marrow transplant from a female donor when you were younger, which is why the authorities were duped into thinking you were a woman," Cailan signed.

"Yes, I developed leukemia twelve years ago. My twin sister is like me, one of the little people and she was a match. Thus, my blood makes me appear to be female."

"And you took out five men bare-handed?" Mirlinda asked.

"Non, I had these." Two knives magically appeared in his hands. "I also used a wire garrote on one of the men."

"One of the men was shot," Mirlinda said. "Was that you, Brook?"

"Nope. Henri gutted the first gunman and caught his pistol when he dropped it. He shot one of the guys through his eye."

"Holy shit," Mirlinda whispered. "So, you're a freelance assassin?"

"Non, like you, Mirlinda, I work exclusively for American and British foreign intelligence agencies."

"What do you mean, 'like me?'" Mirlinda asked.

He pursed his lips and reached for his coffee. After taking a sip, he cocked his head at her. "As I understand it, Sasha Nesti only hunts for the FBI, CIA, and MI6. No independent work." He took another sip of his coffee and held up an index finger, telling her to wait a minute.

"Your next question will be, 'How do I know that?' My answer is how do I know what each customer at Les Deux likes to eat and drink? How can I recognize when someone needs cheering up by delivering a special treat? Or ask Brook how I know what types of clothing she prefers and her sizes without her telling me?"

Mirlinda frowned at Brook. "He knows that?"

"Yep, but don't ask me how."

"How is because over the years I have finely tuned my observational skills. In several cases, they've kept me alive." He shrugged. "Plus, Brook told me."

"Did you know the CIA director was a Russian agent?" Cailan signed.

"Yes, I was actually in Geneva to kill him. His work with Paradox and Circe put a price on my head. I knew Lagunov would probably draw

CIA and MI6 agents tasked to kill him and that it would also draw Paradox because she blamed those two organizations for the death of her lover, Circe. I was watching Paradox when purely by chance I saw her enter the bar and take a seat next to Brook."

"And at that point, you became my guardian angel," Brook said.

"Forgive me, but I've known you were an agent of either the U.S. or Britain for two years. But I also knew you had no idea who Paradox was and what her capabilities are."

"She's still out there," Brook said.

"I know and she's probably watching you," Henri said.

"What about you?" Mirlinda asked. "What if she sees you?"

Henri popped the last of his croissant in his mouth and wiped his hands with a napkin. "Brook, when I warned you about Paradox at your hotel bar, did you see me?"

"No."

"That's because no one notices the little people. We're invisible, which leads me to my plan to kill Paradox, but it means using you as bait."

"Bait?"

"Yes, but she will have to get close to you, so no worries about a sniper shot."

"And where will this take place?" she asked.

"On the train platform of the Magenta RER off Gare du Nord."

"Do you want us to back you up?" Cailan signed.

"*Non*, Paradox will be very careful when she goes after Brook. She has probably seen you and knows you're connected to Brook. I will handle her, and I won't let her hurt Brook."

"Are you sure you want to do it this way?" Mirlinda asked.

Brook took a deep breath. "If Henri says he can do it, I'm game."

"You can say that again," Mirlinda said.

Brook gave her a quizzical look.

"You're game, all right. Big game."

Chapter Forty-Four

Friday, April 14th; Paris, France; The Magenta Train Platform, Gare du Nord

Brook gently probed her wound with her fingers. The skin was no longer inflamed but it itched. She rolled her arm around in a circle several times to check her mobility. The arm wasn't sore, but she could feel a slight pull where the scar tissue was forming. She'd been doing a series of stretching exercises to keep it loose and it seemed to be working.

She leaned on the bathroom counter and stared at her reflection in the mirror. Henri's plan was extremely dangerous. She had to take the subway to the Gare du Nord, but he couldn't follow her, because he'd stand out. Instead, he would be waiting at the choke point where if all went according to plan, Paradox would be concentrating on Brook, allowing Henri to kill her.

The operative words were "according to plan."

They didn't even know if the assassin even knew she was back in her apartment. Because of his various disguises, Cailan was running surveillance for her. He was wearing one of them and was roaming the neighborhood between Brook's apartment and where she would catch the train. He'd alert her if Paradox followed. Brook was acting as if she was on her way to receive her next assignment and they hoped that the assassin would follow. But with someone like Paradox, there was no telling if she'd bother with that or just kill her outright. The first obstacle was making it from her apartment to the metro station. The second was getting to the Gare du Nord and the RER's Magenta station. If she survived that long, the last was hoping Henri could kill Paradox before she killed Brook.

"Gotta do this," she said.

She left her apartment bathroom and went to her bedroom to get dressed. She dressed in the clothes Henri had purchased for her, namely black cargo pants and a gray mock turtleneck. She laced up a pair of gray Under Armour Valsetz tactical boots. She threaded her belt through a Craft Quick-Draw back-of-the-waist holster and checked to see that her FN509 had a full 15+1 load. With her arm not yet at one hundred percent, her knives would be of little use. She pulled on a black Patagonia fleece hoodie and checked to make sure it covered her gun.

She took a deep breath. "Rock and roll, Brook."

She grabbed her keys and locked up her apartment then headed for the metro. She kept her head on a swivel and her ears attuned to her surroundings for any sign of someone following her, but the street was still busy at 10:00 at night. Not surprising since Paris never slept. But she prayed the assassin wouldn't try a sniper shot.

As she walked toward the St. Michel-Notre Dame station, an old man in an olive green military field coat and a black beret came out of a side lane and paralleled her on the opposite side of the street. He used a blackthorn cane as he walked and sent her a one-handed sign message.

"Tall woman. Hands in her pockets. No threat yet."

That had to be Paradox, so it looked like she'd taken the bait. She probably wouldn't try anything until Brook was more isolated, but with Cailan's heads-up, she was now even more alert. She continued walking to the station and trotted down the stairs. She used her monthly pass to get through the turnstile and waited on the platform. Paradox was nowhere to be seen as the train arrived. Brook tried not to look behind her as she boarded but heard rapid footsteps and caught a blur of a black figure entering the car behind her. The assassin made it just in time. Her phone buzzed with a text.

"She's in the car behind you."

"Yeah, I saw her," she whispered to herself.

The car was half full, so she didn't expect Paradox to come after her yet. The next stop was Chatelet/Les Halles, and half of the passengers got off, and several more got on. Brook was still safe. The next stop was Gare du Nord where she disembarked. The station was always busy so again, Brook wasn't concerned with Paradox trying anything here as long as she was cautious. She took out her cell phone and texted Henri.

"At Gare du Nord. Ready to head for the Magenta platform."

"The next train leaves Haussman St. Lazare in fifteen minutes. It should be the next one to you. Second to last car."

Brook saw there was a Starbucks in the station, so she ordered a small black and headed for the stairs up to the entrance to the Gare Magenta. She took the stairs down to the platform and stood near two policemen who were wearing body armor and Glock 19s. After several terrorist attacks, the police had increased their presence in the train stations, which was comforting for Brook.

The platform started to vibrate, and the sound of the approaching train echoed off the concrete walls. Brook watched it slow and pass her. When it came to a stop, she walked quickly to the next-to-last car and entered. The only one in the car was Henri who was curled up in the corner to her right, pretending to be asleep. She went left toward the other end of the car and took a seat as the train pulled out. She reached behind her and drew her gun then took a suppressor from her pocket. After she fixed it onto her gun, she placed it slightly under her right thigh.

The train pulled into the Pantin station and the doors opened, but no one got on. As soon as it pulled out, the door that led to the third to last car opened and Paradox strolled in. She glanced at Henri but didn't consider him a threat, so she walked toward Brook aiming a suppressed pistol at her. She fired one shot that Brook felt as it passed by her face.

"Use your left hand and place your weapon on the floor then kick it away," Paradox said.

Brook reached slowly across her lap and raised the gun by its barrel. She leaned over and placed it on the floor then pushed it away with her foot. Paradox held one of the poles with her right hand while keeping the gun in her left aimed at Brook.

"You're quite difficult to kill, Ms. Payne. Or should I call you Eliana Azarolla?"

"Whichever you prefer, Ms. Allard, or should I call you Paradox?"

"I thought I had you in Geneva, but you seem to be healing well."

Brook smiled. "Almost good as new."

Paradox clucked her tongue. "You're quite impressive, Ms. Payne. You wiped out two five-man teams made up of former special forces operators even though you were wounded. My hat's off to you. You are truly special, and the CIA is going to miss you."

She took a step closer and lowered the gun as the train pulled into Noisy le-sec. When no one got on, she raised the gun.

"You were quite difficult to locate. It took a lot of searching, but the nearer I got to finding you, the hotter my spirit of revenge burned. Do you know what it's like to lose someone you love, Ms. Payne?"

"I do."

"But what if they're unjustly murdered?"

"I know that, too."

"Who did you lose?"

"My father was murdered by a group of anti-vaxx fanatics."

"Ah, so you know what it feels like to wake up in the morning, knowing your loved one is gone, but the people responsible are still alive and free. Tell me something, Ms. Payne, are the ones who killed your father still out there?"

"That depends on what you mean."

"Where are they now, Ms. Payne?"

"Dead."

"I see. By your hand?"

"Some, yes."

"And how did you feel after you killed them?"

She paused as the train stopped at Rosny-Bous-Perrier. It stayed for two minutes and then pulled out.

"In answer to your question, it didn't bring my father back, so in the end, I'm not sure what I accomplished."

"Ah, well, I believe in revenge. Do you know why?"

"Nope."

"Because I am a romantic and romantics believe in revenge because we love harder, suffer losses more bitterly, and hold onto grudges that have shattered our hearts."

The train slowed and pulled into Rosny-Sous-Bois. The station looked deserted, so the doors barely opened and closed before it departed.

Paradox checked her watch. "Oh well, it's been interesting talking to someone of your caliber, Ms. Payne."

"I wish could say the same but tell me something. I'm trying to figure out if you're on too many drugs or not enough of them. Which do you think it is?"

Paradox sneered at her. "Time to die, bitch."

"I couldn't have said it better myself," Henri said.

Paradox started to turn, but Henri put three .22 rounds through her head before she barely moved. The beauty of the small caliber bullets was that they didn't exit her head, so blood loss was minimal. He holstered his gun under his jacket then motioned for Brook to help him move her body under the seats.

The train started to slow for the Val de Fontenay station. "This is our stop," Henri said. "We take the next train back to Chatelet/Les Halles then transfer to a blue line train that will take us back to St. Michel-Notre Dame."

"She was an interesting person," Brook said as they stepped off the train.

"No, she was a sick bitch who had a mental orgasm every time she killed someone."

"Well, it's over." She leaned over and pecked Henri on the cheek. "Thanks, big brother."

"Why, any time, little sister. You should text Cailan and Mirlinda and tell them Paradox is dead."

"I will and how about we meet them at the Prescription Cocktail club for a celebratory nightcap?"

"Champagne," Henri said. "We must have champagne."

"And as Jack Higgins character Sean Dillon would say, 'Krug non-vintage.'"

"Mais bien sûr"

Chapter Forty-Five

Friday, April 28th; Paris, France; Les Deux Magot

Brook took her usual table against the windows of the café. The afternoon sun bathed the buildings in warm sunlight. She closed her eyes and smiled as she felt a breeze caress her face and ruffle her hair that while still short, had grown back to where she wore it fashionably styled. Her arm was about eighty percent back to normal, but Andrew McGill had given her a month off and hinted that he was okay if she felt she needed to retire after being shot.

Henri appeared, carrying a warm *pain au chocolate* and a crème cafe, and bowed. "Ah, Eliana, it is good to see you again. I trust you've had a good week?"

"Thank you, Henri. I have had a good week. Just resting, reading, and exploring Paris. I've never had time to check it out before because I was always busy."

"And now you are free?"

"For at least a month. My boss said I'd accrued quite a bit of vacation, so I took him up on his offer to use some of it."

"I have your usual for you."

"As always, you know just want your customers want."

"*Oui,* I have exceptional observation skills."

Brook laughed. "Don't I know it."

"So, what did you do during this glorious week?"

"This may sound strange for someone who's lived in Paris for five years, but I'd never explored the Louvre."

"*Mon Dieu,* you are right. It is very strange. And you are an art aficionado, are you not?"

"Yes, but most often I'm drawn to the Musee d'Orsay and its impressionists, expressionists, and pointillists, but I thought I'd take a week and explore Paris' crown jewel."

"And how have you found it?"

"A bit overwhelming. There's so much to see."

"Well, I should think a week would help you experience much of it." He checked his watch. "I'm finished here in two hours. Can I take you to lunch?"

"What did you have in mind?"

"Aux Lyonnais. It's a landmark Paris bistro that first opened in 1890, but it spent many years without a noteworthy menu. However, Alain Ducasse and Thierry de la Brosse have relaunched it and have raised the bar by offering an updated take on the cuisine. Have you ever had quenelles à la lyonnaise with sauce Nantua?"

"No, I have not."

"Ah, they are a must. Quenelles Nantua is a legendary dish and one of the highlights of French cooking. They are feathery light, fluffy fish dumplings bathed in Nantua, the queen of sauces. It's an aromatic essence of crayfish extracted by simmering the shells with a mirepoix of onion and carrot, white wine, and fish stock and finished off with a swirl of butter."

He kissed his fingers. "You can die a happy death after you have tasted them."

"It sounds wonderful. I'll just sit here and enjoy the day until you're finished."

"Excellent." He disappeared into the café.

Brook shook her head and chuckled. Henri truly was like a big brother, and very protective. Of course, she still couldn't believe he was the assassin known as Enigma. But then, she never would have guessed Mirlinda Dzafer was Sasha Nesti. Amazing how her circle of friends had expanded to include three of the deadliest people on earth.

But the more she thought about it, she wondered if she was cut out for this anymore. For the first time in her career, she'd been shot and if it hadn't been for Henri, a group of five ex-special operations agents would have killed her, to say nothing of Paradox. Brook had operated solo for so long that it was beginning to wear on her. She once told Cailan and his wife Maggie that she'd never been a people person and that her job as an independent SOG operator was well suited to an extreme introvert like herself. But the events of the past month, had her questioning that view of herself.

Three times she'd worked with Cailan and the fact that he and Mirlinda had been willing to help her and, most of all, Henri's care for her when she was injured spoke of something she'd never experienced before—real friendships. She was thirty-eight years old, and she'd never had anyone she could call a real friend. Maybe it was time to reevaluate her life and profession. She had plenty of money in a dozen accounts in several customer-friendly countries, so that wasn't an issue. Plus, her mother was a billionaire, achieved from the sales of the rights to the vaccines and the company that she and her father had created. Henri was the perfect person to advise her. After all, he was a former SOG contractor who'd gone into semi-retirement.

Her thoughts were interrupted by Henri's appearance. She checked her watch.

"Wow, I didn't realize I'd been sitting here for two hours," she said.

"Time flies when you're having fun. He was holding a motorcycle helmet. I have my scooter. Are you okay to ride?"

"I'm almost good as new."

"Then shall we go?"

She stood and followed him to a short alley behind the cafe where several scooters were parked. He handed her a second helmet that was strapped to the back of the scooter and helped her on. He pulled on his helmet and started the bike then pulled out of the alley into traffic. Fifteen

minutes later they parked, and he led her to Aux Lyonnais. The maître-
d greeted them as they entered.

"*Bonsoir*, Henri, *comment ça va* ?"

"I'm excellent, Jean. May I introduce you to my sister, Eliana?"

Jean took her hand and kissed it. "You are his sister?"

She smiled. "Adopted."

"Ah, well welcome to Aux Lyonnais. Please, follow me."

He led them to a table for two against a back wall where they could
both see the entire restaurant.

"Henri has already ordered for you. For starters, we have Escargots
de Bourgogne followed by the quenelles Nantua. And to accompany
your food, I've selected a Champagne Cuvée Prestige Diebolt-Vallois."

"Everything sounds wonderful," Brook said. Jean bowed and retired.

"Henri, this is crazy. You didn't have to do this?"

Jean returned with the champagne, opened it, and poured some into
a Riedel High-Performance Champagne glass. Henri checked its color,
bouquet, and taste and nodded.

"Excellent, Jean."

He poured for them both then placed the bottle in a stone cooler.
Henri raised his glass and offered a toast.

"To decisions."

Brook frowned but touched her glass to his. "What do you mean
decisions?"

"Are you not struggling with what to do with your life, Eliana?"

"How—?"

"Observation, my dear. I read it on your face earlier as you were
sitting at Les Deux."

"Geez, Henri, how do you do that?"

"Years of experience and because I've gone through the same things."

"Like what?"

"When I first started in this business, I was a very angry young man,
wanting desperately to prove that I was as good as any normal-sized man.
I had no friends, and the only thing that kept me going was a drive to
succeed. At the age of twenty-four, I became a contractor for your

company and one in Britain. I thought I was Robin Hood, righting the wrongs done by evil men and women."

"Is that why one of your instruments of choice was a crossbow?"

He sipped the champagne. "Yes."

"Did you know that it is one of my favorites?"

His eyebrows rose. "No, I did not. So, that is one more thing we have in common. But after five years of contracting for the CIA and MI6, I was diagnosed with leukemia. I had no friends to turn to and realized I was all alone in the world. Fortunately, my sister and I have maintained a relationship over the years, and she not only turned out to be a match, but she donated her marrow to me. It took me a year to go through the procedure and recover, and it was an excruciating process, especially when you're alone. When I recovered, I took a job at Les Deux Magots. It was my first real interaction with people who, once they got to know me, didn't view me as odd but rather as more of a confidant than just a waiter."

He chuckled. "You would not believe the things people tell me."

"Actually, I can. You have an air about you that speaks of caring and trust."

Henri started to tear up. "Thank you. You have no idea what that means to me to hear you say that. Anyway, I went back to the business, but my heart was no longer in it and for people like us that's very dangerous and leads to mistakes."

"Is that how your blood was left at the scene of one of your jobs?"

"Yes, your organization had tasked me to remove a Swiss banker who was laundering money for the Bratva. He made a trip to Helsinki to meet with the leaders of the organization and stayed in the Hotel Kamp. When he went out to dinner, I broke into his room and waited for him to return. What the intelligence brief missed was that he was an expert in Paranza Corta, the Italian knife fighting system often associated with assassins. For someone who was essentially a banker, he was quite good, but not good enough."

Henri pushed up his right sleeve, exposing a long scar. "He cut me badly before I took him down. I cleaned up in his bathroom, but there was no way I could remove all my blood. But as I thought about it, I realized it would throw anyone looking for me off track, because they'd be looking for a woman."

"That happened when I was thirty-two. I continued as a contractor for five more years, but I so enjoyed my work at the café, that I stopped taking jobs and fell off the grid."

"And you don't regret it?" Brook asked.

"Not at all. I have friends like Jean the maître-d here and many of the patrons of Les Deux. I enjoy reading and visiting the art galleries. I even have a vacation home in Limone sul Garda, a picturesque village on the shores of Lake Guarda in Italy's northern Lombardy region with a population of just over one thousand. It's my mental health get-away."

"It sounds wonderful," Brook said. "I would love to have that life."

"Why can't you?"

"What do you mean? The SOG—."

"Will get along fine without you. You've served them for more than a decade, correct?"

"Yes."

"And you were injured and almost killed on your last venture for them, correct?"

"My boss Andrew McGill hinted that it might be time for me to consider retirement. He indicated he'd support me. He might even use me in an intelligence capacity rather than what I do right now."

"Well, there you have it," Henri said.

"But what would I do? I'd get bored just sitting around."

Henri raised his champagne glass and sipped. When he set his glass down, he wore a mischievous grin and folded his arms across his chest. "You could work at Les Deux."

Brook raised her glass. "That would definitely be cool, but I doubt if they'd hire me. I don't have any experience."

"But I'd hire you, and you could learn."

"How are you going to do that? Do they just let you hire anybody you want?"

He cocked his head at her. "Well, seeing as how I'm the owner, I don't see a problem."

Brook choked on her champagne and had all she could do to keep from spraying it across the table.

"You own Les Deux Magots?"

"I do. I bought it four years ago. And if you're interested, I know of a very nice villa in Limone sul Garda that's for sale."

Brook stared at her glass but didn't say a thing for several minutes. "Wow, me a waitress. Now there's a change."

"You could have all the *pain au chocolate* you want, and it would be on the house."

"Seriously?"

"Of course. I take care of my employees."

"And the villa?"

"I can make a call right now." He leaned forward and touched her arm. "No offense, but you need to get out before a mistake kills you."

"What's Limone sul Garda like?"

"It's the northernmost spot where lemons grow naturally, hence the name, and it has an exceptionally mild climate, considering it's located at the feet of the Alps. And, of course, the lake is beautiful."

Brook picked up her champagne glass but caught herself scanning the restaurant for threats. She couldn't turn off what she called her "battle readiness." Even when she relaxed in a café like Les Deux Magots, her senses were on high alert, and the problem was, she wasn't sure she could ever turn them off. Nothing like a paranoid waitress constantly scanning every patron who walked in the door for someone who might want to kill her.

"How do you turn it off?" she asked.

"Turn what off?" Henri said.

"The constant counting of the exits, scanning for threats, and judging people as they come in Les Deux?"

Henri leaned back and turned his glass as he admired the champagne. He sipped then stared out the window.

"There is a short hall to your left that leads to the washrooms and a back exit. The kitchen entrance is just beyond it and has a door that leads into the alley. There are sixteen people in the restaurant besides us. Eight are couples on lunch dates. Six are here on business. The two loners are a man by the front window and a woman at the opposite corner table. No telltale bulges under the men's coats. While the women could have a weapon in their purses, it's unlikely except for the single lady in the corner. But because I judge her to be in her early to mid-sixties, I don't think she's a threat. I have a Benchmade Infidel fighting knife in a sheath on my left forearm and a Sig P365 SAS in an ankle holster just in case I'm wrong. But that has never happened."

He sipped the champagne. "So, in answer to your question, I don't."

"Then how do you relax?"

"Working at Les Deux has sharpened my observational skills immeasurably and I've learned to hide them behind the facade of a friendly waiter who only wants to meet his customer's needs, all while sizing each one up." He cocked his head at her. "Le Deux will hone your skills to the point that you will do it unconsciously."

"I'd be worried about being recognized."

Henri leaned forward and smiled. "I assume you have several passports that your agency is unaware of?"

"A dozen."

He sat back and his eyes widened. "*Mon Dieu,* you are very paranoid."

"Well, after what just happened, I think I was right to be."

"Choose one that you like and style your hair to match. Since you almost always sit outside and I'm the only one who ever waits on you, you can slip right into a new identity and work at Les Deux without any of the staff being any wiser to who you were."

"How long did it take you to normalize?"

He chuckled. "As if that term could ever be applied to you and me. But I think within three months, I was happily serving food and drinks and, most importantly, making friends." He shrugged. "Now, I don't think about it, but don't mistake that for a lack of vigilance.

Brook reached into one of her cargo pockets and withdrew a maroon booklet with the words, "Europese Unie, Konenkrijk Der Nederlander" written in gold across the front. She passed it to Henri.

He opened it and saw the picture of Brook with stylish short blond hair. The passport was in the name of Anki van Dijk, a Dutch citizen.

"*Oh, c'est magnifique.* Your agency doesn't know about this identity?"

"Nobody does, except for you, of course. I've never used it."

"*C'est parfait!* So, I will have to start calling you Anki." He raised his glass and offered a toast. "So, what do you say to my idea?"

Brook grinned and raised her glass. "I say let's toast to a villa in Limone sul Garda and all the *pain au chocolate* I can eat."

They clinked and sipped.

"I'll probably get fat," she said.

"From what I know of you, I seriously doubt that."

She put her hand over Henri's. "Thanks, big brother."

"You are most welcome, little sister."